HER FIRST
CHILD

BOOKS BY SHERYL BROWNE

The Babysitter

The Affair

The Second Wife

The Marriage Trap

The Perfect Sister

The New Girlfriend

Trust Me

My Husband's Girlfriend

The Liar's Child

The Invite

Do I Really Know You?

HER FIRST CHILD

SHERYL BROWNE

bookouture

Published by Bookouture in 2022

An imprint of Storyfire Ltd.
Carmelite House
50 Victoria Embankment
London EC4Y 0DZ

www.bookouture.com

ISBN: 978-1-80314-331-6
eBook ISBN: 978-1-80314-330-9

To all my friends and readers.
Thank you for inspiring me.

Silence isn't empty, it's full of answers.

Unknown

PROLOGUE

The man walking the length of the corridor towards me looks out of place, purposeful. People are generally not like that here, often walking around randomly, mumbling to themselves. Or else very quiet, stuck in their heads, staring off into space. It's usually quiet. Sterile. No clutter or mess, the walls all painted in calming soft pastels or white. I don't like white walls. I find them far too impersonal and clinical. You would have thought the people who designed the building would have thought about that, the association between hospitals and the frightening situations those who are unfortunate enough to be there find themselves in. I can't bear clutter. I keep my room scrupulously tidy. It's sparsely furnished, with just two chairs, a nightstand and a small dressing table – no place to hide things, but I'm fastidious about cleanliness. You are, aren't you, when you have a sick child to care for?

I shrink back in my chair when I realise the person the man has come to see is me. 'Hi.' He smiles, a short, troubled smile, as he stops in front of me. 'How are you?' He's strikingly handsome, soulful brown eyes, mournful almost. I feel I should know him, but I'm not sure that I do.

My son studies the man, and my heart bleeds for the little boy. He's always wondering, hoping that one day his father will come. I ease him close, kiss the top of his head and shush him gently. *One day soon, sweetheart.* I make him a promise I'm not sure I can keep.

'I brought you some things,' the man says, the furrow in his brow deepening as he sweeps his eyes over my child and then back to me. 'Some fresh clothes and a new notebook and crayons. I'll leave them on the table, shall I?' He indicates the recreational table, a utility table with soft, rounded edges lest anyone should walk into it and injure themselves.

I feel my son's excitement at the prospect of new crayons. We've almost used up all the ones we had, making pictures of magical places to brighten up the white walls.

A woman approaches. My eyes swivel towards her as she joins him. *His wife?* I wonder. They make a striking couple.

'How is he?' she asks, nodding to the little boy in my arms, and I hug him still closer. My instinct, as any mother's instinct would be, is to protect him, but I'm not sure what it is I have to protect him from. It's there somewhere, something dark and indefinable, floating on the periphery of my memory. Is it something to do with her? Do I know her? A teasing recollection taunts me, two little girls sitting together under the shade of tall trees, but it's gone before I can capture it, disappearing like a wisp of smoke.

Narrowing my eyes, I scan her face carefully and a chill of apprehension creeps through me. She's smiling, and her expression is sympathetic, but there's a spark of triumph in her eyes as she reaches out to stroke my little boy's soft silicone cheek.

ONE

PRESENT

Eve

Eve was with a young patient when her phone alerted her to a text. Quickly she checked it. *Your mother's here*, she read, and her heart stopped dead. She'd come to her house? A knot of dread tightened like a hard fist inside her. Why? After all these years? But Eve knew why. She should never have spoken to her on the phone. She should have ended the call immediately when she'd realised it was Lydia. Her mother had had a reason to contact her, a valid one, but Eve knew what her real motive was. She would not allow it. After a childhood that had left her with the worst kind of scars, internal scars that would never heal, she would die before she allowed that woman access to her child. She needed to get back home. Now.

'I'm so sorry. It looks like I'm needed to attend an emergency.' She quashed her panic rather than break the tentative bond she'd built with the small patient in front of her. Offering the mother an apologetic smile, she addressed the child directly.

'Do you think it might help to talk to someone, Jasmine?' she asked, greatly concerned for the girl's welfare. She was apparently struggling with her reading and communication skills, and was bed-wetting too, which, having ruled out an infection, was worrying in a seven-year-old. Eve felt for her. She knew how isolating it was to start school without being able to understand pictures in a book. To see other children talking to each other and making friends while you sat alone not knowing how to fit in. She was desperate to help Jasmine and her mother if she could.

'Sam wouldn't like that.' The girl's mother spoke for her, another jarring reminder of Eve's own childhood, where her despicable father's word was law and she was never allowed a voice. Sam, the woman's partner, who was also one of Eve's patients, was a moody, abrupt man, and Eve considered he might possibly be the source of Jasmine's problems.

'Perhaps we could organise for just the two of you to chat to someone?' she suggested, thinking it would be a start. The general practice counsellor they referred young patients to was shrewd. She might pick up on signs that weren't immediately obvious, get Jasmine or her mother to open up a little. 'It can sometimes help to talk, and the professional I have in mind is really lovely.'

The woman looked her over warily. 'I'll think about it,' she said.

'Great. You can give the surgery a call any time and they'll pass a message on to me.' Eve gave her an encouraging smile. 'Meanwhile, could you make Jasmine another appointment for a few days' time? I'd like to repeat the urine test, just to be sure.'

The woman nodded, her expression still wary as she took hold of her daughter's hand and stood up. Eve watched them walk out, and her heart bled for the little girl. Her shoes were too small. Eve guessed they were skinning her feet.

Swallowing back a lump of emotion, she made a note on

Jasmine's file to follow things up if the woman didn't get in touch, then, quickly texting her husband to say she was on her way, gathered up her bags and coat.

Noticing her colleague's open office door, she knocked and peered around it. 'Sorry, Jen, I have to dash off early. Emergency on the home front. Do you think you could cover for me? I just have one patient left for a medication review and a blood pressure test.'

'No problem. Nothing too worrying, I hope.' Jenny frowned in concern.

'No,' Eve assured her, though she *was* worried. She didn't imagine that Lydia would reveal things to her husband that might implicate her, but she simply didn't want her there, in her home, in her life. She wanted her gone, as far away as possible from her family, from her innocent son. 'Just a burst pipe. The kitchen's flooded and Dom's struggling to cope.' Citing her husband as incompetent, which he wasn't, she gave Jenny a knowing smile.

Twenty minutes later, she pulled up on her drive and braced herself to go inside. Might her mother have changed, she wondered, found a conscience? She realised she'd been nurturing that hope as she'd driven back. Their phone conversation had been short. After so long with no contact, they had nothing to talk about. Her mother had felt obliged to contact her to tell her that her paternal grandmother had died, which evoked no emotion in Eve other than anger that she had to be reminded of her father at all. It was a forlorn hope, she realised. Lydia would have to have changed considerably, and Eve really didn't think that was possible.

Dom came to meet her in the hall as she let herself in. 'Sorry,' he murmured, leaning to kiss her cheek. 'I wasn't sure what to do when she just turned up. I thought I should text you.'

'It's okay. I was seeing my last patient anyway,' Eve assured him.

Dom was aware she and her mother didn't get on, but no more than that. There were things she couldn't bring herself to tell him, secrets about her family she would never want him to know. She'd survived her past, worked so hard to bury it and reinvent herself. She didn't want it all dragged up again to colour his perception of her, her perception of herself. Her competence was a veneer, but he didn't realise it. Underneath, she was still the frightened child she'd once been, waiting for bad things to happen. And now that Lydia had surfaced, they would happen, she was sure of it. There was no way, though, to convey any of this to Dom without telling him everything.

'How's Kai?' she asked, searching his face. He knew how reluctant she'd been to return to work after her maternity leave. He hadn't said anything, but she suspected he was put out that she'd appeared not to trust him to look after their son.

'He's fine. Sleeping.' He smiled reassuringly. 'He's learned a new word today. It's unintelligible, but he looked pretty delighted with himself.'

Eve smiled back, some of the tension leaving her. The smile faded from her face, though, as Lydia appeared from the kitchen. Seeing her mother's pinched and worried face, her eyes skittering away from her in that way they always had, she was immediately put in mind of a fragile bird. Outward appearances were deceptive, though, she reminded herself. Delicate-featured and petite, Lydia had always had an air of frailty about her. No one would ever suspect what she was capable of.

'Eve.' She smiled uncertainly. 'How are you?'

Scared, Eve thought. *Of why you're here.* 'Fine,' she said, appraising her carefully. 'You?'

'I'm actually not feeling too well.' Lydia's hand fluttered to her chest.

Her complexion was definitely pale, and Eve felt a flicker of concern. But then, recalling how adept her mother was at feigning illness, she dismissed it.

'The strain of your grandmother's death, I think,' Lydia went on weakly, to Eve's astonishment. Lydia had hated her mother-in-law. From what Eve remembered, the woman had been awful to her, undermining her, never supportive of her. 'I thought a little lie-down might help,' she added, heading towards the stairs.

TWO

Eve watched in disbelief as her mother made her way upstairs and along the landing to the spare room. Bewildered, she turned to Dom. 'She's staying?' she asked, though as her mother seemed to know where she was going, it was apparent that she was.

'She had an overnight bag with her.' Dom shrugged awkwardly. 'She came on the train. I assumed she wasn't planning on travelling back to Shropshire tonight.'

Of course he would have done. He would also have assumed that Eve wouldn't dream of letting her travel back. It wasn't his fault. She managed a faint smile in his direction, but he clearly saw through it.

'I do good cuddles, I'm told,' he said quietly, moving to circle her with his arms. 'I'm sensing someone might be in need of one.' His decadently dark eyes caressing hers were so reassuring, so full of genuine concern, Eve felt her throat tighten. She'd found what she needed in him, a good, caring man whose gentle nature was her saviour. He wasn't outwardly macho as some men felt they needed to be, but he had a quiet inner strength she knew she could depend on. She'd never mentioned her brother, but she had told him a little about her past, as much as she'd dared. That her mother had struggled with her maternal feelings for her, that her father had been distant. She'd learned to live with it, she'd said. But she hadn't. There would always be a cold hollowness inside her where a mother's love should be.

In turning up at her front door, it was as if Lydia were driving that fact home. There was nothing Eve could do about it this evening, though. She could hardly demand she leave without Dom asking questions she wasn't emotionally prepared to answer. Taking a breath, she shrugged out of her coat and headed towards the kitchen to warm Kai's feed. With her mother upstairs, she didn't want to leave him for too long.

Dom followed. 'How about I make us one of my speciality mocha coffees?' he offered. 'We'll put extra chocolate sprinkles on and indulge ourselves.' He stopped as the sound of Kai waking reached them from the baby monitor on the worktop. He was just gurgling, but still Eve's nerves were immediately on edge, and she cursed the fact that she hadn't yet installed the new digital video monitor she'd purchased. The Wi-Fi monitor was good, but she could only check the live footage on her phone.

'He's okay,' Dom said as she dug the phone from her bag and flicked to the app. 'I'm sure he'll let us know when he's not.'

Busy checking the video footage, Eve didn't answer. Reassured when she saw that Kai actually was fine, his little arms moving, his eyes wide and alert, she looked back to Dom. 'Sorry, I can't help worrying. New mother syndrome.' She tried to make it sound like a joke, but with her own mother here, she couldn't rid herself of the feeling that her worry was justified.

Dom smiled indulgently. He looked tired. He was bound to be, Eve supposed, with a crucial deadline to meet. The position he'd been offered at Frontier Brand Creatives, a leading graphic design company, depended on him coming up with innovative ideas, but working from home couldn't be easy with a new baby in the house and she knew he was worrying about meeting the deadline. 'I'll go and fetch him,' he offered. 'You take five minutes and wind down.'

'No, I'll go.' Eve stopped him, then, seeing his crestfallen face, immediately regretted it. 'I've missed him,' she explained with an apologetic shrug. 'I haven't seen him all day.' She was only back part-time, but even so, three days seemed too many to be away from her child.

'I know. I get it.' Dom sighed. 'It's just...'

'Just?' Eve searched his eyes.

He looked hesitant. 'I can't help feeling you're shutting me out sometimes. Not just with caring for Kai, but generally. I don't want you to feel you can't confide in me, Eve.'

She felt a pang of guilt. 'I don't mean to shut you out,' she said, pressing a hand to his cheek. 'I just...' *Can't let you in.* There was no way she could do that completely. If she told him all there was to know about her past, he would be horrified. Only Chloe, her friend since primary school, knew everything. Without her, Eve would have felt so lonely as a child. She would now, despite having such a caring man in her life. The fact was, though, she'd known him for only a short time. They'd been going out together for just six months or so when she'd fallen pregnant. Dom had been over the moon at the prospect of fatherhood and was adamant he wanted to marry her, convincing her that he loved her and that he'd been working up to asking her anyway. She loved him too, her love for him growing a little more every day she was with him, but Chloe was the only person who really understood her.

'You need to check, just in case,' he finished, mustering a smile.

'You could warm his feed for him,' she suggested. Her need to constantly check on Kai wasn't Dom's fault either. She tried to resist but found it impossible. It would be even worse now, with her mother having gained access to her.

Going quickly up the stairs, she glanced through the open door at Lydia lying on the bed in the spare room. Seeing the rise and fall of her chest, Eve wondered whether she really was sleeping. Her mother had done that so often, taken to her bed and ignored her. Why *had* she come? It was possible that her mother-in-law's passing had stirred up emotions she was struggling to deal with; she might even be feeling lonely. Her husband had been a monster, but there'd been no one else in her life since, as far as Eve knew. But then she'd been damaged by a marriage that had been made in hell. That much had finally become obvious to Eve. She herself had been damaged too, and now she wanted no part of her past creeping back to harm her family. Lydia would know this. She would know that she simply wouldn't take that risk. So why was she here?

Hurrying on to the nursery, Eve found Kai still contentedly gurgling, his little arms flailing excitedly as he reached for the clouds and stars on his musical mobile. 'Hello, my gorgeous baby boy,' she said, smiling down at him, and then, seeing his gummy smile of delight, his huge beguiling eyes, she reached to pick him up and breathe in the special sweet, innocent smell of him.

She would keep him safe. She would never allow anything or anyone to hurt him. Her mother would know this too.

Squeezing him close, she carried him across the room, kissed the top of his soft, downy head and then laid him gently down on his changing mat. Kai didn't fight her as she changed him, trusting her completely to tend to him, as a mother should tend to the needs of her child. As *her* mother should have tended to hers and to Jacob's. Her heart twisted as her thoughts went to her brother, and she tried hard to push them from her mind. She needed to concentrate on what was happening now, on getting through tonight and then getting her mother out of her life.

When she brought Kai downstairs, she found her mother had made a sudden recovery and was talking to Dom in the kitchen. 'Busy,' she heard Dom saying as she walked in. 'Which I might not be if I don't get this commission in on time.'

'Ah, your magazine project.' Lydia nodded. Dom had obviously already spoken to her about it. 'Who's it for again?' she asked, an almost maternal look on her face as she glanced at him.

Eve was surprised that her mother seemed to be genuinely interested in Dom and what he did. But then Dom, with his easy nature, would soon have won her over. Fleetingly, she wished Lydia had ever been interested in her and anything she did, but dismissed the thought. She didn't want to dwell on her past. She was happy now. She had Dom and Kai and Chloe. As for her mother, she wouldn't miss what she'd never had, she told herself firmly. She wasn't sure, though, that she believed that.

Dom smiled in her direction as he saw her. '*Here Now* magazine,' he replied to Lydia as he walked across to Eve. 'It's aimed at challenging gender roles and behaviours, so it needs a brand that's innovative, edgy, sophisticated and contemporary. I think I've finally got the ideas sorted. Now all we need to do is to put it all together, don't we, little man?' Smiling, he reached for Kai.

Eve hesitated, feeling somehow that she might be stripped of her armour if she handed him over. Realising how that would look to Dom, though, she reluctantly allowed him to take him.

'You are clever.' Lydia sighed in admiration. 'I don't have an artistic bone in my body.'

Going across to the worktop to collect Kai's bottle from the warmer, it struck Eve that her mother looked much the same as she always had. She was thinner, and her short copper-coloured hair was peppered with wisps of grey, but she was still an attractive woman. Eve's hand went to her own hair, which still hung in dark coils down her back, and a shudder ran through her as an image of her mother coming menacingly towards her wielding a pair of scissors flashed through her mind. She didn't think the terror her parents had instilled in her that day would ever leave her.

'Eve was never very artistic either,' Lydia went on, jarring her from the painful recollection. 'Were you, darling?'

Eve tugged in a tight breath. 'No. I was more interested in science,' she answered shortly.

'Always had her nose stuck in a book, barely communicated sometimes.' Lydia sighed indulgently.

Recalling her mother's silences, which had been incomprehensible to her as a child, Eve was hard pushed not to laugh in complete disbelief. 'Books were my only company, weren't they, Mother?' She shot her a loaded glance. 'But I think that's a subject best left for another time. Don't you?'

Lydia looked hurriedly away. 'So who's this beautiful little boy going to take after, I wonder?' she continued after a pause. 'Daddy, obviously. I can't believe he's so like you, Dominic.'

Dom looked Kai thoughtfully over. 'I actually think he's more like his mum. He has her pretty Cupid lips, don't you, Kai?'

'Yes, but all babies have pretty Cupid lips,' Lydia pointed out dismissively. 'Don't they, little dot, hmm?'

Eve glanced back to see her mother taking hold of one of Kai's hands and making kissy faces at him, and suppressed a sudden overwhelming urge to cry. If only for appearances' sake, why couldn't her mother have made an effort to relate to her even in the smallest of ways?

'Would you like me to feed him?' Lydia offered as Eve went across to retrieve her child, who was chuckling happily at the woman who seemed to be attempting to bond with him.

Eve felt herself tense. 'No,' she declined flatly. 'I like to give him his evening feed myself,' she added, catching Dom's curious glance as she reached to take Kai from him. 'It's his bath time. Our quiet time together.'

'Oh.' Her mother looked deflated for a second, then seemed to pull herself together. 'Right, well, why don't I make myself useful and get dinner on?'

'Sounds like a plan. I'll give you a hand,' Dom said, and Eve thanked her lucky stars for a man who was intuitive enough to step in and deflect the awkward moment.

With Dom keeping the conversation flowing, dinner turned out to be not too much of an ordeal. Lydia avoided any further revelations about Eve's childhood. She'd clearly gathered from Eve's barely veiled warning earlier that it was a subject she wanted kept closed. She didn't make much eye contact across the table, but given their history, Eve didn't wonder at that. After a glass of wine, and Dom expertly massaging her shoulders once they were in the privacy of their bedroom, she felt almost relaxed.

'You've missed your vocation. You should have been a masseur,' she said, snuggling into him and resting her head against his chest, where she could listen to the reassuring thrum of his heartbeat.

He wrapped an arm around her. 'You know, I reckon you're right. I could charge a fortune in between projects for home visits to needy mothers. I'd be rolling in— *Ouch!*' He winced as Eve tweaked one of his nipples. 'On the other hand, maybe I'll give it a miss. Don't fancy waking up with body piercings I hadn't planned on having.'

'You're mad.' Eve snuggled closer.

'I know,' Dom pressed a soft kiss to her hair, 'but you're the one who married me. Try to get some sleep tonight, hey?'

Eve smiled. She wouldn't get much sleep. She would check on Kai several times, particularly with Lydia here. She did love Dom for trying to take care of her, though. She had no idea how she would survive if she ever lost him. He really did seem to think the world of her. And he loved his son with his very bones. Things would be all right. Lydia would never open the can of worms that was their past. She would know that everything would come tumbling out. She would never risk that happening.

THREE

1997

Lydia

David hadn't come home on time, again, leaving her with a fractious two-month-old baby, a Caesarean scar that hadn't healed properly, and a wilful nine-year-old child. When he did arrive, he would cite some emergency at work while wearing that agitated expression he'd had ever since she'd left the hospital with their premature baby. As if it were him who nursed Jacob when he cried through the night.

She had begun to wish he would never come home. She was too tired to tiptoe around him. Whenever he was here, he was moody, 'exhausted from overwork', he was fond of saying, as if Lydia sat around all day with her feet up. Chance would be a fine thing. Even before Jacob was born, she'd juggled working part-time in his business with childcare and housework. He hadn't been pleased when she'd told him she was pregnant again. 'I thought you were on the bloody pill,' he'd said, his expression accusing. She'd tried to explain that the tummy bug she'd had had made the pill less reliable, but he hadn't been listening. With his construction company struggling to undercut local competitors, finances were tight, and she'd known he hadn't wanted another child. She'd hoped, though, that once he saw his son, he would change his mind. He clearly hadn't. He seemed indifferent to Jacob, who, with his ebony hair and impossibly dark eyes that seemed to watch her every move, was the image of his father. She prayed it was in looks only.

Seeing Jacob's eyelids finally close as he stopped fighting sleep with every ounce of strength in his body, she breathed a sigh of relief and crept to the nursery door. Trying to balance her weight lest the creaking floorboards wake him, she was closing it quietly when a crash from the kitchen below shattered the silence, causing him to bellow out a raucous cry.

Lydia felt her patience stretch to near breaking point. A sharp lump clogging her throat, she went back into the nursery, pausing inside the door and inhaling slowly. It didn't help. Jacob's cries grated on the inside of her skull. She was so tired, exhaustion seeming to seep through to her bones. She didn't think she could do this, cope with a recalcitrant daughter, a husband who undermined her in every way possible, and a baby who never slept. Yet what choice did she have? With her GP next to useless, telling her that the way she was feeling was perfectly normal, she had to pull herself together, as David's mother, who'd given birth to three sons and 'never had any trouble with any one of them', had suggested she should. She had no idea how to, though. Having lost her own mother to breast cancer three years ago, there was no one else she could confide in.

A wave of grief crashed through her as she thought of her mother. Concerned that Lydia might find herself trapped in an unhappy marriage as she herself had been, she'd wanted her to finish her studies, become a nurse. Lydia hadn't finished her studies. Pregnant with Eve, instead she'd married David, who'd

convinced her to work alongside him, helping him build up and
run his company. She'd actually been his secretary, and not a
very well paid one at that. He gave her a small allowance while
claiming to the tax man that, as a partner in the company, she
drew a large salary. He had her tax allowance too, of course. All
of which offset the company tax liability.

She'd let her mother down. She'd let herself down. Now
she was trying to make the best of it, to do her best, but whatever she did, she just didn't feel *normal*. She'd wanted to
scream it at the doctor, David too. Tell them that she wanted
to go back to work, but not with David. She wanted to find
her own job. It would have to be part-time, but still, it would
allow her to take a little of her independence back. She
wanted to go out with her friends occasionally, even if David
didn't like her to, imagining her gallivanting off with some
other man – as if she would have the energy. She just wanted
to be normal. She hadn't said anything in the end. She didn't
have the energy for the inevitable consequences of her daring
to complain when he claimed to work his fingers to the bone
for her.

Wiping her wet face, she went to the cot, took another shuddery breath, then bent to pick Jacob up. David's mother had
told her to leave him to cry, insisting she was setting a prece-
dent, but she couldn't just leave him like this. David would be
beyond irritable, and there would be nothing she could do to
appease *him* either. 'Be quiet, Jacob, *please*.' She pressed him to
her shoulder, shushed him and soothed him. Still he bellowed as
if he were being murdered.

Squeezing him closer, which only made him cry harder, she
picked up his comfort blanket and headed back out to the stairs.
She was part way down when another loud crash reached her.
God, that girl! Every time she put Jacob down, something would
wake him, usually Eve making a racket, thumping up and down
the stairs or going into the nursery, which Lydia had told her

under no circumstances to do. She would swear she did it on purpose sometimes to draw attention to herself.

Frustration and anger building inside her, she hurried the rest of the way down, thrusting the kitchen door open to find Eve and her friend Chloe on all fours on the floor. 'What are you *doing*?' she asked, her tone sharp.

The girls jumped to their feet and Eve dropped her gaze guiltily to the broken crockery in her hand.

'We were washing up, Mrs Lockhart,' Chloe answered, in the absence of anything forthcoming from Eve. 'The dish slipped out of my hand. Sorry.'

'Twice?' Lydia's gaze travelled accusingly between them as she placed a bottle in the warmer and jiggled Jacob in her arms.

'It wasn't Chloe's fault. We were only trying to help.' Eve's brow creased into a scowl as she finally spoke up in defence of her friend. 'We dropped the bits while we were picking them up. We didn't do it on purpose.'

Lydia sighed. 'You can help by being *quiet*,' she said despairingly.

Eve said nothing, exchanging embarrassed glances with Chloe instead, which irritated Lydia further. She'd seen David exchange that same glance with his mother around her, and she was getting sick of it. She was beginning to feel alienated by everyone.

'Isn't it time you went home, Chloe?' she asked her. 'Your mum will be wondering where you are, and Eve needs to make sure she's ready for school tomorrow.' Seeing Eve's scowl deepen and feeling very close to losing her temper, she turned away to check the bottle warmer.

Hearing the girls place what was left of the casserole dish on the table and then shuffle to the door, Lydia stayed where she was, making up the formula she was forced to feed Jacob because her milk had dried up. She felt like weeping with frustration. Surely Eve could see she was at the end of her tether?

Minutes later, following much whispering in the hall, Chloe shouted goodbye, and Eve reappeared in the kitchen. 'We have a school trip tomorrow,' she announced.

Lydia breathed deeply, her patience now stretched paper-thin. 'And you're only just telling me this *now*?'

'There's a letter on the table in the hall,' Eve mumbled. 'We're going to the Birmingham Museum and Art Gallery,' she went on, despite the fact that Jacob had ramped up his cries to an ear-piercing shriek, meaning Lydia could hardly hear herself think. 'I don't need a packed lunch or anything. Miss Grantham said they have a café there where we can buy sandwiches.'

'And did Miss Grantham have any bright suggestions as to what you might buy these sandwiches with? I don't have any money in my purse, Eve,' Lydia pointed out angrily. She never had any money in her purse. The allowance David gave her was barely enough to feed them and clothe the children, and she had to account for every penny. He was always reminding her to produce her receipts so he could make his company accounts tally. Lydia didn't really understand how everything worked, but she daren't question him. His moods could be dark. It was safer to just give in and go along with things.

Noticing that Eve's gaze was glued to the floor, she shook her head in exasperation. She did wish her daughter would try to make life a little easier for her. 'You'll have to ask your father,' she said. Depending on what time he came home, of course. Running his own company was full on, she was aware of that. The fact that he hadn't been home most evenings since early into her pregnancy, though, was a great big red flag to Lydia. That, plus his lack of interest in her, and his hurtful comments. He'd been horrible to her before that, though. Vile and aggressive when the mood took him.

A shudder ran through her as she recalled how, when she'd inadvertently under-ordered the amount of concrete fibre needed for a major job, he'd lost his temper in front of several construction workers. Lydia had fled, crying hot tears of humiliation as she'd waited on the canal bank that backed onto the industrial estate. He'd followed her, clutched the back of her neck, his fingers digging hard into her flesh. 'You're useless,' he'd hissed, so close to her ear she'd felt his spittle spatter her cheek. 'I ought to drown you and your fucking sprog.'

She should leave him. She *would*, just as soon as she could find a way. Anger rose hotly inside her. But how would she find a way? Where would she go without a penny to her name?

'Do you want me to hold him while you make his feed?' Eve asked tentatively behind her.

'No. Go and shower and go to bed,' Lydia snapped, glancing at her to find Eve looking utterly crestfallen, which did nothing to improve her own mood. 'I'll have a word with your father,' she added, her stomach churning as she imagined what his reaction would be to her not budgeting prudently.

Eve nodded and turned to the door. Listening to her trudge up the stairs, Lydia sighed again and collected up the bottle. She would feed Jacob on her bed, she decided. He was less irritable there, and she could keep an ear out for Eve coming out of the bathroom.

Once on the bed with the baby nestled in the crook of her arm, she attempted to entice him to take some of his formula. Jacob, though, only screwed up his face and spat the teat out. Desperate to quieten him as the inevitable raucous bawl followed, she clutched him tightly to her. Leaning back on the pillows as his crying, muffled and heart-wrenching, continued, she allowed her own tears to fall. *Why won't you feed? Why in God's name won't you sleep?* she mentally begged him.

After a minute, his cries subsided to a hiccuping stop. Lydia stayed where she was, hoping, praying. She wasn't sure how much time had slipped by when the bathroom door opening jerked her upright. Jacob didn't stir. By some divine miracle, he was finally silent. A prickle of apprehension running through her, Lydia scrutinised him briefly, then, rather than risk waking him, eased him to the middle of the bed and hurried to the landing to warn Eve that her father was due home any minute. The last thing she needed was her daughter banging around up here, which would be bound to rile him.

'Jacob's asleep in the main bedroom,' she whispered as Eve headed for her room. 'Whatever you do, do *not* go in there and wake him, do you hear?'

The girl's step didn't falter.

'Eve?' Her forehead creasing into a frown, Lydia took a step towards her. 'I'm speaking to you.'

Still Eve said nothing, walking mutely on and closing her door behind her.

Scarcely able to believe her bare-faced insolence, Lydia stared after her. Her daughter was ignoring her quite blatantly. She couldn't do this. Hot tears of frustration and anger sprang to her eyes. She just *couldn't*.

She went to the phone in the hall. She would call David's mother, beg for help if she had to, because though the woman practically bristled with pride at how faultless her sons were, David simply wasn't. He was making her life a nightmare and Lydia couldn't cope any more. She needed some time away from him, away from the children, if she was going to hold onto her sanity.

Praying that the woman would pick up, willing herself to be strong and tell her how things were, she started when David came through the front door.

'Talking to anyone interesting?' he asked, squinting quizzically at her as she fumbled the phone back into its cradle and spun around to face him.

She hesitated. But then, knowing she had to try to make him understand how desperate she felt, she blurted it out. 'Your mother.'

A look of incredulity crossed his face.

'I need *help*, David.' Lydia forced herself on. She couldn't bear this any more. She felt unseen, unheard. She had to have a voice. A *life*. 'You're never here, and—'

'Because I'm at *work*.' He cut angrily across her.

'I know. I know you are, but...' She faltered in the face of his obvious anger. 'No one's listening to me, David. *You're* not listening to me. I can't cope!'

'And you think my mother is the person to talk to? To *help* you? A woman who's incapable of accepting anything less than perfection?'

'Yes. No.' Lydia grew flustered. 'I don't know. I—'

'The answer's *no*, Lydia!' David grated, slamming his hand so hard on the hall table that the ornaments jumped. 'You do *not* talk to my mother about our personal life. Not *ever*. Do you hear me?' His face was thunderous as he locked his gaze hard on hers. 'In fact, you don't bloody well talk at all unless *I* tell you to!'

Lydia recoiled, her stomach twisting in confusion and fear. 'David, s-stop,' she stammered, her throat closing. 'Please don't do this.' A sob escaping her, she stepped back as he continued to glare at her, a vein popping tellingly in his temple, his thick-lashed eyes so dark they were almost black.

'Can you not understand a basic instruction?' he seethed, moving toward her. 'I just told you not to—'

'Mum!' Eve shouted from the landing. 'Something's wrong with Jacob!'

FOUR

Something changed in David's eyes as Eve screamed again from the top of the stairs, 'Mum! You have to come *now*!' As if a switch had been flicked, fear flooded his features and he turned to the stairs, taking them two at a time.

Her heart in her mouth, Lydia flew after him, reaching the landing as he banged the nursery door open and stepped in, reappearing a second later.

'Where is he?' he asked Eve, who stood on the landing, tears streaming down her cheeks. 'Where *is* he?' he yelled when she didn't answer.

'*Your* room!' Eve choked out a sob. 'He's on the bed.'

'David.' Lydia followed him as he stormed towards the main bedroom. '*David!*' She bobbed behind him, trying to get past him as he bent over Jacob.

'He's not breathing,' he whispered hoarsely, sliding his big hands underneath him.

Lydia's heart stalled as he held Jacob clumsily to him. 'Put him down,' she murmured, fear gripping her stomach like a vice as she recalled how she'd left him.

'He's not *breathing*.' His face was filled with abject terror.

'David! Put him back down and get out of my way!' she screamed.

For the first time ever, he did as she asked. Pushing forcibly past him, she stooped over the little boy, lowered her face to his and felt for a breath. There was nothing. *Nothing.*

Oh dear God, what had she done? Her hands trembling, she tipped his head back, groped through her memory for what she knew she should do. *Please breathe*, she willed him as she blew gently into him. *Cry, Jacob! I won't be cross. For pity's sake, please cry!*

David stood back as her nurse's training kicked in, the training she'd given up to marry him, bear his children, run his business, appease him. Accepting that she knew what she was doing, he allowed her to try to resuscitate their son. Lydia worked diligently, prayed fervently. When Jacob took his first breath, she allowed herself to breathe in again.

Other than to mutter, 'Thank Christ,' David didn't speak as she eased Jacob from the bed, nestling him to her and carrying him to the landing.

She could hear voices downstairs in the hall and realised Eve must have called 999. One of the paramedics who'd arrived was talking to her. 'He's upstairs,' she heard Eve say tearfully. 'He wasn't moving, but my mum breathed into him and then he started crying. He's only two months old and I didn't know what to do.'

'You did the right thing calling us,' the man assured her.

'Absolutely the right thing. Well done,' a woman said behind him.

Lydia met them at the top of the stairs. She didn't want to part with Jacob. They would have to monitor him, assess him. They would blame her. They all would.

David didn't say much in the ambulance, other than to ask

her throatily whether she was all right. She was surprised he was concerned about her, that he actually didn't seem to be blaming her. Taken aback when he took hold of her hand. He did love his child, she realised. What might have been the cruellest of catastrophes had woken him to that fact.

Once in the hospital, she watched in fascination as he wept. She hadn't realised he was capable of that kind of emotion. 'I'm sorry,' he mumbled hoarsely. His eyes were those of a haunted man, his hand clutching hers so tightly as he watched the medical staff working urgently on their baby that Lydia winced. She could feel the fear emanating from him, fear for the little boy he'd spent so little time with. He breathed a sigh of palpable relief when the doctor turned to smile at them reassuringly.

'He's stable,' the man said. 'We'll be admitting him for observation and running some more tests, but for now he's doing fine.'

David wiped a hand across his eyes. 'Can we go to him?' he asked hopefully.

'Absolutely.' The doctor nodded them in Jacob's direction. 'We'll be moving him to the paediatric intensive care unit shortly. I'll leave you to spend some time with him. One of the nurses will alert you when we're ready for him.'

David looked uncertain and bewildered as he approached his son, more like the man Lydia had fallen in love with. She couldn't put her finger on when it had started to go wrong between them, when he'd started noticing all the things she apparently did wrong rather than all the nice things she tried to do for him. When he'd stopped seeing her as a human being. It had happened day by day, drip by drip, until she felt as if who she was had been washed away.

She watched a swallow slide down David's throat as he took Jacob's tiny hand in his own large one. She could see he was struggling. 'I do love you, Lydia,' he said, his voice thick with emotion. 'I'm just scared you'll end up going off with someone else.'

Lydia was speechless. He was like a different man. As she continued to watch him, she found herself praying for a way to make this softer side of him stay.

FIVE

PRESENT

Eve

Eve knew there was something wrong the second she opened her eyes. Scrambling from the bed, she hurried along the landing to the nursery. There were no gurgles from Kai's cot when she walked in, no excited flailing of little limbs as he reached excitedly for his musical mobile. The silence was profound, petrifying. Panic tightened like a hard fist inside her, and she flew to the cot, where she found him lying on his tummy, his little face turned towards her. He was perfectly still. No movement at all. 'Kai?' She placed a hand on his back.

A millisecond passed before her world shattered around her, each piece striking her heart like a knife. 'Kai!' She scooped him out, bringing him to her and pressing an ear to his mouth, searching desperately for the reassurance of soft breath on her cheek. *No!* She glanced at the ceiling, railing at a God she struggled to believe in. *Don't you dare!*

'Dom!' Fear crackling through her like ice, she screamed for him as she carried Kai to his changing mat, where she laid him carefully on his back. *Don't do this, baby. Please don't do this.* Praying with all of her being, she placed a trembling hand on his forehead, gently tilting his head then lifting his chin. *Wake up, Kai. Please wake up.* She gulped back a ragged sob and placed her mouth tightly over his nose and lips, breathing softly into him.

'Dom!' she shouted again as she eased back to place two fingers on Kai's tiny chest. *One. Two. Three.* She counted the compressions, her own heart thudding painfully with each one.

'Eve?' She heard Dom behind her, his voice wary. 'Jesus Christ, what's happened?'

'Call an ambulance!' she screamed.

'But—'

'He's not breathing!' *Fifteen. Sixteen. Seventeen. Breathe. Breathe. Breathe.* She prayed harder.

'Fuck!' Dom muttered, and she sensed him whirl around.

She kept her attention fixed on her baby. *Twenty-eight. Twenty-nine. Thirty.* She placed her mouth back over his, breathed softly, ignored her mother as she appeared like a bad omen beside her.

'Eve? What's wrong?' Lydia's voice was a terrified whisper.

One. Two. Three. Eve went back to her compressions, willed herself to keep calm.

'*Eve*, talk to me!' Lydia demanded her attention, that shrill edge to her voice Eve had heard so many times growing up.

She didn't answer, concentrating instead on the pressure she was applying to her baby's chest.

'What happened?' Lydia asked tremulously – and Eve wanted to scream, *Go away! For pity's sake, please just go away.*

'They'll be here soon.' Dom was behind her, his voice choked, his hand massaging her back, his focus on their baby. Eve could feel him willing him to breathe. *Please respond, Kai. Please.*

'Wait!' Dom said urgently. 'He moved. I'm sure he did.'

Eve snatched her gaze to Kai's face, and seeing the tiniest flutter of his eyelashes, relief crashed through every vein in her body.

'Thank God,' her mother murmured, stepping closer.

'No!' Eve's heart jolted as she noticed Kai's legs jerking upwards towards his tummy, indicating a seizure. Shoving her mother away, she lifted him, turning him gently onto his side, and then looked frantically around for something to support him. 'Dom, his blanket.' She gestured towards his cot. 'Roll it up.'

Dom moved swiftly, grabbing the blanket, rolling it and passing it to her. 'Okay?' he asked, his voice hoarse with palpable terror as she tucked the blanket tight to Kai's body.

Eve nodded and bent to kiss her baby's soft cheek. 'It'll be okay, Kai,' she whispered. 'Mummy's here, sweetheart.'

Lydia still hovered behind her. 'I don't understand,' she said, seemingly impervious to the fact that Eve didn't want her there. 'He seemed fine when I came in earlier.'

Eve snapped her gaze towards her, a combination of bewilderment and terror surging through her. 'You came into his room? In the middle of the night?'

'I needed the bathroom.' Lydia's eyes skittered down and back. 'I just wanted to check on him. I am his grandmother.'

Grandmother? She didn't have any right to that title. She didn't have the right to call herself a *mother*. Eve bit back the anger bubbling up inside her. 'I think you should go.'

Her mother didn't reply for a second. Then, 'Don't be like this, Eve,' she said, her tone now a mixture of hurt and confusion. 'I only want to be here for you. If you won't let me in, though, how—'

'You made my life a misery!' Tears spilled from Eve's eyes. 'You were *never* there for me!'

'I wanted to be,' Lydia protested sorrowfully.

Then why weren't you? Eve's blood thrummed. She wasn't going to discuss this. Absolutely *wasn't*. 'I want you to *leave*.' She grated the words out.

Lydia inhaled sharply. 'Why are you doing this?' she asked. 'Why won't you talk to—'

'I think that's enough, Lydia, don't you?' Dom intervened, his voice tight with anger. 'Eve doesn't need this. Kai's desperately *ill*, for Christ's sake.'

'But he was fine when I came in. I swear he was,' Lydia insisted feverishly. 'After what happened with Jacob, I would have noticed if—'

'Just *stop*!' Eve cried, her chest tightening. She hadn't told him about Jacob. She hadn't told him anything. It was all too unbearable.

'Jacob?' Dom looked between them, confused.

'Eve's younger brother,' Lydia went on, peeling the lid painfully back on Eve's past. 'I tried to tell them about the seizures, about his sleep apnoea and how sick he was. No one listened. Right up until the end, I tried to tell them.'

'He *died*?' Dom asked, aghast, and Eve felt her heart fold up inside her.

SIX

PRESENT

Chloe

Hurrying along the hospital corridor, Chloe stopped as she saw Dom sitting in the waiting area, his face ashen. The poor man looked dreadful. How in God's name had this all happened? She hadn't been able to believe her eyes when she'd seen Lydia climbing out of a taxi outside Eve's house yesterday. What was Eve thinking allowing her anywhere *near* her? Her mother had blighted her life, and now here she was wrapping her tentacles around her again. Chloe had to speak to Eve, make sure for everyone's sake that she had nothing to do with the woman. She also needed to alert Dom that to allow Lydia access to his family would place them in jeopardy, if it hadn't already. It might also have serious consequences for Chloe herself. She wasn't sure what she would tell him, but she had to try to warn him.

Watching him approach one of the doctors, she hung back a while, deciding to grab him once he'd finished talking to her. It would also be an opportunity for her to try to glean exactly what had happened. With Lydia here, it was her business too, after all.

'I'm afraid we don't have anything conclusive yet, Mr Howell,' she heard the doctor say. 'We're still waiting for his blood and urine tests to come back, but as I think you already know, his MRI and EEG were normal. We found no abnormalities on the structure of the brain or abnormal electrical activity. We'll probably repeat the MRI at around one year of age if the seizures continue.'

'Is that likely?' Dom asked. Chloe heard his voice catch and felt for him. He loved his son. You could see it in his eyes whenever he looked at him. Eve was overprotective of Kai, possessive sometimes, unsurprisingly. Chloe knew that Dom had noticed and clearly didn't understand why. Eve excluded him, perhaps without even realising she did. She'd certainly aimed to exclude Lydia from any contact with Kai, or with Dom, which was why this made no sense. Why, after all these years, would she invite the woman into her life and risk secrets coming out?

'I really can't say at this stage.' The doctor looked him over sympathetically. 'Some babies will continue to have seizures as they get older, but some will never have any more. It really depends on the type of seizures they have. We'll be doing a lumbar puncture to check for infection or metabolic and chemical disorders.'

'Right.' Dom sucked in a breath. He was devastated. Obviously out of his mind with worry. How worried would he be if he knew it might be history repeating itself?

'Don't worry, Mr Howell.' The young doctor, who Chloe imagined couldn't fail to be affected seeing such a handsome man close to tears, reached to place a hand on his arm. 'As I'm sure your wife will tell you, it doesn't hurt that much. The needle is more likely to make him cry than the procedure, and he's been a very brave little boy so far.'

She was trying to reassure him, but Chloe suspected he

wouldn't feel very reassured. He wouldn't want Kai to have to be a brave little boy. She felt her heart break for him, wished she could go to him and wrap her arms around him.

'Might it be inherited?' Dom asked, no doubt wondering about Eve's little brother. When Eve had called her earlier, she'd told her that Lydia had blurted it out. Why she would have done that, Chloe couldn't comprehend. It couldn't fail to have triggered all sorts of questions in Dom's mind. He'd already asked Chloe about Eve's past, seeking her out at a barbecue she'd organised when she'd been trying to maintain the facade and pretend everything in her marriage was fine. She'd been hoping that if she tried hard enough, it would be. It hadn't been. Steve wouldn't notice however hard she tried. He'd been too busy looking elsewhere. Dom wasn't like that. He was caring and attentive. Eve had landed on her feet when he'd made a beeline for her in the pub the first time they'd set eyes on him. It had been immensely peeving at the time. Chloe had wondered what Eve had that she hadn't, but she'd tried to get over it.

He'd been worried about Eve when he'd approached her at the barbecue. Apparently he'd tried to coax information about her childhood from her and she'd closed up like a clam, telling him she found it difficult to talk about. He'd said he wouldn't push her, but he was obviously upset, because it appeared she didn't trust him. He was upset now. With what had happened with Kai, he would want to know more, of course he would, which was why Lydia's presence was dangerous.

The doctor considered what he'd asked her. 'Assuming there's some family history, it is possible,' she answered. 'But the risks are very low. For now, I think our best course is to assess all the initial tests and record his EEG while administering vitamin B6. If he does have a B6 deficiency, then his seizures are very treatable.' She gave him a supportive smile. 'Try not to worry.'

Dom nodded tightly. *Easier said than done*, Chloe thought.

She stepped forward and called his name. 'Eve rang me,' she said as he glanced towards her, looking confused for a second, and utterly exhausted. 'I came as fast as I could. I had to wait for Steve to come home to watch the kids. He has a job he has to get back to, as usual. I'm sure he thinks the responsibility for the children is all... Sorry, you don't need to hear my problems.' Realising she was going on, as she always did around Dom, she stopped and searched his eyes. They were filled with such anguish she felt her breath stall. He was broken inside. Naturally he would be. 'How is he?' she asked.

'He's doing okay,' Dom said with a sharp intake of breath. 'Whether he actually is okay, we'll have to wait and see.' He glanced down, looking very close to tears.

'Oh Dom.' Chloe leaned in to give him the hug he obviously badly needed. 'I'm so sorry,' she said, squeezing him before easing away. 'You must be so worried.'

'I'm terrified.' Dom swallowed. 'I need to ask you something, Chloe,' he said, his gaze going towards the door behind him. 'About Eve, her family.'

Chloe braced herself. She'd guessed he would ask, but she didn't have her answers ready. She needed to speak to Eve first.

'Eve's brother,' he fixed his gaze on her, 'how did he die exactly?'

Chloe glanced down and back. 'I'm not sure Eve would want me sharing things about her past, Dom,' she answered guardedly. 'You should talk to her.'

He nodded, as if he'd expected she might say that, then kneaded his forehead. 'I have to know, Chloe. If what happened to him has some relevance to Kai's seizure, then...' He looked back at her, quiet desperation in his eyes. 'I can't get anything much from Eve. She told me her brother was sick, but even then she seemed reluctant, not meeting my gaze. We've barely had time to talk since. There's no one else I can turn to.'

Chloe agonised. She couldn't possibly tell him everything,

but she had to find a way to put him on his guard. 'She's my best friend, Dom,' she said, wanting him to realise that anything she did tell him was also with reluctance.

'I know.' He blew out a sigh. 'I understand. I'm asking you to break a confidence, compromising you, which I don't mean to do. It's just that I can't help thinking she's been keeping things from me around her brother's illness, and if there's even the slightest chance the same thing could happen to Kai...'

Chloe scanned his face cautiously. 'There isn't,' she said. 'What happened to Jacob couldn't possibly happen to Kai, I promise you.'

Dom narrowed his eyes. 'And you know this because...?'

Her eyes flicked towards the door. She really didn't want to talk to him behind Eve's back, but if she were to tell him at least part of what happened, it might ease his concern. In any case, Eve couldn't hope to keep him completely in the dark now. Chloe paused to wonder at that, the irony of Lydia turning up, this happening, which meant that Dom would be bound to be concerned about Kai and would insist on knowing more. Bracing herself, she took a breath. 'You're right, Eve is keeping things from you,' she said. 'If I tell you, though, you have to promise not to say it came from me.'

Dom nodded, his expression wary.

'What happened with Jacob,' she started, then faltered, her gaze shooting past him. 'What the bloody hell is *she* doing here?'

Dom glanced to where Lydia was coming along the corridor. 'She's staying with us.' He looked cautiously back at Chloe. 'She arrived yesterday.'

'I gathered that,' Chloe growled. 'But why?'

Dom frowned, clearly perturbed. 'There's been a family bereavement,' he said. 'Eve's paternal grandmother. She and Lydia talked on the phone and Lydia obviously decided to pay a visit.'

So they could share the grief of their loss? Reminisce

together about happier times? Chloe didn't think so. Lydia had an agenda, she could feel it in her bones.

'Well, I have no idea how Lydia managed to guilt Eve into talking to her at all when her particular form of torture was *not* to talk to her daughter,' she seethed. 'But if you want to keep your family safe, Dom, get that woman out of your house.'

SEVEN
PRESENT

Lydia

Lydia's step faltered as she realised it was Chloe in the hospital corridor. Seeing the look on her face, one of ill-disguised disdain, she stopped walking, panic unfurling inside her as she watched her lean closer to Dominic. What was she telling him? It was clear they were talking about her, but surely Chloe wouldn't discuss anything to do with Eve's past with him?

Her breath stalled as her mind hurtled back to the bleakest day of her life and the horror that would be ingrained on her memory forever. She was right there in the hall, looking up at her daughter at the top of the stairs, Jacob in her arms, his weight almost too much for a twelve-year-old girl to bear. 'Get out of my way,' Eve had hissed, her eyes desperate and hostile.

'Eve, go back,' Lydia had begged her, glancing frantically towards the lounge. The television was booming out the regular evening soap, a woman's voice screeching, a male voice bawling, fingernails scraping on the inside of her skull. David was in one of his dark moods. Nothing would shift it, Lydia knew. It couldn't end well.

Nausea swirled inside her as she watched her daughter take another defiant step down. 'Eve, you have to take him *back*,' she warned her, her gaze darting again to the lounge.

'You need to let her get by, Mrs Lockhart.' Chloe appeared behind Eve. 'She's coming to my house. She's bringing Jacob with her so we can look after him.'

'*You?*' Lydia had stared at her in disbelief. 'Don't be ridiculous. He's not well.' She clutched the stair rail and started determinedly upwards.

Eve descended another step. 'I *said*, get out of my way,' she growled, her face distorted with an anger Lydia had never seen before in her daughter.

'For goodness' sake, *stop* this, Eve.' Lydia continued to climb the stairs, and then froze, her blood turning to icicles in her veins as the lounge door crashed open, spewing a cacophony of noise into her head. Theme music, loud, mournful. Jacob crying, coarse, grating sobs. David bellowing, 'Lydia!'

'Lydia? Lydia, are you okay?' She snapped her eyes open, relief flooding through her as she realised the hand on her arm wasn't David's, but Dominic's. 'Are you okay?' he repeated. 'You look pale.' His eyes were kind, she noticed, concerned as they searched hers. There was no anger there, no reproachment or disdain, and she realised that Chloe hadn't told him. She couldn't imagine him looking at her with the slightest compassion if he knew all there was to know.

'I'm fine,' she assured him. 'Just a bit shaken.'

'You and me both.' Dominic massaged the back of his neck. He seemed tired, preoccupied, as he obviously would be.

'I came to see how Kai was,' she started, 'but—'

'He's okay,' Chloe cut in, striding across to stand next to Dominic. 'The doctor's with him. So is Eve. So now you know, you can just bugger off again, can't you?'

Lydia looked away. She didn't want to argue with Chloe. It wouldn't achieve anything. 'I don't intend to stay, Chloe, don't worry,' she assured her.

'Good. The exit's that way.' Chloe nodded back along the corridor.

Lydia buried a sigh. She shouldn't have come. Even with David gone, what was broken between her and Eve could never be fixed. She'd been too hard on her daughter. Her childhood had been cruel. There was no way to undo any of it. Ignoring Chloe, who had eventually become a barrier to any communication with her daughter, the person Eve would rather confide in, she turned to Dominic. 'Please give Eve my best wishes. She knows where I am if she needs me,' she added, smiling sadly and turning away.

'She doesn't *need* you. You were never bloody well there when she *did*,' Chloe threw after her. 'What is wrong with you? Why would you come here now, dragging Eve's miserable past along with you?'

Lydia's step faltered, but she didn't turn back. There was little point. It was too late to try to reach out to her daughter now. Eve would reject her advances, as she already had. She didn't want her here, anywhere near her or her family. Who could blame her?

'You're not welcome here, Lydia.' Chloe reiterated that fact. 'You destroyed your children's lives. Stay away from her.'

EIGHT

PRESENT

Eve

Eve looked up as Chloe came into Kai's room, her expression livid, Dom close behind, looking confused. After all that had happened, he would have questions. Questions Eve had no idea how she would answer. She glanced at Kai, who was sleeping softly, his small chest rising and falling.

'I just saw Lydia,' Chloe said, walking across to her.

Eve's gaze snapped back to her. 'She was here?'

'She was, unbelievably.' Chloe's expression softened as she looked down at Kai. 'How is he?'

'He seems fine.' Eve followed her gaze, her heart turning over as she relived the moment she'd first set eyes on him this morning. 'They're going to be running the tests I spoke to you about on the phone. All we can do for the moment is keep a close eye on him.'

Chloe nodded. 'What *is* Lydia doing here, Eve?'

Eve shrugged evasively. 'She just turned up.'

'What? Completely out of the blue?' Chloe looked sceptical.

Eve took a breath. 'We spoke on the phone,' she admitted. 'She rang to tell me my father's mother had died. Maybe I gave her the impression I wanted to see her. I suppose I hoped we might finally talk.' For all her denials, part of her *had* hoped they might. That, after years to reflect, Lydia might answer the questions Eve badly needed her to: *Why did you allow him to diminish you? Why did you then do that to me?* Most of all she wanted to know why Lydia's first instinct hadn't been to protect her children at any cost, as Eve's was to protect Kai.

She could feel Chloe's incredulous gaze on her as she reached to take hold of her baby boy's hand, marvelling at his small fingers, his tiny nails, how perfect he was.

'To a woman who used *not* talking to you as a tool to control you?' Chloe asked her, aghast. 'Are you mad?'

Eve winced inwardly. She knew her friend hadn't meant to be unkind. It had been Chloe who'd noticed the bruises from the many accidents she'd had, the cuts she'd told everyone were from a fall against the glass in the back door. Chloe, whose arms she'd cried in when her mother, rather than do what Eve had desperately wanted her to do and talk to her, had taken her to their GP. She'd been scared when he'd referred her to a psychiatrist, and had looked at her mother sitting next to her in the surgery, willing her to take her hand, to reassure her. Lydia hadn't so much as glanced in her direction. That had been the loneliest day of Eve's life.

'Possibly,' she answered with a sad smile.

'I'm sorry, Evie.' Clearly realising what she'd said, Chloe reached for her hand. 'I didn't mean...' She stopped as Dom approached, having hung back to give them a moment to talk.

'Why don't you two go and grab a coffee?' he suggested, sliding an arm around Eve. 'I'll stay with Kai. Don't worry, I'll call you straight away if there's any need to,' he promised, clearly noting her reluctant expression.

Sighing with a mixture of guilt and exhaustion, Eve leaned into him and nodded tiredly. She needed to show him that she trusted him. And she and Chloe did need to talk.

'We won't be long,' Chloe said, smiling at Dom as Eve broke away from him to hook an arm through hers.

Chloe made no secret of the fact that she liked Dom. She'd been there when Eve had first met him. He'd come across to their table at the pub while Chloe had nipped to the loo. He was visibly nervous, his mesmerising dark eyes flecked with uncertainty. Eve would never forget what he'd said. *You're going to think this is the corniest chat-up line ever, but I think you're beautiful.* Smiling hopefully, he'd passed her his phone number, telling her he would think he'd won the lottery if she called, and that was it. Chloe had returned from the loo, watching him with interest as he walked back to his friends. 'He's a bit gorgeous, isn't he?' she'd said, looking curiously at Eve. 'What did he want?'

'Me,' Eve had replied, slightly gobsmacked.

Chloe had definitely approved of him when Eve had introduced them properly over a meal at the local curry house weeks later. Eve recalled how she'd looked him over appreciatively. 'Well, he ticks all my boxes,' she'd said, arching her eyebrows. 'Dark, good-looking, caring, healthy.'

'Healthy, anyway.' Dom had laughed self-consciously. 'I'm not sure about the other attributes.'

'*And* modest.' Chloe feigned a swoon. 'I'd hang onto him if I were you, Evie. Men like him don't grow on trees, you know.'

Steve hadn't been pleased about Chloe being quite so gushing about Dom's qualities, Eve remembered. She'd been doing it on purpose, Eve had guessed, flirting a little to get Steve's attention. She'd felt for Steve, but couldn't really blame Chloe, who'd confided in her that he'd had an affair. She didn't

think he'd strayed since, but Chloe was obviously hurting and
wanted to hurt him in return. She still didn't trust him, but Eve
couldn't blame her for that either.

Once they were a little way down the corridor, Chloe
stopped and turned to her. 'I don't actually have time for a
coffee,' she said. 'Steve has a job he has to get back to, some old
woman who's going to be without her heating if he doesn't, so
he says. He wasn't thrilled about having to come back early. I
need to know what's going on, though.' She scanned Eve's face
worriedly. 'Why on earth didn't you send Lydia packing as soon
as she arrived?'

'She is my mother, Chloe,' Eve pointed out.

'Right,' Chloe said flatly. 'She obviously never got the job
description.'

'She arrived while I was at work. Dom let her in,' Eve
explained, well aware of why Chloe would be concerned. 'I
doubt I would have. It was a bad idea to let her stay. I should
have driven her back myself.'

'It was,' Chloe said bluntly. 'You should have nothing to do
with her, Eve. It's too risky.'

'She wouldn't do anything that might damage my life now.
Or yours,' Eve said, but she didn't sound confident.

'Are you sure about that?' Chloe asked, narrowing her eyes.
'Look, I don't know why she would turn up. Perhaps with her
mother-in-law dying she decided she needed to try to clear her
conscience. As far as I can see, though, the very fact that she's
here means she's trying to gain access to your life. And allowing
her that is dangerous, Eve. You know it is.'

Eve nodded. She understood what Chloe was getting at, but
her mother would know that to say any more than she already
had would be extremely unwise.

'She always said your father was manipulative,' Chloe
reminded her forcefully. 'But wasn't she equally as manipula-

tive? Look at what she did to you. She made you so miserable you were suicidal.'

'It wasn't all her fault.' Eve was surprised to find herself defending Lydia. 'My father was unpredictable, volatile. She was always having to tiptoe around him.'

'And *you* had to tiptoe around them both.' Chloe reminded her of that too.

'I know.' Eve sighed and fiddled nervously with her watch strap. It wasn't actually her parents who'd sent her spiralling into such a pit of despair she'd wondered whether she wanted to live any more. It was thinking that Chloe had deserted her, that she had no one in the world who would love or understand her. Chloe had been filled with remorse when she'd told her. She'd known how much Eve had needed her support.

'All I'm saying is that if she worms her way back into your life, she'll have control over you all over again,' Chloe pointed out in exasperation. 'Don't let her in, Eve. For your family's sake, as well as your sanity.'

Chloe didn't need to add that she was as desperate as Eve was to keep a lid on the past. There would be implications for her too if the secrets they'd kept came spilling out. The fact was, though, Lydia was already in. What *had* she been doing in Kai's room in the middle of the night? Cold foreboding prickled the length of Eve's spine as she recalled what her mother had said. That she'd gone in to check on him. Had she? Eve couldn't believe that she would have done any more than glance at him from the door. She needed to look at her video footage.

'Look, I have to go.' Chloe shrugged apologetically. 'I'll call you later.'

Feeling suddenly alone, as she had so often growing up, Eve wished she had told Dom everything at the outset. Shame had stopped her; of her history, her abnormal family. And now, how could she?

'I'm always there for you, Evie. You know that.' Chloe leaned to give her a hug.

As she eased back, Eve searched her friend's face. They'd made a pact to draw a line under the past, never to talk about it. To be there for each other and move on with their lives. 'I know.' She nodded. She did know. They'd had a bond since school. Another memory floated into her mind: her and Chloe sitting cross-legged at the foot of a gnarled oak tree in Chaddesley Woods, bees humming busily in the air, thin spring sun filtering through the branches. Chloe had gone first, slicing the craft blade across her finger, and then Eve. 'Together forever.' Chloe had pressed her bloodied finger to hers.

That was the promise they'd made each other. Later, that bond had been strengthened. They'd finished school together. Gone to university together, though Chloe had eventually decided she wasn't clever enough to study medicine and given up. They'd even liked the same boys, one in particular, which had almost broken the trust between them. Now they lived a short distance apart, Chloe having convinced Steve to purchase the property diagonally opposite Eve's, as Eve had suggested, so they could stay close. Eve was so glad she had. Sometimes the secrets felt so unbearably heavy, she struggled to carry them on her own.

'I'll be fine,' she assured her, mustering up a smile as she gave her friend a hard hug back. The smile slid from her face, though, when she turned around to find Dom a few feet behind her at the water cooler. How much had he overheard?

NINE

'The video monitor's working,' Dom said, meeting Eve on the landing as she came quietly out of their bedroom after settling Kai. They'd moved his cot in there. It hadn't been something they'd even had to discuss. Neither of them wanted to leave him on his own. 'It's pretty clear.'

'Thanks for doing that.' Eve smiled, hugely relieved. The live footage from the Wi-Fi app was good, but she hadn't realised she had to subscribe to the cloud to store the videos, or else purchase a camera with a memory card slot. That meant they had no footage of Lydia going into Kai's room to check on him. She wouldn't allow her mother in the house again, but still she didn't feel safe without eyes on her baby twenty-four hours a day.

'He's my son. You don't need to thank me,' Dom reminded her as she had a last glance over her shoulder before pulling the bedroom door partially to.

'No, I know. Sorry.' She headed towards the stairs. 'I'm glad that you care enough to do things without me badgering you, though.'

'Your father didn't, I take it?' Dom commented, following her down.

Eve's step faltered. 'No,' she answered cautiously. 'No, he didn't. Why do you ask?'

'I heard you and Chloe talking,' Dom admitted, as she led the way to the kitchen. 'Something about him being controlling.'

Eve's heart missed a beat and she worked to get her thoughts in order as she walked across to the monitor he'd placed on the worktop. 'He was,' she said simply, guessing he would want more.

'Yet Chloe thinks your mother is controlling too,' Dom added, his voice a mixture of confused and wary.

Eve felt him watching her as he waited for her to answer, and she looked for a distraction. 'Coffee?' she asked him, moving to the kettle.

He emitted a long sigh. 'No thanks. I could use something stronger, but I'm thinking that's not a good idea given the situation with Kai.'

'It's okay.' Eve smiled over her shoulder. 'I doubt I'll be able to sleep, so I'll be keeping an eye on him, don't worry. I've contacted Jenny Beecham from the surgery and she's agreed to take over my patients so I can have some extra leave. It's a shame, because there's a young girl whose communication skills are worrying for her age,' she hurried on, her heart pitter-pattering with nerves as she attempted to deflect the conversation away from her history. 'I was hoping to build a relationship with her mother, but if she comes in while I'm away, I'm sure Jenny will handle it.'

Dom was quiet for a second, then, 'Did you ever consider that your own communication skills might need some work?' he said, surprising her. Dom had never criticised her. Not ever. That was one of the reasons she felt so safe with him.

Spooning coffee shakily into a mug, she scrambled for something to say.

'What's going on with you and your mother?' he asked bluntly. 'I get that you two aren't close, that what happened with your brother drove some sort of wedge between you, but I need to know what it was.'

She clanged the spoon down and went back to the monitor.

'He's fine. You can see him moving,' Dom assured her. 'You need to talk to me, Eve. Why is Chloe insisting you should have nothing to do with Lydia?'

Eve had no idea what to say, how to even begin to explain, and nor did she want to.

'Talk to me, Eve.' Dom sighed again, exasperated. 'At least look at me.'

She turned reluctantly to face him. She'd hoped never to have to tell him the things she'd tried to forget. She'd worked hard to keep her past and her dysfunctional family from damaging her own little family, and now, because Lydia had resurfaced like some long-buried nightmare, it was all creeping back to haunt her.

Dom studied her, a long, searching look. 'I need to under-stand, Eve,' he implored her. 'What went on between you two that's so terrible you can't confide in me? Whatever it is, I wouldn't judge you. Surely you know me well enough to know I would never do that.'

Eve scanned his face. He looked exhausted, dark shadows under his eyes. He'd been working hard on the commission that would secure a well-paid position, meaning he could pull his weight financially, which she knew was important to him. He'd been distraught at what had happened to Kai, cried quiet tears of heart-rending fear as their little boy had been rushed to hospital. She had to try to allay some of the fears that would undoubtedly be running through his mind now. Swallowing back a sharp stone in her throat, she took a breath. 'Jacob had epilepsy,' she whispered, deciding to tell him only as much as he needed to know. 'Diagnosed at about six months. He was just two months old when he had his first seizure.'

'Shit.' Dom stared at her, clearly staggered. 'So there might be a chance that Kai has it too?'

'The risk is low,' Eve provided quickly. She reeled inwardly as her mind flashed back to the hospital ward she'd become so familiar with, and the last time Jacob had been admitted before God had taken him for an angel. That was what her mother had told her. She'd lied. She'd lied about everything.

'Is the hospital aware of this?' Dom asked, his face a mixture of shock and confusion as he moved instinctively to check the monitor.

'Yes,' Eve assured him. 'You weren't there when Dr Salama and I discussed it. I should have mentioned it, but with so much going on, it slipped my mind.'

Dom stayed where he was, his shoulders visibly tensing. 'Yes, you damn well *should* have mentioned it,' he grated, turning to glare at her – and Eve's heart missed a beat. She could feel the anger emanating from him. It was palpable, justifiable, but she'd never seen him like this. Never known him lose his temper.

He drew in a breath, massaged his forehead. 'What else haven't you told me, Eve?' he asked tersely.

She saw the disillusionment in his eyes as he looked at her, and her heart plummeted.

'Kai's my son,' he reminded her tightly again.

Knowing she had no choice, Eve nodded. He had a right to know everything that was pertinent. Kai had had a plethora of tests. Thank goodness his blood and urine tests and his EEG and MRI scans were normal. The doctor had told them what she already knew: that brain injuries causing seizures could be impossible to pinpoint, especially those associated with microscopic damage occurring during pregnancy. He'd been scheduled for regular follow-ups and prescribed vitamin B6, which was believed to help with the development of the brain. Now it was a case of time would tell. If there were no more seizures, it might indicate a vitamin B6 deficiency. Eve prayed that that was the conclusion they would reach.

'Jacob had sleep apnoea,' she said, her breath catching as another stark image assaulted her. She was right there, looking down at her little brother lying still and unmoving while her parents argued downstairs. She couldn't believe it at first. Knowing he was on their bed, she'd crept in because she was sure he would start crying when he heard raised voices, and then her father's anger would be so much worse. She'd tried everything to wake him, even pinching him, her childhood reasoning telling her that couldn't fail. He would cry then, scream probably, but at least she would know he was all right. He hadn't murmured. Just like Kai, he hadn't fluttered even an eyelash.

Her life had been pretty miserable up until that night, but she'd understood, as much as a nine-year-old could, that her mum had been tired after having a baby. Afterwards, though, following a brief reprieve when her dad's temper had improved, it had become unbearable. His good moods never stayed.

She watched Dom carefully, saw the myriad emotions that crossed his face as he processed her words. 'You mean he stopped breathing in his sleep on a regular basis?'

She answered with a small nod. 'He had asthma, too, but that wasn't picked up until months later,' she went on, glancing towards the window, where the rain trickled like teardrops down the glass, reminding her of all those tears she hadn't allowed herself to cry as a child. 'She blamed me,' she added tentatively.

'Who, Lydia?' Dom sounded incredulous. 'For what?'

Eve wavered. 'I'm not sure. For the fact that I existed, I think, which was pretty amazing when I spent most of my time trying to be invisible. Jacob needed a lot of care, and my father's mood swings made her life horrendous. She couldn't cope. I realise that now, but it still hurts.'

Dom didn't respond for an interminably long moment. Then, 'I see now why you don't have much to do with her. It really is a fractured relationship, isn't it?' he said, working visibly to contain his emotions.

'Very.' Eve glanced down and back.

Dom looked her over, as if assessing her. His forehead was still creased in confusion, but there was sympathy in his eyes as he walked across to her. 'You should have told me, Eve,' he said, taking her hand and running a thumb gently over her knuckles. 'I can see why it's difficult for you to talk about, but if there's anything else that might impact on our son's life, I need to know.'

She looked down at his hand holding hers, a strong hand, long fingers, clean fingernails. He *was* a good man. Dependable. She needed him now more than she'd ever imagined she could. 'There's nothing else,' she told him, guilt twisting inside her. She wanted to tell him everything, but she couldn't risk losing him.

TEN
1997

Lydia

Lydia sensed someone watching her as she nursed Jacob in the chair David had found at a second-hand shop, bringing it home as a surprise the day after Jacob had been discharged from the hospital. Looking up, she saw her husband standing hesitantly at the nursery door. 'I'm making some tea. Shall I bring you a cup up?' he asked – awkwardly, because he rarely offered to do anything that might be deemed remotely domestic.

'I'd love one, thank you.' She smiled in surprise, still unable to believe the change in him since Jacob had been taken ill. It was as if he'd realised what was important in his life. She hoped so. Prayed fervently it would last. She was still wary of riling him, but she no longer felt as if she were walking around on eggshells, frightened of doing or saying the wrong thing, of Jacob crying in the night and waking him, which was always a trigger for one of his dark moods. She was even toying with the idea of suggesting he make a doctor's appointment while he seemed approachable, subtly hinting that he might be depressed, that he might benefit from talking to someone, but she sensed that might be pushing her luck.

'He seems content,' he said, nodding at Jacob and walking across to her. He wasn't exactly smiling as he reached down and tentatively took hold of one of Jacob's hands, but he wasn't scowling, or worse, wearing that inscrutable expression he some-times did. Those were the times she knew that the fuse inside him might be about to blow.

She would speak to him about seeing the doctor, she decided, but not yet. Jacob did seem more content. Was it possible a miracle had occurred? That her life might even be less stressful on a daily basis? She wasn't holding her breath.

'It'll be ready in two minutes,' David said, gently extracting his hand from where Jacob's tiny fingers had been curled around one of his and heading back to the door.

Lydia got to her feet as he went out. It was a bit much to expect another miracle, but you never knew. Jacob's eyelids looked heavy as she carried him across to his cot to lay him care-fully down. Setting his soft toy mobile in motion, she backed away, praying silently as she did.

She braced herself on the landing. There was hardly a sound. No more than a contented gurgle. Scarcely able to believe it, she allowed herself to relax, and then, in urgent need of the loo, snatched a moment to go to the bathroom.

Creeping back to the nursery to find Jacob actually sleep-ing, she blinked in astonishment, checked to make sure she could see the steady rise and fall of his chest, then went to the main bedroom, where she could keep an ear out for him.

Walking towards the bed, she paused before the dressing table mirror and sighed at the sight of herself. With no time or energy, and little incentive, she'd made no effort with herself since having Jacob. She couldn't do much about the dark circles under her eyes and the excess weight, but she could at least apply a bit of make-up. After hitching her hair up, which she felt made her look slightly less haggard, she was halfway through a slick of lipstick when the phone rang. She froze, awaiting the inevitable distressed wailing that would normally accompany the sound. When none came, she dropped her lipstick and, her heart wedged in her throat, raced back to the nursery.

Jacob was still asleep. Needing to convince herself he was all right, she peered into the cot to check, and then, almost in a stupor, crept out again. Hearing David on the phone, she headed for the stairs, intending to fetch the tea rather than have him bring it up and disturb Jacob, then stopped and listened warily.

'She's doing fine,' she heard him say, that curt edge to his tone that she had learned indicated he didn't want to discuss whatever the subject was further. There was a pause, then, 'No, Lydia's decided that allowing Jacob to cry himself to sleep isn't a good idea. She's doing a good job of taking care of him,' he went on. 'You should try showing her a little more respect.'

Lydia was staggered. He could only have been talking to his mother. She watched in bemusement as he put the phone down without even saying goodbye. He'd stood up for her. Defended her, his wife, against his perfect mother, the woman who'd given birth to three children and 'never had any trouble with any of them'. He'd changed since Jacob had been taken ill. He really had.

She was about to go down and thank *him* for showing her some overdue respect when there was a racket from the kitchen. Eve and Chloe coming through the back door from the side entry, she realised, and making absolutely no effort to be quiet.

She started agitatedly down, and then stopped again,

flinching as David slammed his hand against the hall table. Her heart sank as he spat out a curse and banged through the door into the kitchen. God, that *girl*! Could Eve not at least try not to rile him? She was well aware of what the consequences could be if his mood shifted.

ELEVEN

1997

Eve

I'm not sure what's going on between my dad and my mum. They're actually being nice to each other. That is, my dad's being nice to my mum. He suggested we all go out together, which is something we rarely do. 'Go on. Go and play.' Wearing a smile that looks out of place on his face, he glances between me and Chloe as we sit at the table in the pub garden, and I'm glad Chloe's here with me. I begged my mum to let her come, and she relented eventually. 'I suppose it will keep you from under my feet,' she said, sighing and looking at Chloe in that way she does. I'm not sure she likes Chloe. She says I spend too much time with her, but I don't take any notice and Chloe says she doesn't care. Chloe's mum has to work hard running her recruitment agency, and we're both lonely on our own. I always feel safer when Chloe's with me at my house, like when my dad banged furiously into the kitchen earlier. I'd thought we must be in big trouble, but he just stopped in front of us and glared.

'Sorry,' I mumbled. I had no idea what I was supposed to have done, as we'd only just come through the back door, but from the furious look my mum was also giving me, I figured I must have done something.

My dad didn't answer, just kept on looking at me. His face was tight, like it sometimes is before he goes into one of his dark moods, and I didn't know what else to say, what to do. I hoped my mum might say something, but she didn't, and I was sure he was about to explode. My mum must have realised he might, because she tugged on his arm to make him look away. 'They're just overexcited, David,' she said. 'I'm sure they're going to make an effort to be a little more respectful now, aren't you, Eve?'

Seeing the warning look in her eyes, I knew I'd better make an extra-special effort to be good. I was scared of my dad, but truthfully, I was also scared of my mum, never knowing how she would be with me either, especially since Jacob was born. Chloe was holding my hand and she gave it a squeeze. She was scared as well. I could tell.

'She needs to act her age,' my dad said after a worrying pause.

'She is only nine,' my mum reminded him, frowning at me, and I scrambled through my brain trying again to work out what I'd done, what it was I kept doing that annoyed her so much.

My dad looked me up and down, and I'm not sure why, but I felt goosebumps pop up on my arms. It felt as if he was assessing me, like some of the girls do at school. 'Old enough to show some respect,' he said. He didn't look angry any more. He just looked like he didn't like me very much. It seems to me sometimes that neither of them do. I try to tell myself I don't care, but I do. I want them to like me.

'I'll be having sharp words with her, don't worry,' my mum assured him. 'Go on, Eve,' she said, her eyes sliding towards the kitchen door. 'Upstairs to your room, but don't let me hear any noise, do you hear?'

I nodded fast and skirted around them, still hanging onto Chloe's hand. I half expected my dad to start bellowing behind us, but he didn't. It was really weird. *This* is weird, too. I look from my dad to my mum, who's sipping the drink my dad bought her. Chloe's sucking her Coke through her straw, but I haven't touched mine yet. I'm wondering what the catch is.

'Go on, Eve.' My mum smiles – a smile that looks as out of place as my dad's does – and places her glass back on the table. 'There's a climbing frame over there. Why don't you go and play like your dad suggested?'

Do as he says, I guess she means. We're too old for the climbing frame, which is for little kids, but I suppose she's just trying to keep the peace. 'Okay.' I shrug, catch hold of Chloe's hand and get to my feet.

'We can make daisy chains and tell stories,' Chloe whispers as we walk away. I'm actually glad I don't have to sit there any longer, where I feel as if my dad is watching my every move.

'Don't you go flirting with any boys,' he calls after us, and Chloe and I swap embarrassed glances. We know what he's talking about, but we don't even like boys. Not the boys at school, anyway, who are as bad as the mean girls who are always poking fun at me.

'Don't be daft, David. She's far too young,' I hear my mum tell him, and I wish they'd just stop. All the tables are full and I'm sure everyone is looking at me.

'They're never too young,' my dad growls, and I feel my cheeks burning deep red, which I hate.

'Don't go too far, Eve,' my mum shouts.

Chloe rolls her eyes. 'Don't worry about it,' she says, giving me a reassuring smile and tugging me across to a sunny spot by the fence where my mum and dad can see us. There are lots of daisies growing there at least.

We've made the longest chain ever, while making up a story about a secret upside-down forest where all the animals are magical and there are no bullies allowed, when I notice my dad get up from the table. He's collecting glasses, going to get another drink, I guess. After a while, I notice a man who's passing the table stop to pick up Jacob's Peter Rabbit, which must have fallen from his pram. He hands it to my mum, who takes it and pushes it back in the pram. The man says something to Mum and then leans to look at Jacob, making a funny face at him. He seems quite friendly. I think he would be allowed in the forest.

My mum smiles at him as he straightens up. She looks nice today. She's wearing make-up and jeans with a white flowy top. I notice how she tucks her long hair behind her ears as she speaks to the man and I think it makes her look less cross, more carefree and pretty. I wish she could be like that all the time, even though I know that wishes don't come true. It doesn't stop me wishing, though.

My dad comes back from the pub after a minute. I see him stop as he walks towards the table, looking from my mum to the man and back again. The man looks up as he approaches, nods at him, looks again at Jacob and then walks away with a wave.

Watching the man go, my dad takes hold of my mum's arm and leans to say something close to her ear, and I start to feel the butterflies taking off in my tummy. He's looking at me now, his face tight. My eyes flick to my mum, and I can tell by her fearful expression that she's as scared as I am.

TWELVE
PRESENT

Eve

Eve was getting hot and flustered. It was Chloe's birthday, but she had been adamant she wouldn't leave Kai with the babysitter. She was a lovely, conscientious, caring girl who'd been recommended by Chloe and also one of the receptionists at the surgery. Kai had been fine with her the one time they had left him, but that had been before the hospital episode. Before Lydia. It had only been a week since then. It was too soon, Eve had told Dom, and he'd agreed he wasn't comfortable leaving him yet. She'd been relieved. She would have to leave him sometime, but for now, she felt she needed to keep a close eye on him. She was beginning to regret inviting Chloe and Steve here instead of going out for a meal, though. She was hopelessly behind with everything. Ah well, it wasn't the end of the world. Having two children herself, Chloe would understand.

Dom walked up behind her as she lifted the lid to peer at the one-pot chicken Provençal she'd opted to make, the idea being that it was easy. She hadn't bargained on having to season the chicken overnight and then fry it, and all the chopping involved, tomatoes, herbs, celery. She'd been tempted to throw the onions and garlic in whole. 'It's not too late to change your mind and go out for a drink with Chloe, you know,' Dom suggested as she replaced the lid and blew her sweat-saturated fringe from her forehead, her mind half on the pudding she'd taken out of the freezer too late and half on whether she actually had time to do anything with herself. 'Me and Steve can always have a beer from the fridge and watch some rugby.'

'Meaning you'd be nowhere near the baby monitor,' Eve pointed out. 'And what will you eat while you're watching the rugby?' She arched her eyebrows enquiringly.

'I think I can manage to follow the recipe and finish making dinner,' he said with a semi-amused smile.

She pressed a hand to his cheek. 'I don't doubt it,' she said, although she wasn't so sure. His attempt at a veggie bake for their last get-together had gone swimmingly until he'd realised he'd forgotten to actually put it in the oven. Still, she was grateful for his light-heartedness, which there'd been precious little of lately, and his support.

She'd tried not to let it show, but she'd been constantly on tenterhooks, with Lydia having rung the landline twice over the last few days. She'd told Dom they were sales calls, after hurriedly banging the phone down. Finally she'd rung her mother back on her mobile, telling her outright never to call her again. 'I just want to talk, Eve,' Lydia had started. 'I don't want to interfere in your life, but—'

'It's too *late*!' Eve had snapped over her. 'I don't *want* to talk to you. I don't want to *see* you. Why would I, for God's sake?'

Lydia had paused, then, 'You're a mother now, Eve,' she'd said, unbelievably. 'I know how difficult that can sometimes be, how lonely, and I just wanted to—'

'*What?*' Eve had laughed, now utterly incredulous. 'Impart

your pearls of wisdom on parenting? Unburden yourself? Bring up the past when you know I want no part of it?'

'I just want to help.' Lydia had sounded tearful, and Eve had felt angrier than she'd felt since she was that terrified twelve-year-old child on the stairs.

'You're a liar, Mother. You're trying to get close to my child. You know you are, and I will never allow it. I don't need you. Do you hear? Stay away from me. Stay away from my family. Digging up the past will do you a damn sight more harm than it could do me, trust me.'

With that, she'd hung up, prayed that that would be an end to it. The cold, creeping certainty inside her, though, told her it wasn't.

'Go and grab a shower,' Dom said as she turned to the fridge to grab the ingredients for the green salad. 'I'll see to this.' Relieving her of the lettuce, he slid an arm around her waist and gave her a squeeze. 'And don't worry, I'll keep an eye on the monitor while you're in there, I promise.'

Eve looked up at him. His rich brown eyes were filled with a mixture of concern and kindness. The man hadn't got a bad bone in his body. 'You're lovely, do you know that?' She pressed a soft kiss to his lips.

'So I'm told.' His mouth twitched into a smile. 'And charming and witty and good-looking and—'

'Now you're over-egging it.' She gave him a mock scowl.

'Well, maybe not that charming.' His smile widening, he drew her to him, kissing her softly, then cursed as the doorbell rang. 'They're early. I'll go. You slip upstairs while I dazzle them with my wit.'

Eve laughed, marvelling at how he always managed to make her do that, even when she felt like crying. 'Tell you what, you finish up our haute cuisine and I'll let them in. Chloe won't mind fixing her and Steve a drink while I make myself presentable.'

Determined to make it a nice evening despite feeling frazzled, she swung the front door open. 'Hey, birthday girl,' she said, pulling Chloe into a hug as she stepped in. 'I hope you've had lots of lovely surprises.'

'Oh, definitely. Steve's full of them, aren't you, Steve?' Easing away, Chloe shot him a glance that was nothing short of murderous as he shuffled in behind her, a bottle of wine in his hand and a weary expression on his face.

Perplexed, Eve looked at Chloe and was alarmed to see that her eyes were red-rimmed and watery. She'd tried to hide it with make-up, but it was obvious she'd been crying. From the whiff of alcohol Eve had got as she'd hugged her, she suspected she'd also already had one or two drinks. 'Chloe? What's wrong?' she asked anxiously.

'Nothing.' Chloe breathed in hard through her nostrils, snatched the wine from Steve and fixed a smile in place. 'We had a few words, that's all. Let's not spoil the evening because my husband's a prat. Where's Dom?'

Taken aback, Eve glanced at Steve, who shrugged disconsolately. She turned back to Chloe with a troubled frown. 'He's finishing the meal while I go upstairs for a quick freshen-up. I haven't had a chance yet.'

'I know that feeling well. With two children and a husband who's forgotten they're also his, I scarcely have time to pee.' Giving Steve another withering glare, Chloe headed on down the hall. 'Yours, on the other hand, is a gem,' she called back as she reached the kitchen door. 'Worth his weight in gold. Hold onto him, Eve. Don't let that bloody mother of yours poison his mind against you with her disgusting lies.'

For God's sake, be quiet, Eve pleaded silently. Hurrying into the kitchen behind Chloe, she met Dom's quizzical gaze and her heart dropped. He had obviously heard her.

'I'll pour us a drink,' Chloe said, waggling the wine bottle and heading straight for the cupboard where the glasses were kept, a slight weave to her walk as she went. 'You go on up and make yourself gorgeous. I'll give Dom a hand finishing up here, not that he doesn't look extremely competent, as always.'

Dom glanced at Eve, his brow knitted in consternation, then went across to where Chloe was extending an arm expectantly towards him. 'Evening,' he said drily as she pulled him into a neck-breaking embrace. 'I take it you've been celebrating?'

'Absolutely,' she said as he extracted himself, now looking slightly peeved. Eve guessed he would be. After all that had gone on recently, the last thing he would welcome was being in the middle of an argument between Chloe and Steve, something that seemed to be looming. 'On my own, unfortunately. Steve's been busy, haven't you, Steve?' Another loaded look in his direction as he stood awkwardly just inside the kitchen door. 'Would you like to share what you've been busy doing, *darling*?' Eve heard the acerbic edge to her tone, and her stomach knotted with trepidation. This wasn't going to go well.

Steve glanced apologetically towards Eve. 'Leave it, Chloe.' He sighed. 'Now's not the time. Eve's gone to a lot of trouble.'

'Would you like to know what my birthday surprise was?' Chloe went on anyway, to Steve's obvious dismay. 'It was a biggie. Huge.' She gave her husband another derogatory glance. 'But he's right. Now's not the time to share. Eve clearly has been working hard. And Dom, too.' She looked him over appreciatively as he reached to open the bottle of wine she'd been struggling to unscrew. 'You know what you are, don't you?' she asked him, threading an arm around him.

'Not a master chef, that's for sure.' He smiled awkwardly. 'Chicken's a bit on the well-done side.'

'Ah well, see, that doesn't matter.' Chloe waved a hand. 'Because you *try*. You're helpful and caring and attentive, good-looking, the whole package really. One in a million, I'd say. I told Eve to make sure she hung onto you the minute I saw you.'

'For Christ's sake, Chloe, pack it in, will you?' Steve muttered. 'You're embarrassing everyone.'

Chloe whirled around to gawk at him. 'Are you serious?' She laughed. 'If *anyone's* embarrassing anyone, it's—' She stopped as a wail from the baby monitor grabbed their attention.

'I'll go.' Eve, who'd been nervously watching proceedings, headed quickly for the hall. 'Won't be long,' she called back, nausea roiling her stomach as she flew up the stairs. Alcohol loosened tongues, and Chloe had consumed a fair amount of it. She was emotional, and clearly not thinking straight. What else might she say that would be bound to raise questions from Dom?

Her heart banged, nerves churning inside her, as she hurried into the nursery. 'It's okay, gorgeous boy.' Needing the reassurance of her son's small body close to hers, she picked him up and gathered him to her, breathing in the special smell of him as she pressed a soft kiss to his head. 'Mummy's here, sweetheart. Don't fret, little one.'

Immediately reassured, he gave her a beautiful gummy smile. As she laid him on his mat to change him, her heart swelled with pure primal love for him. She would kill to protect him. She would never let anything or anyone hurt him, not ever.

'There we go,' she said brightly once he was clean and dry. She would take him down, feed him while Dom served the food, she decided. That way she could keep an eye on things.

Picking him up, she headed back to the landing. She didn't bother freshening up, going straight back down instead. Steve gave her another apologetic glance as he seated himself at the far end of the table. She offered him a small smile back. She cared deeply for Chloe, but she couldn't help but feel for Steve, who looked as if he would rather be anywhere else right now.

Chloe came across, glass of wine in hand. 'Hello, little fellow. You really are gorgeous, aren't you?' Gazing down at Kai, she took hold of one of his hands and pressed her lips to it.

'Sorry,' she murmured, her eyes swimming with tears as she looked at Eve.

'It's okay.' Eve scanned her face, concerned. 'What's happened, Chloe?' she urged her.

'Talk later.' Chloe nodded to where Dom was busy at the cooker and, with some effort, mustered up a reassuring smile.

Once Kai was fed and safely by her side in his baby bouncer, Eve finally sat down at the table. The others picked at the pâté and baguette Dom had produced as a starter, but she had no appetite. The conversation was stilted, Chloe going from talking animatedly to hardly speaking at all while Dom tried to chat to Steve about the latest rugby news. Steve, although a keen rugby fan, didn't seem very enthusiastic, his eyes constantly travelling to Chloe.

Wishing the evening was over, Eve caught Dom's eye, smiling at him as he fetched the main course from the cooker and placed it on the table. Disconcertingly, he didn't smile back, breaking eye contact with her instead and turning his attention to their guests.

'Right, leg or breast?' he asked, lifting the lid from the pot and picking up the serving spoon.

'Breast for Steve,' Chloe said, shooting her husband yet another killer glance. 'He likes a bit of juicy breast, don't you, Steve?'

Breathing in hard, Steve pushed himself away from the table and stood up. 'I've had it with this,' he muttered with a despairing shake of his head. 'Sorry, guys. I think it might be a good idea if I leave.'

'Had it with what?' Chloe asked bitterly. 'Me calling you out for what you are, a cheat and a liar?'

'It was one photograph, Chloe,' he retaliated angrily. 'Taken ages ago. I'd forgotten it was on my phone, for Christ's sake. I made a mistake. One. I am *not* cheating on—'

'She *rang* you!' Chloe yelled over him, causing Kai to start.

'You complete *bastard*!'

'What?' Steve looked stunned. 'When?'

'It doesn't bloody matter when!' Tears springing to her eyes, Chloe shot to her feet. 'I'm sorry, Evie,' she mumbled, then turned and headed for the door.

'Chloe!' Eve jumped up to follow her and rushed into the hall, but Steve was faster. Eve watched from the open front door as he caught up with her halfway across the road. Chloe's progress was precarious on her high heels, and he put an arm around her to steady her. She attempted to shrug him off, but eventually, as she reeled dangerously to one side, he managed to get hold of her, supporting her and steering her towards their own house.

'Leave them,' Dom said from behind her. 'They'll need some space to sort things out.'

From what she'd heard, Eve didn't think things were sortable, but she guessed he was right. Poor Chloe. She'd obviously been in bits but had come tonight anyway rather than let them down. She would have to call her tomorrow. Chloe would need to talk, and Eve really needed to find out what on earth was going on.

Watching until she was sure her friend was safely at her front door, she went back inside to find Dom nestling Kai close to his shoulder.

'So, are you going to tell me what's going on?' he asked, searching her face questioningly.

Noting the deep suspicion bordering on disillusionment in his eyes, Eve knew he wasn't asking about the situation with Chloe. 'I thought it was pretty obvious,' she answered evasively.

'Not to me.' He held her gaze, his own unflinching. 'I'm talking about Lydia, as you know very well. I heard what Chloe said about her before she came into the kitchen. What disgusting lies might she tell me, Eve? If we're going to have a future together, I think you need to start being straight with me.'

THIRTEEN

Eve felt her heart sink. She had no idea what to say to him. 'It's history, Dom. I've moved on, closed a lid on it. Chloe had been drinking or she would never have brought it up. She knows I'm not comfortable talking about it to anyone.'

'I didn't think I was just anyone,' he replied, his eyes full of hurt.

She glanced away. 'I just can't talk about it, Dom. Not now,' she said, avoiding eye contact with him as she eased Kai from his arms.

'I guess that tells me all I need to know,' he said quietly as she started up the stairs. 'Clearly you don't feel able to confide in me. I suppose that's your prerogative,' he went on as she faltered. 'There's no law that says you have to share your past with the person you're married to, is there? After what happened with Kai, though, I'm struggling to understand. Why can't you bring yourself to trust me, even with my own child?'

Hearing the dejection in his voice, Eve felt her throat close. She glanced down from the landing, watching him as he dropped heavily to the foot of the stairs and buried his head in his hands, clearly upset and utterly frustrated.

Her heart aching for him, she carried Kai to the bedroom, hugging him close to her as she rocked him in the chair while singing softly to him. He loved 'Amazing Grace'. It seemed to soothe him more than any other lullaby. He would study her while she sang, his gaze as intent as his father's, until his eyelids grew heavy and sleep claimed him. She had no idea why she'd chosen the song. Out of the blue, she'd found herself singing it one night, her mother's voice drifting into her mind as she did. Dom had overheard her. He'd said he'd almost been moved to tears. He'd been close to tears just now.

He'd promised her he wouldn't pressurise her, but how could she expect him to keep that promise, knowing what he did now? He'd said he would always be there for her, but how could he be if she kept pushing him away?

Seeing Kai's eyelids flutter closed, she continued humming softly to him for a while, her chest swelling with unbearable sadness. It was clear that Dom didn't think they could have a future together without complete honesty. He was the only man she'd ever felt she could trust not to hurt her, not to humiliate or scare her. If she lost him because of all of this, she didn't think she could bear it.

Kissing her sweet, innocent boy's downy head, she carried him to his cot and laid him gently down, wiping away a tear that spilled down her cheek. She had to talk to Dom, tell him something to placate him. And then she had to end this, the uncertainty, the threat that she felt hung constantly over her. Somehow she had to find a way to bury her past once and for all.

Dimming the night light, she went quietly to the landing, pulling the door partially to behind her. Dom was sitting at the kitchen table when she went down. 'Has he gone off?' he asked, glancing in her direction.

Eve nodded and smiled tentatively. 'Out like a light,' she assured him. 'All the excitement probably.'

'It's definitely been an interesting night.' He couldn't keep the weary facetiousness from his voice. It was clear that he'd had enough. He was tired of trying to break through the walls she'd so carefully erected around herself. How could she blame him?

'I thought I might make us some hot chocolate,' she offered, hoping to deflect the conversation they would inevitably have to have. 'Do you fancy some?'

'No, thanks. I have a beer.' Getting to his feet, he nodded towards where it stood on the table; a fresh bottle, Eve noted, on top of the several he'd already had this evening.

She headed for the kettle. 'Thanks for clearing up,' she said.

Dom sighed heavily behind her. 'Why do you keep thanking me?' he asked. 'As if I shouldn't pull my weight around the house.'

Eve furrowed her brow, confused. 'I don't, do I?'

'All the time.' He picked up his beer and took a swig. 'You thanked me when I installed the baby monitor.'

'Did I?' She focused her attention on making the chocolate. She did thank him, possibly too often, but only because she was grateful that he took the initiative without having to be prompted. That he showed he cared. She didn't mean anything by it.

'Do you not realise that I need to know Kai's okay too?' he asked her.

'Of course I do,' Eve answered falteringly. 'I just—'

'That my heart almost gives out every time I imagine he might have stopped breathing? He's my *son*, Eve,' Dom went on forcefully. 'I love him more than my life. I never believed it was possible to love a child so much, so fiercely. I would die to keep him safe. You must realise that.'

He was angry. Eve glanced at him warily. 'I know you would,' she answered quietly.

'Do you?' Dom pressed. 'Do you know me at all, Eve?

Because if you did, it strikes me that you should know I would never judge you.'

Eve didn't answer. She wasn't sure how to.

'Do you love me?' he asked.

She felt her heart jar. 'You know I do.'

He fell silent for a second. Then, 'Why do you make such an effort to please me?' he went on, confounding her. 'You don't need to. In fact, it would please me more if you would just stop trying so hard.'

Eve eyed him in surprise. She hadn't realised that trying to please someone was a crime.

'It would certainly please me if you would allow me to help more with my son.' He got to the point. '*Do* you trust me, Eve?' he asked, and waited.

She swallowed. 'Of course I do,' she said, glancing away and back again.

Dom swirled his beer contemplatively around the bottle, then placed it down. 'So why won't you talk to me?'

Eve hesitated. 'About?' He'd been drinking. This wasn't a discussion they should be having tonight.

He shook his head in despair. 'Fine,' he said. 'You clearly *don't* trust me, do you?'

'Dom,' she walked towards him, 'I do. I just...' She stopped and pressed her fingers against her forehead. 'Can we not do this now? I'm so tired.'

'Me and you both,' he snapped, a mixture of frustration and anger in his eyes. 'I'm scared to death, Eve. I lie awake most of the night listening for the slightest sound from Kai. I feel sick to my gut when I remember my worst nightmare is *not* hearing the slightest sound.'

Eve felt her heart break for him. 'I know you do.'

'Do you?' He raked a hand through his hair. 'We don't talk, Eve. *You* don't talk to me. How do you think that makes me feel? Do you realise I keep playing what happened to Kai that morning over and over again? I can't get it out of my head.'

'I know.' She struggled for the right thing to say. 'Of course you would. You're bound to.'

'Do you know what sticks in my mind most?' He searched her eyes, his own curious, and something else – guarded. She'd never seen that look before. 'Your expression. You were terrified when you realised Lydia had been in Kai's room.'

Eve turned away. 'That's ridiculous. I was terrified for Kai. My attention was on him.'

'Terrified and furious.' Dom wouldn't let it drop. 'As if you blamed her.'

She busied herself washing up the few things that hadn't gone in the dishwasher. Anything but look at him.

'What went on that I don't know about?' he asked. 'You have to tell me.'

'I'm too tired for this now, Dom. I need to go to bed.' Her gaze averted, she turned from the sink to hurry past him to the door.

'Eve...' He sidestepped, preventing her from leaving. 'I need to *know*.' Agitation obvious in his voice, he reached for her arm.

And Eve's heart missed a beat. 'Let go of me,' she whispered, images from her childhood clicking graphically through her mind. Her father's huge hands curled into fists, slamming into surfaces, furniture, doors, tables. Fingers digging mercilessly into soft flesh. The accusations, the pitiful denials, the quiet sobs, she could hear them, echoes of her past; she was desperate to escape them. The unendurable silences that followed, that was the most abiding memory of all.

'Why can't you just talk to me?' Dom begged. 'For pity's sake, Eve, I—'

'Let go of me!' She tore her arm away from him and flew stumblingly from the room.

FOURTEEN

1997

Lydia

The girls were huddled together as they waited for David to fetch the car from the car park, colluding in that way they did. 'You should put a pillow over his face while he's sleeping,' she heard Chloe whisper. Her gaze, definitely murderous, travelled to the car as it approached, and Lydia felt a shudder run down her spine. Eve's gaze, as it swivelled from Chloe to the car and then to her, was petrified. Lydia guessed her daughter knew she'd heard. She chastised her with no more than a warning glance. She wasn't sure who was influencing who, but with her mind on David and what was going through his head, she couldn't worry about that now.

David was silent all the way home. His gaze fixed forward, wearing that inscrutable expression she'd seen before, which made her sick to the pit of her stomach, he drove without uttering a word. Eve and Chloe were as quiet as mice in the back, her daughter whispering goodbye to her friend as they dropped her off. Even Jacob didn't cry. Where once Lydia might have prayed that he wouldn't, this time she'd have welcomed the distraction, been grateful for an excuse to disappear straight up to the nursery with him once they arrived at the house.

Pulling up on the drive, still David didn't speak. Climbing out of the car, he strode straight to the front door, leaving her to lift Jacob's seat out and carry him in on her own. Eve tried to help, fetching the changing bag from the footwell. 'What's wrong, Mum?' she asked, eyeing her with trepidation as Lydia steeled herself to go inside.

'Nothing.' Lydia pushed through the front door and stepped warily into the hall. 'Go up to your room,' she instructed her, lowering Jacob's carrier carefully to the floor. 'And don't make any noise. Not a squeak, Eve, do you hear?'

Eve lingered for a second, studying her worriedly; then, seeing her father emerge from the lounge, she headed quickly for the stairs, glancing over the rail at David with a mutinous scowl on her face as she went. Lydia prayed David didn't see it, because there would be no way he wouldn't blow.

She smiled in his direction as he loitered in the hall. 'I'll just take Jacob up,' she said, trying to keep her tone light; to keep the peace, as if she could. 'And then I'll make us some tea while I get his feed ready.'

Still David said nothing. He didn't have to. His expression, as dark as thunder, said it all. Lydia lowered her gaze and crouched to unbuckle Jacob. He was whimpering, his small fists kneading his eyes, verging on waking. Holding him to her, she went quickly up after Eve.

Once in the nursery, she laid Jacob in his cot, then hummed 'Amazing Grace' softly to him, which seemed to soothe him. Wishing she could love him properly, talk to him naturally as a mother should be able to talk to her child, she stroked his cheek with the back of her hand, then headed quietly to the door. She was amazed he was actually still sleeping. She didn't suppose he would sleep for long, but with her nerves jangling, she was grateful for small mercies.

She hadn't realised David was on the landing until he spoke behind her, causing her to start. 'What were you doing, Lydia?' he asked, with no particular inflection in his voice.

Swallowing back the lump lodged like grit in her throat, she turned slowly around. 'Just putting Jacob down,' she answered cautiously.

He studied her for a long, silent moment. Then, 'Don't be deliberately obtuse,' he said quietly.

Lydia saw the flash of anger in his eyes and knew exactly what he was referring to. 'I was just saying thank you,' she murmured. 'Jacob's rabbit fell out of his pram and that man picked it up, so naturally I would thank him.'

David considered, his eyes narrowing as they travelled languorously over her. 'And smile at him.'

Lydia didn't respond. How did one say thank you without smiling? she wondered.

'Flirting,' he stated, as if it were a fact. 'That's what you were doing, Lydia.'

'No!' Nausea churned inside her. 'He was looking at Jacob. Talking about his own children. He has a daughter the same—'

'Making eyes at him. Flicking your fucking hair back! Do you think I'm *blind*? Stupid? Is that it?' His hand shot out like a viper's tongue, catching hold of her arm and dragging her towards the bathroom before she could blink.

'Open it,' he said, his fingers digging spitefully into her flesh as he shoved her towards the cabinet.

Lydia twisted to stare at him in bewilderment. What was he going to do?

'I said, *open* it!'

Her heart jolting, she did as he instructed.

'Scissors.' He nodded towards the pair she kept there.

Her stomach twisting in confusion and fear, she glanced at him again, saw the spark of fury in his eyes and, with trembling fingers, lifted them out.

He tightened his grip on her arm. 'Cut it,' he commanded, steering her to the sink.

Lydia froze.

'Are you deaf? I said *cut* it.' Moving swiftly, he grabbed her long, flowing hair with his free hand, yanking it tight and pulling it sideways.

Her stomach lurching, Lydia stared at herself in the mirror. Surely he couldn't mean it? She hadn't cut her hair since she was sixteen. He *wouldn't* do this. Her eyes travelled pleadingly back to his. There was nothing there but simmering anger. No care. No compassion. The switch had flicked and his dark mood had taken over, all-consuming, unforgiving of her imaginary sins. In that moment, she realised that this was her reality. That the reprieve had only been temporary and this was how it would be for the rest of her life with him. Deep, visceral anger swirled inside her. She wouldn't allow it. She would *not* cower and succumb to him. Not this time. A jolt of pure rage shooting through her, she lifted the scissors and plunged them hard into the back of the hand that held her.

He didn't even murmur. Lydia's blood turned to ice in her veins. Time stood still for an agonisingly long second. With no sound at all but the slow drip of the bath tap, it was as if the world had stopped turning.

And then he moved, swiftly, releasing her hair and gripping the back of her neck like a vice. 'Do it,' he hissed, his mouth so close she could feel his breath on her cheek. It reeked of the beer he'd swilled back at the pub. 'Do as I said, or I'll snap your scrawny little neck like a twig, understand?'

He jerked her painfully forwards when she didn't respond. 'Do you *understand*?'

'Yes!' Lydia squeezed the word from her throat. 'Yes,' she choked, bitter defeat compounding her shame.

Shaking all over, she reached to extract the scissors. He didn't wince. Didn't seem to feel it. The adrenaline rush he was getting from her humiliation had made him immune to it. She should have known. She'd fought before. She hadn't won then. She could never win. With nothing to call her own, he had her trapped like a moth in a bell jar.

Closing her eyes briefly, she lifted her ineffectual weapon, took hold of her hair and started cutting, jagged, coarse snips, until her shoulders and neck were bare, nothing but the hand he still held there.

She felt as if part of her had died inside as she looked down at her shorn locks filling the basin, her tears and his blood soaking into them.

He didn't speak, merely breathed deeply, and she dared to hope that his need to inflict cruelty had been satiated. 'Good,' he said after a contemplative second. 'Now hers.'

Eve? Shock coursing through her, Lydia met his eyes in the mirror. Dark eyes, cold and uncompromising.

FIFTEEN

1997

Eve

I froze as my dad's gaze met mine in the bathroom mirror. His eyes were dark pinpricks of pure hatred. He hadn't flinched when my mum had plunged the scissors into the back of his hand. They'd been sticking straight up in the air, rich red droplets of blood trickling down his arm to plop starkly onto the white rim of the sink, and it was as if he didn't even know they were there.

He held my gaze for a long, petrifying moment, and then he turned slowly back to my mum, who looked like a startled bird, her huge green eyes wide, like glassy marbles, her hair... gone, sitting in the sink, hanging over the side like curly copper snakes.

I knew before he spoke that he was coming for me. My stomach clenching painfully, I backed slowly away from the door. 'She's getting older,' he was saying to my mum. 'Moody and hormonal. Her figure's filling out. If she's anything like you, it won't be long before blokes come sniffing around and her belly's filling out too. Can't have that, Lydia.'

I retreated along the landing as they emerged from the bathroom, my dad shoving my mum ahead of him, his big hand tight around the back of her neck. I watched my mum wet her lips with her tongue, her eyes darting this way and that before landing on me. She was going to do it, I could see it in her expression. It was that same look she fixed me with whenever she told me not to make a noise, warning me what the consequences would be if I dared to disobey. I backed further away, but there was nowhere to run, nowhere to hide.

'David, wait!' my mum cried as they neared the nursery. 'Jacob,' she stammered, 'he doesn't sound right. He's wheezing.'

My dad's step faltered, and my heart boomed against my chest. I could feel my blood pumping and I was sure I was going to faint like I almost did once in school assembly. I watched as his gaze slid towards the nursery door. 'See to him,' he grated, steering my mum in that direction.

My mum flew through the door in an instant. 'He needs water!' she shouted. 'Fetch his water from the fridge, David. *Now.*'

Terrified, I watched for a second as my dad debated, then almost wilted with relief as he headed for the stairs, taking them two at a time. Squeezing my tears back, I turned quickly towards Jacob's room but found the door slammed in my face.

'Mum?' I whispered, pressing the palm of my hand against it and suppressing a sob. I wanted to go in. I wanted to tell her. I *had* to tell her before they cut off my hair that it wasn't me. I hadn't woken him. I *hadn't.*

Hearing my dad thundering back up the stairs, I tried desperately not to cry, not to breathe, taking my chance to flee as he pushed his way into the nursery. I was halfway down when I heard my mum screaming behind me, 'He's sick! We have to get him to the hospital!'

SIXTEEN

PRESENT

Eve

'Eve! I'm *sorry*,' Dom called after her as she flew to the lounge. Stopping in front of the window, she wrapped her arms around herself and tried to calm herself down.

'I'm so sorry, Eve,' he repeated, his voice anguished as he approached her. 'I had no right to grab hold of you like that. I was just trying to stop you walking away.' He paused, sighing heavily. 'I shouldn't have done that either. You clearly don't want to confide in me. I don't understand why, but I guess I'm going to have to try to accept it.'

Eve squeezed her arms tighter. If only he knew how much she did want to confide in him. She'd convinced herself she could cope, have a normal life, a family, a career, and up until now she had managed it. Perceived as calm and competent at work, which she had to be in order to do what she did, being the best wife and mother she could be at home, she'd achieved all she'd ever dreamed of. She'd only done that, though, by burying her past; pretending to herself that it didn't exist. Lydia had reminded her it *did* exist, that no matter how hard she tried to reinvent herself, she couldn't run away from it. And now it was catching up with her. She didn't feel as if she was coping any more. She felt as if her life was unravelling. Emotionally, she felt as if *she* was unravelling. Somehow she had to keep a grip on things before her world spiralled out of control.

'Why were you so scared just now, Eve?' he asked cautiously.

'I wasn't. I...' She faltered. 'You took me by surprise, that was all.'

'You were.' Dom didn't sound convinced. 'You were scared of me. I could see it in your eyes. You must know I would die before intentionally hurting you. I know I have, but I honestly didn't mean to. Please tell me how I can make this right. I don't want to lose you.'

He sounded so dejected, so bewildered, Eve felt her heart break for him. *Make me a different person*, she thought. *Someone who doesn't feel like a fraud. Someone you can love honestly.* The deep loneliness she'd felt as a child enveloped her at the thought of a life without him, the man who loved her, or at least this confident version of her. A man who'd been content with their relationship and felt no need to pry into her past. They'd been happy together. They would have stayed that way if it hadn't been for Lydia crashing into her world to tear down her walls.

She wished there was a way to avoid this, but wishes didn't come true, did they? She'd wished so hard as a child that she would wake up one day and things would be different. That her mother would look at her without admonishment in her eyes, that she would smile at her, talk to her when the house fell frighteningly silent. That she would have clean socks for school and just fit in. She never had. She had no choice but to tell him now, some of it at least, enough to explain her disproportionate reaction. He hadn't hurt her. She'd simply been reacting to the fact that he could have done if he'd chosen to.

Taking a tremulous breath, she steeled herself. 'My father,' she started, and stopped, wondering how she would explain the impact his behaviour had had on her life, her mother's life, the devastating consequences for Jacob.

'Was he violent?' Dom asked, his voice tight.

Eve supposed that depended on how you measured violence. She closed her eyes, her heart jarring as she recalled the incident that was scorched indelibly on her mind, when her father's anger had been worse than she could ever remember, his simmering fury, born of jealousy, spewing over. She caught her breath, seeing again his impassive face in the bathroom mirror, her mother's face, terrified, defeated, as she'd scrutinised the woman looking back at her, her hair hacked from her head as if by a child. Her determined expression as she'd come towards Eve wielding the scissors. Would she have gone through with it? Eve had thought she would. She'd felt the fear in her bones.

'Eve,' Dom urged her. 'Talk to me.'

She swallowed hard, feeling sick to her very soul. 'He was controlling,' she told him, finally. 'He controlled my mother. She controlled me.'

He looked at her, confused. 'Controlled how? *Why?*'

'She punished me with silence,' Eve answered, her voice dropping to a whisper. 'It was her way of making sure I was quiet. Looking back, I should have spoken out. There were people who would have listened.' There had been. Her teachers would have listened to her, talked to her. *I could have saved Jacob.* Her heart broke all over again, this time for the child who was too small and defenceless to save himself.

SEVENTEEN

She was frantically weaving locks of hair together, like Rapunzel desperate to escape her prison, but hers was Jacob's nursery and the hair wasn't attached to her head, and suddenly it was a daisy chain, and Eve knew it wouldn't take her weight. Still she lowered it, perching herself on the window ledge to climb down after it. She could make it. If she was really quiet, she would be invisible and she wouldn't weigh more than a feather. The butterflies fluttered frantically in her chest as she heard the stairs creaking, scissors snipping. She had to get away. But the daisy chain was breaking, the petals folding up and slipping back through the stems like cotton through a needle. The butterflies were turning to wasps, and they were crawling, crawling under her skin right up to her scalp. She had to go back, but she didn't want to. She couldn't...

'Eve,' someone whispered. '*Eve*.' The whisper grew louder, insistent, urgent.

'No!' Eve woke with a jolt, her heart thrashing as she felt a hand on her shoulder.

'Eve, it's me,' Dom said, leaning over her. 'Are you okay? You were dreaming.'

She blinked, disorientated for a second, before realising she was in Kai's nursery and not the place that had haunted her childhood dreams and haunted her still. Her gaze shooting in the direction of Kai's cot, which after much deliberation they'd decided to move back in here, she wrenched herself from the rocking chair she'd obviously fallen asleep in, about to go across to him, when Dom stopped her.

'He's fast asleep,' he assured her. 'Dreaming peacefully judging by the contented look on his face.' He looked her over, a concerned furrow forming in his brow. 'You've been here most of the night. I'm guessing you could use some coffee.'

Eve nodded gratefully and rolled her shoulders, attempting to ease the crick in her neck. Unable to sleep, she'd gone into the nursery around two o'clock, desperate to keep her baby safe from the threat she knew would always be there. She *had* to keep Lydia out of her life. Focus on being the best mother she could be, on her family and her job. These were the people who needed her. Chloe, too. She had to remind her friend she was there for her. They needed each other, to support each other, just as they always had.

Following her out of the nursery, Dom reached to gently massage her shoulders. 'Better?' he asked after a minute.

'Much.' Eve smiled. Trying to oust all thoughts of her mother from her mind, she turned to him, wanting him to know how much she needed him too, wanting him to know also that her trust issues weren't because of anything he'd done. Having suffered at the hands of the people who should have loved her and been there for her, she'd doubted him. She shouldn't have. 'I'm sorry...' she began.

'I'm sorry about...' Dom said at the same time. 'Great minds,' he added with a faint smile.

Eve noted the shadows under his eyes and felt for him. He looked as sleep-deprived as she was. 'I overreacted last night,' she said, wanting to put things right between them. 'Ghosts treading over my grave, I think.' Despite her attempts not to dwell on things she couldn't change, a cold chill prickled her skin as she pictured a grave that would never bear a headstone. A place that she'd never visited nor ever would.

Dom nodded, his eyes narrowed thoughtfully. 'You had every right to react the way you did. I shouldn't have been aggressive. That was unforgivable.'

'You weren't,' Eve said quickly. He'd been reactive, just as she had, but not aggressive. She'd never known him to be that. She doubted he was capable.

'I think I was.' Dom glanced awkwardly down and back. 'I care about you, Eve. I love you. Nothing will change that. I know you think my family are pretty perfect as families go, but I can assure you they're not. We have skeletons in our cupboards. Everyone does. Please don't think there's anything you can't tell me. We're married, for better or worse. There's nothing that could be that bad, is there?'

'No,' Eve answered cautiously. She didn't know his family well, but she doubted very much it could ever be as imperfect as hers, that his skeletons could be as terrible as hers.

'Please keep talking to me, Eve. I don't want us to drift apart.'

As his eyes searched hers, flecked with uncertainty, she leaned to kiss his cheek. 'I will,' she promised.

He held her close. 'I'll go get that coffee on,' he said.

Eve followed him to the stairs. 'Actually, do you mind if I leave mine for half an hour?' she asked.

Dom glanced curiously back at her.

'I thought I'd go and check on Chloe while Kai's still sleeping. I suspect she'll be in need of a shoulder.'

'More than likely.' Dom frowned thoughtfully. 'Take your time. I can't promise not to call you if Kai wakes up, though. I'll probably be in a complete panic wondering what to do with him.'

Noting the small smile curving his mouth, Eve shook her head. 'I'm sure you'll figure it out.' She gave him a smile back and headed for the main bedroom to pull on some clothes and then to the bathroom to quickly brush her teeth. She had to ease back a little and let Dom take the reins more often.

She did need to check on Chloe. She was concerned about her. She'd drunk too much yesterday. Obviously she had good reason, but she was acting erratically. Eve wanted to be there for her, but she also had to remind her that there were things Dom didn't know. Warn her that there might be dire consequences if he did.

EIGHTEEN

1997

Eve

I'm sitting in the hospital corridor while I wait for someone to come and tell me how Jacob is, listening to music on my Mini-Disc player. Chloe lent it to me, then she'd said I could keep it because she'd had a new one for Christmas. She can be really kind sometimes. I wish she wouldn't tease me, though, saying she's going to be best friends with Kirsty, the queen bee of the mean girls at school. When I'm close to crying, she puts her arms around me and says she was only joking, that she was just testing to see if I cared. I don't know why she does it. She knows how much it upsets me. I don't think I would want to wake up if I didn't have Chloe.

I see the shoes first as someone stops in front of me, shiny, polished men's shoes, and I know it's someone important. Slowly I look up to see the doctor who was in Jacob's room looking down at me. With my earphones in, I can't hear what he's saying, and the butterflies go frantic in my tummy. When I see him smile, though, I feel a huge wave of relief and I pluck my earphones out and pay attention.

'I hear you called the ambulance,' he says, and I nod uncertainly. I did. I knew it was urgent and that someone had to do it quickly, so while my mum and dad were upstairs, I grabbed the phone in the hall and dialled 999. I felt safer when the paramedics came the last time.

'I was scared,' I mumble, not sure if I should be talking to him. He doesn't look strange, he looks nice, but he is a man, so I suppose I shouldn't, especially after what happened to Mum.

'I imagine you were,' he says with another kind smile. 'You did the right thing, though. Well done, Eve.'

I feel my cheeks heat up. They always do when I'm embarrassed, but I also feel my chest swell with pride. No one ever says that to me, apart from Miss Grantham at school sometimes, and then I wish she wouldn't because the horrid girls always sneer and repeat it in soppy tones at playtime. *Well done, Evie. Well done, Evie.* They're like buzzing wasps in my head and I wish I could swat them.

'She did good, didn't she, Dr Kelman?' The nurse who was here last time, whose name is Liam, smiles, coming across from the desk. 'I'll have to watch her. She'll be after my job.'

I smile back. I can't help myself. Liam is chatty and nice. He looked after me last time, showing me the big computer behind the desk and then taking me on a tour and explaining to me about all the equipment and what it's used for. They're both nice, but I don't want my hair cut off for smiling at them, so I straighten my face pretty quickly.

'I'd better get on. Lots of patients to see,' Dr Kelman says. 'Well done again, Eve. You might well have saved your brother's life. Your parents should be proud of you.'

I drop my gaze as he walks away, a sinking feeling now inside me. I don't want Jacob to die.

Liam sits down next to me. He doesn't say anything straight

away. I think he knows I'm sad. 'So what do you want to do when you leave school, Eve?' he asks after a while, sounding as if he's actually interested. 'I bet you'd make a good nurse.'

I think about it. 'I'd like to be a doctor,' I say, making my mind up. I'm not sure why I want to be a doctor. Watching them helping Jacob, pressing his small chest and putting the oxygen mask on his face and the drip into his arm, and everyone being relieved when the doctor said Jacob was okay, made me wish I could do that, make miracles. My mum and dad were really relieved and grateful, my dad especially. He cried the first time it happened, because he felt guilty, I think. 'I'm not sure I can be, though.' I sigh, realising it's like wishing I could fly and that wishes don't come true. 'I'm not clever enough.'

Liam frowns thoughtfully. 'You were clever enough to know to call the ambulance. Don't be so down on yourself.' He gives my shoulders a quick squeeze, and I know my dad wouldn't like it after what he said to my mum, but I don't care. It makes me feel good. Feel good about me. 'I'll let you into a little secret, shall I?' he goes on. 'I didn't think I was clever enough to be a nurse, but then I just kept telling myself I was. You can be anything you want to be, Eve, if you believe in yourself and study hard enough.'

I search his face interestedly, wondering whether I really can. How, though? Where would I start? If we can't afford socks, I doubt we can afford books. The library, that would be the place to go. And Chloe has the internet. She can't use it too often because it's expensive, but she did say I could have a go sometimes. I can try. At least see if I can learn stuff.

'I noticed your mum has a new hairdo,' Liam says after a minute.

My eyes spring to his. Is he joking?

He's looking at me curiously. 'I cut my own hair once,' he says, reaching to fluff it up. 'Made a right mess of it.'

He rolls his eyes and I laugh. 'You have nice hair,' I tell him, and I'm not lying. It's spiky, with blonde streaks in it. It really suits him.

'Thanks.' Liam pats it bashfully. 'Takes me forever to do it. Your hair's lovely,' he adds, nodding towards it. 'So long and curly. I bet it took you ages to grow it.'

His gaze drifts past me. Noticing the scornful look in his eyes, I twist to see my dad coming towards us, and anger bubbles up inside me. I take a breath and make sure to look right at him. 'It did,' I say, feeling brave with Liam sitting beside me. 'I like my hair long. I'm never going to cut it. Not *ever*.'

NINETEEN
1997

Lydia

Once they'd pulled up on the drive, Lydia turned to unfasten Jacob's carrier. Eve was sitting on the other side of the carrier. Noting her daughter's wary expression as she studied the back of her father's head, Lydia guessed she was trying to gauge David's mood, wondering whether the storm had passed. Had it? David hadn't spoken much on the way back from the hospital. She'd noticed him adjusting his mirror to look at her. She hadn't been able to read his expression, but he'd softened while they were at the hospital, and just as she had before, Lydia had seen remorse and guilt in his eyes. How long would it last?

Stuffing her own remorse deep down inside her, she reached to take hold of one of Jacob's hands, feeling the smallness of it in her own. Her heart squeezed as she bent to look into his eyes and saw that, despite his tender age, he too seemed wary. Of her.

She started as David pulled open the door beside her. 'I'll

bring him,' he offered. 'You go on in and put the kettle on. I think we could all do with a cuppa.'

Lydia was astounded when he helped her out of the car. Standing on the drive, she hesitated, uncertain. She wasn't sure he actually knew how to lift the carrier out. He raised an eyebrow curiously, clearly wondering why she wasn't doing as he'd suggested. 'I need Jacob's bag,' she improvised, indicating where it sat in the footwell.

He nodded. 'Eve will bring it,' he said, leaning into the car. 'Grab the bag, Eve,' he instructed her. 'And then go on in and give your mother a hand. She'll be tired.'

Lydia stared at his back in bemusement, and then, her chest palpitating, turned towards the house. The dark mood had passed. Relief surged like a tidal wave through her. It wouldn't last, she knew it wouldn't, but for now, they were in calmer waters.

He was mopping the gravy up on his plate, congratulating her on a tasty meal, when she chose her moment to approach the subject.

'I've been meaning to make a doctor's appointment,' she said, collecting his plate and carrying it across to the sink.

'Oh yes?' David glanced at her, his expression mildly interested.

Rather than look at him, Lydia turned her attention to the apple pie she'd taken out of the oven. It was just a shop-bought one, but it was his favourite pudding. His mother had served it when she'd first met her, telling her that the best way to a man's heart was through his stomach. 'My boys do like their puddings,' she'd said with a fond smile at David, and Lydia had guessed she'd never be able to compete with 'Mother's home-made'. Still, she hoped David might appreciate that she'd made an effort. 'I thought he might be able to help with my weight problem,' she said, placing the pie on the cooling rack.

'Good idea.' David nodded, and Lydia supposed that even though she'd barely touched her dinner and her stomach was rumbling, she should forgo her slice of pie. 'I wondered whether it might be an idea for you to make an appointment too,' she said, attempting to keep her voice casual. 'I thought you could have a chat with him.'

There was a long pause behind her. Then, 'About?' David asked, a suspicious edge to his voice that sent out a warning signal.

Still she pushed on. If there was to be any hope of a future where she wasn't living in dread of his unpredictability, she had to make him see that he needed help. 'Well, I know you've been struggling with work pressures and a new baby in the house,' she said carefully. 'I thought the doctor might be able to give you some advice about relaxation techniques, or possibly prescribe something to help you sleep. The pills he gave me a while back are very good.' She left it there. What she really wanted was for the doctor to prescribe something for his mood swings, even refer him to a counsellor.

David stayed silent, and Lydia felt a familiar knot of tension tighten her stomach. She didn't dare look at him as she stirred the custard simmering on the hob, but she heard him push his chair back.

She jumped when he spoke directly behind her, his voice low and filled with such malice she felt the hairs rise icily over her skin. 'The trouble with you, Lydia,' he growled, 'is that you always have to spoil things by having an opinion on something you know nothing about.'

'It was just a suggestion,' she stammered, attempting to take a step sideways away from him.

He stopped her, slamming a hand down on the worktop. 'Shut up,' he seethed, close to her ear. 'Just keep quiet until I tell you to do otherwise. You don't speak to anyone. You don't even murmur, do you understand?'

'I was just trying to help.' Lydia heard the quaver in her voice and hated herself for it. 'I know you don't sleep well and I—'

'Least of all to that daughter of yours, who looks at me with nothing but scorn in her eyes.' David spoke over her. 'Just like her fucking mother!'

Lydia twisted to face him, confusion and fear churning inside her. 'I can't not talk to Eve,' she dared to argue with him. 'I have to communicate with her, David. I'm her mother, for goodness' sake.'

David studied her, his eyes dark pools of cold contempt. 'She needs to learn her place. Show some respect,' he said.

Lydia almost laughed; but for the fuse she could hear sizzling, she might have done. 'I need to get past.' She tore her eyes away from his. 'I have to see to Jacob.'

'You don't hear very well, do you?' David didn't move.

Lydia didn't have time to react before he snatched up the saucepan.

Ten minutes later, she lay on her bed, struggling to breathe past the excruciating pain in her chest. A slow tear sliding down her cheek, she lifted her hand to her shorn hair, which was still sticky with the custard that had scalded her scalp. He'd told her the custard was lumpy. That if she wasn't too stubborn to follow his mother's recipe, it wouldn't be. She laughed, a short, hysterical sound that turned into a sob. Any hope she might have had that he would seek help vanished as she replayed the vitriol-filled words he'd hurled after her as she'd fled, humiliated, from the kitchen. 'Do something with that hair,' he'd snarled. 'It looks a right fucking mess.'

She should never have said anything about him seeing the doctor. Desperation had driven her. Naïvely, she'd thought that while he was calmer, he might be more approachable, but she should have known better. He was succeeding, wasn't he? His latest attempt to reduce her to less than nothing was working. She was acquiescing to his desire to silence her. Fear gripped her afresh, fear of the unknown if she were to leave him. Fear of the known. She'd told herself he was depressed. That his mood swings were because he was overworked and worried about the business. That stress got the better of him. She'd always done that, lied to herself, made excuses, covered up the bruises. Stress didn't cause his mood swings. The fact was, he had no respect for her or for any woman.

Thinking his little boy was ill, though, he'd changed. In his obvious concern for him, he'd become human. It had been short-lived; the fuse had soon blown again. What could she do? She couldn't pretend Jacob was ill every time her husband's temper reached tipping point. She squeezed her eyes closed, prayed hard to God to help her, and then started as she heard a creak on the landing. Eve, she realised, hearing the tinny sound of music emerging from the MiniDisc player her daughter constantly listened to. Feigning sleep, Lydia hoped she would go away. She couldn't talk to her. To do so would invite the wrath of her husband, a man she didn't love any more but had no choice but to live with until she could find a way to escape. The danger was, she almost believed she did still love him when he was kind to her.

TWENTY

PRESENT

Chloe

Coming downstairs with a miserable three-year-old in her arms, leaving her son upstairs sulking because she'd told him off for tormenting his little sister, Chloe found Steve in the kitchen. He looked as dreadful as she felt. She recalled the horrendous argument they'd had after arriving home from Eve and Dom's and felt like bursting into tears all over again. The evening had been a disaster. Once the babysitter had left, they'd both drunk too much, while verbally slating each other. Steve had slept on the sofa, and she'd finally fallen into bed around 3 a.m. So much for her birthday celebration.

'I suppose you're going to rugby practice?' she asked, talking to Steve's back. It was Sunday. He was bound to be. Nothing kept him away from his rugby.

Steve emitted a heavy sigh. He didn't answer her, picking up his coffee instead and swigging it back.

Chloe felt her temper simmering. Was he really going to

just waltz off, leaving her and his children upset? How had this happened? How was it that she failed at everything she attempted, whereas Eve, who'd had no confidence whatsoever, succeeded at everything? Eve had sailed through her degree, secured a position as a GP. Landed the perfect man, who actually Chloe had had first dibs on. Yes, she'd been married, but suspecting that Steve had been cheating on her even then, she'd felt so lonely. Dom had been looking at her as she'd waited for Eve to arrive at the pub. He'd been interested in *her*. She recalled how his eyes had drifted to hers over his beer, how his mates had ribbed him because he kept missing bits of the conversation. He'd even smiled at her. And then in came Eve, no longer the scruffy, skinny little thing she once was, but groomed and immaculate in her work clothes, the shy ugly duckling turned into a beautiful swan. Dom had obviously chosen his moment to speak to her when, desperate for a pee, Chloe had finally risked a trip to the loo. And there they were when she came back, sitting at the table together, eyes locked. It was like something out of a crappy romantic movie, everyone else in the pub fading into the background. They were so mesmerised by each other they might as well have been bathed in soft light.

What had happened? Why did Chloe end up with all the shitty luck? What had she ever done that was so wrong? Right from day one, when Miss Grantham had asked for a volunteer to take the newcomer to the school under their wing and Chloe had put up her hand, she'd supported Eve. Admittedly, she'd wanted the praise Miss Grantham had heaped on her initially – with her parents both being more interested in their jobs than in her, she got precious little attention at home – and she had liked the fact that Eve had needed her and looked up to her. She didn't seem to be looking up to her now. She hadn't even bothered to make sure she got home all right last night, which Chloe would certainly have done if their positions had been reversed. The fact was, Eve hardly ever seemed to have time for her, and that hurt. Just like Chloe's parents had been, she was too busy with her job, too busy with her cosy little family to even go out for a drink with her any more. That wasn't fair when Chloe had stood by her, kept her secrets. She had no choice but to, of course, but still it hurt.

'So you are going then?' she asked Steve as he dumped his mug in the dishwasher and collected his keys from the island.

'I can't let my teammates down, Chloe,' he answered wearily.

'Oh no, we can't let our *mates* down, can we?' she retorted, lowering Rose to the floor. The little girl went immediately to lock her arms around Steve's leg. Chloe's heart wrenched for her. The children had been in bed when they'd got back last night, but once the row had kicked off, their raised voices had woken them, and they were both tired and fractious this morning. Chloe was absolutely fed up and heartbroken. She couldn't believe he was willing to throw his family away for the thrill of illicit sex with some cheap tart whose plumbing he'd serviced, satisfactorily obviously, since he'd clearly been servicing her ever since.

Steve shook his head. 'Which means what?' he asked.

'You know very well what.' Chloe went to retrieve her daughter, scooping her up and carrying her to the lounge. If he was doing this to them, he didn't deserve his little girl's love. He knew everything Chloe had been through. He'd been right there when, terrified, thinking her life was over before she'd even hit her teens, she'd ended up sobbing on his shoulder. Two years older than her and seeming much wiser, he'd helped her, Eve too, promised he would be there for her whenever she needed him. It had been several years before they became girl-friend and boyfriend rather than just casual friends, and he'd promised her again then that he would always support her. But once she'd borne his children, he'd obviously got bored of her. Some support, she thought bitterly.

Once Rose was settled in front of CBeebies, Chloe headed back to the kitchen, meeting Steve in the hall. 'Are you even *going* to the sports club?' she asked as he reached for his coat from the pegs. Clearly he couldn't wait to be gone. Would that *she* could just grab her coat and leave.

'For Christ's sake, Chloe.' Dragging a hand through his hair in frustration, he turned to face her. 'I've told you, it's history. I haven't seen Anna in ages.'

'Right. But you kept her photo on your phone for old times' sake, as one does.' Gulping back tears of humiliation and anger, Chloe eyeballed him furiously.

'I haven't *kept* her photo,' Steve denied again. 'I've got hundreds of photos on my phone. I just forgot to delete the bloody thing. How many times do I have to tell you?'

'So her calling you was purely coincidental?' Chloe enquired facetiously. 'A misdial, possibly?'

'I've no idea,' he said with a tight intake of breath. 'Probably.'

'And thinking it was you answering the call, she apologised for ringing you when she'd promised she wouldn't because...?'

He ran a hand over his face. 'I told her not to call me again when I ended it with her. Obviously I would have—'

'Ooh, I know.' Chloe cut across him, blinking in feigned delighted surprise. 'It was to tell you to wish me a happy birthday. How very thoughtful of her.'

'Oh for fu—' Steve banged the heel of his hand against his forehead. 'I've told you until I'm blue in the face, I have no *idea* why she rang!'

'Do pass on my thanks,' Chloe went on. 'You can call her when you leave. As in, permanently.'

'There is *nothing* going on between us,' Steve yelled. 'Why don't *you* call her if—'

'*Now*, Steve!'

'Christ, give me strength.' He sighed. 'Chloe, will you please just *listen* to me? Try to trust me a little.'

'Ha!' was her short retort.

'So after all the years we've been together, you're actually telling me to leave?' Steve asked eventually, his voice choked. 'As in give up my home? My kids?'

'You did that when you first shagged her,' Chloe replied angrily. 'Clearly you don't give a damn about your kids, or me. I gave you a second chance, stupidly. You blew it.'

'This is pointless,' he muttered. He turned to the door, then stopped. 'Do you want to know why I looked elsewhere, Chloe?' he asked, turning back. 'I mean really? I'll tell you, shall I? Assuming you're prepared to listen.'

Chloe folded her arms. She didn't respond.

'Because *you* couldn't take your eyes off your perfect bloody man!'

'*What?*' Chloe's heart jumped.

'Banging on about how wonderful he was and how he ticked all your boxes the first time you met him.'

'Dom?' Chloe laughed nervously.

'Yes, *Dom*, perfection personified, no less,' Steve confirmed, sounding hurt and humiliated. 'I mean, I could accept that you think more of Eve than you do of me, but to keep ramming it home how highly you rate her husband, shoving it down my throat at every opportunity...'

'That's ridiculous,' Chloe muttered, gulping back the lump of guilt rising in her chest. 'I can't believe you could be so immature.'

'And simpering up at him at every opportunity *isn't* being immature?' Steve countered angrily.

'I do no such—'

'"Yours, on the other hand, is a gem",' Steve cut in soppily. '"Worth his weight in gold. Helpful and caring and attentive,

good-looking",' he went on, counting off the things Chloe had
said, '"the whole package really",' he finished, now clearly
furious.

Chloe hesitated. 'I was upset,' she stammered. 'I—'

'I think we all gathered that.' His tone was unimpressed.
'The thing is, what is it you're upset *about*, Chloe? That your
mate landed the perfect bloke and you got stuck with the
wanker?' he asked with a mixture of disdain and defeat. 'That
being the wanker who was there for you, digging you and Eve
out of the shit you'd landed yourself in. Would *Dom* have done
that, do you think? He wouldn't want anything to tarnish his
glowing halo, after all, would he?'

'I *know* you were there for us. How could I ever forget?'
Chloe's voice quavered. 'And I don't think I got *stuck* with you.
I married you because I wanted to.' Unsure what to do, how to
stop this ball rolling now she'd pushed it, with God only knew
what repercussions, she moved towards him.

Steve raised a hand, stopping her. 'Tell me something,' he
said, eyeing her steadily. 'Were you desperate to move to this
house to be near Eve? Or was it Dom you wanted to be
close to?'

Chloe's heart dropped to the pit of her stomach. 'Now
you're really being ridiculous,' she snapped. 'You wanted to
move here too. If anything, you were keener than I was. Perhaps
you were desperate to be near Eve.' Raising her chin, she glared
at him.

'Right.' Steve laughed sardonically. 'So now I fancy every
woman I meet? You really don't rate me at all, do you?'

Chloe sucked in a breath, 'It's *you* who cheated, Steve, in
case you've forgotten.'

'As if you were ever going to let me,' he muttered. 'Do you
really wonder why, though, Chloe?' He studied her narrowly.
'Why I would have looked elsewhere for someone who wouldn't
score me off against another bloke? Note I said *would* have, as in

past tense. I did it. I admitted it. I regretted it. I've tried my hardest since to be everything you want in a man. It's obviously not good enough. Or rather, *I'm* not.'

Dragging his disillusioned gaze away, he turned back to the door. Then stopped. 'You aborted our baby, Chloe,' he said, his voice choked. 'You didn't even consider my feelings enough to tell me. You really couldn't have made it any clearer you don't want to be with me.'

'Steve, *wait.*' Chloe stepped after him as he yanked open the front door and walked out, leaving her reeling. She hadn't done it lightly. She'd been angry, thinking it was *him* who didn't want her. She hadn't done it to hurt him or get back at him either, as he seemed to think. She just didn't want another child tying her down. She already had two under five, for goodness' sake. She wanted a *life*.

TWENTY-ONE

PRESENT

Eve

Feeling like a voyeur, Eve stepped back as Steve emerged from the front door, his face thunderous. 'I just came to...' She trailed off, guessing it was obvious that she'd heard at least some of their argument. 'Is everything all right?' she asked, ridiculously, since it clearly wasn't.

'No, everything's very much *not* all right, but you probably gathered that,' he muttered, storming towards her.

Eve reached for his arm as he strode past. 'She doesn't know about...?'

He moved away from her, shaking his head, and relief swept through her.

'You might as well go in,' he said, running a hand despondently over his neck. 'No doubt Chloe needs you a damn sight more than she's ever needed me.'

'That's not true, Steve. She does need you. She always has.'

He glanced at her, an ironic smile crossing his face. 'Yeah, I suppose she does. You too. But not for the right reason, hey, Eve? I've been used, haven't I? My fault. I guessed it, but my stupid male pride wouldn't let me admit it.'

'Chloe hasn't used you.' Eve tried to placate him. 'She loves you. She wanted to be with you.'

'Right.' He studied her narrowly. 'Why didn't you tell me? That she'd come to see you about an abortion?'

Eve glanced quickly at the front door, then back to him. 'I couldn't. I wanted to, but patient confidentiality doesn't allow me to. You know that.'

He didn't look convinced. 'Anna works at the surgery, doesn't she?' he asked.

'The woman you were seeing?' she checked, though she knew who he was talking about. 'She does, yes. Why?'

He shrugged. 'I just wondered how it was she came to ring me when my marriage was falling apart. It seems odd, that's all.'

Guessing the insinuation, Eve hesitated before answering. 'If you're asking whether I've spoken to her about you, or Chloe for that matter, then the answer is no. I'm a doctor, Steve. As such, I'm very careful about divulging personal information about anyone, be they patients, friends or even just casual acquaintances. I have to be.' She paused as he processed her words. 'It's possible that she may have accessed information on Chloe's file. Would you like me to speak to her?'

'No.' Steve drew in a breath. 'I guess it doesn't matter much now anyway.' Insurmountable hurt in his eyes, he scanned her face, then dragged his gaze away and walked on.

Watching him go, Eve's heart wrenched for him, because as much as she would like to deny it, there was an element of truth in what he'd said about Chloe using him. What would he do now? His relationship with Chloe was clearly broken. Eve had realised that when Chloe had come to see her about the abortion, asking her not to mention anything to Steve. She'd thought then it might better if they went their separate ways. She'd been certain that he would never say anything about the events of their past, but now, seeing how crushed he was, she wasn't sure how he might react.

Deciding she would have to call him, tell him she would be there for him if he needed her to be, she turned back to the house to find Chloe emerging, last night's mascara streaked across her cheeks and still wearing her pyjamas. 'You needn't bother coming back for your stuff,' she yelled as Steve climbed into his car. 'You'll find your bags on the doorstep!'

In answer, he slammed the car door, gunned the engine and screeched away from the house.

'Bastard!' Chloe threw after him.

Eve's insides turned over as her friend burst into tears. Instinctively, she went to her, though her head was booming a warning. She hadn't been sure whether to stay or go when she'd realised they were arguing. In the end, she'd stayed and heard pretty much everything Steve had said. She was trying to dismiss it as a heat-of-the-moment accusation, but she couldn't block out an echo of their university days whispering in her ear: *Evie, please believe that I would never willingly hurt you. I love you.* In her rage back then, Eve had accused Chloe of being jealous. Chloe had sworn she wasn't, but had she been? Was she now? She really did seem to think Dom was the perfect husband, which must rankle given that her own husband had been unfaithful.

No. It was ridiculous, as Chloe had told Steve. But then hadn't what he'd accused her of been true? She *had* said all those things about Dom, right in front of Steve. It was quite obvious that she idolised him. But surely she wouldn't make it so obvious if she... Eve couldn't even finish the thought. Chloe didn't have designs on Dom. She would never do that to her. And neither would Dom.

'Come on, Chloe,' she said kindly, determined to ignore the

suspicion blooming inside her. 'Come back inside. You don't want to give the neighbours a poppy show.'

'I don't *care* about the neighbours,' Chloe sobbed as Eve steered her back into the house. 'I don't care about anything. I wish I was dead!'

Eve's heart jolted. 'Don't say that,' she said sternly. They both knew what death looked like. Chloe might feel there was no future now, but that wasn't what she really wanted. 'You have two children, for goodness' sake,' Eve reminded her, closing the front door and glancing up the stairs. 'Where are they?'

'Thomas is upstairs in his bedroom. Rose is in the lounge,' Chloe said miserably. 'I wish to God I'd asked my mum to have them for the night. They shouldn't have to hear any of this.'

She was obviously upset for them, as she would be, but Eve was sure this was all just knee-jerk stuff and that there was no basis in what Steve had said. Chloe was her best friend, and Dom was a good man. He would never do anything that might hurt her or Kai. *Is he too good to be true, though?* a little voice whispered. She dismissed it.

'They *have* heard it, though, Chloe,' she told her sympathetically but firmly. 'And now they'll need their mum to reassure them.'

Leading her to the kitchen, she sat her at the table, then went quickly to the lounge. Finding Rose watching TV, looking content if a little wary, she gave her an encouraging smile before nipping upstairs. Once she'd made sure Thomas was okay, she went back to Chloe.

Her friend looked awful. Pale and shaken, her newly high-lighted hair in complete disarray, which wasn't like Chloe at all. She always made such an effort with her hair and make-up, too much, Eve had thought sometimes. She was naturally extremely pretty and was obviously struggling with self-image. 'Are you going to be all right?' she asked, concerned for her.

Chloe wiped a hand under her nose. 'Fine,' she said, drawing in a shuddery breath. Eve attempted to place an arm around her, and was disconcerted when Chloe shrugged her off. 'It's just a continuation of the disaster that is my life. Sorry I ruined everything last night.'

'You didn't,' Eve tried to reassure her.

'I did, Eve. You know I did,' Chloe replied with a faint smile. 'Anyway, I apologise. I'll make it up to you.'

'There's nothing to make up,' Eve insisted as Chloe pulled herself to her feet and walked away, giving her the distinct impression she didn't want to talk to her. 'We'll organise another get-together soon and do things properly.'

Chloe shrugged. 'I should get on. I need to shower and get the kids' breakfast. Did you want something?'

Eve knitted her brow. 'I came to check on you. I was worried about you.' *More so now you appear to be giving me the brush-off,* she didn't add.

'Thanks.' Chloe kept her back to her. 'I'm fine, though, honestly, if a bit bedraggled.'

'Right. Well.' Eve wasn't sure what else to say. 'I'll get back then. Kai's due his feed soon and I left Dom putting coffee on.'

'Fresh, no doubt,' Chloe commented, an acerbic edge to her voice. 'You landed on your feet with him, Eve. Like I said, I'd hold onto him if I were you.'

'I intend to.' Eve watched as her friend headed for the kitchen door. 'Chloe, about Dom.'

She turned back, a cautious look in her eyes.

Eve took a breath. Should she mention that she'd overheard the argument, the things Steve had said? She decided against it. Chloe was clearly emotional. It would do no one any good to bring it up now. 'Do you think you could be more careful about what you say in front of him?' She opted to tackle the issue she needed to instead, precisely because Chloe was emotional and wouldn't be thinking straight. 'About Lydia, I mean. I haven't shared much with him, as you know, and after you left last night... Well, he's beginning to wonder, obviously.'

Chloe widened her eyes. 'You are joking, Eve?' she asked, her expression a combination of hurt and incredulity.

Realising she'd upset her even more, Eve felt bad. She hadn't meant to do that.

'I was devastated,' Chloe went on, now sounding angry. 'I'd been drinking, with good reason, as I think you know.'

'I know.' Eve faltered. 'I do know, Chloe. It's just, I'm concerned. Not only for myself, but for—'

'It's all right for you, with everything turning up roses in your life, Eve, but some of us are not quite that lucky.' Chloe almost glared at her. 'And you have been lucky, you know, sailing through your degree, landing a prime job as well as the perfect man. And now you come here finding fault with me when I've done nothing all my life but support you. Nothing *with* my life, in fact, because you needed that support and I put myself last.'

Eve was stunned. Where was this coming from? She could feel the hostility emanating from her friend, and it scared her. Chloe had never been like this with her before. And it seemed that she hadn't finished.

'And while we're on the subject of Dom,' she went on, 'since he *is* so bloody perfect, perhaps you should *share* with him.' She made quotation signs with her fingers. 'I mean, he's so supportive and sympathetic, he's bound to understand, isn't he?'

Eve was shaken to the core. Chloe was looking at her as if she hated her. 'Chloe, what's going on?' she asked, hurt and confused. 'Have I upset you in some way, because if I have, I have no idea how?'

Chloe tipped her head to one side. 'You really haven't a clue about how your life impacted on mine, do you?' she asked, scrutinising her through narrowed eyes. 'Even when we were in school, I always had to look out for you.'

'You did not,' Eve refuted, her chest constricting.

'But I did, Eve.' Chloe was vehement. 'I wanted to at first. I liked looking after you. But you became so clingy, so needy, I didn't dare not be there for you. I didn't want you constantly as my shadow, though. I wanted some space to breathe. But then after what happened with Jacob and your bloody father, I had no choice but to stay close. It's suffocating me, Eve. I'm not sure I can do this any more.'

Eve swallowed hard, her heart hammering frenziedly as her mind hurtled back to the school playground and the first time she'd felt betrayed by her best friend. She hadn't known what she'd done then either, but it had hurt so badly as she'd watched Chloe whispering with the cliquey girls. She been so confused, felt so uncertain and so very lonely. She'd lain in bed that night, the night of her own birthday, wishing she were dead. Chloe had been mortified when she'd told her how she'd felt, promised her she would never abandon her, but Eve had sworn no one would ever have that power over her again. And yet here she was, feeling as if her heart was being ripped slowly from inside her.

Why was Chloe being like this? Eve had been the best friend she could be in return for Chloe supposedly looking out for her. But in staying close to Eve, and to Steve too, come to that, Chloe had been looking out for herself. And *that* was the truth. Not this. This was all lies.

'You don't have any choice, though, do you, Chloe? Not if you want me to keep looking out for you too.'

TWENTY-TWO

1998

Eve

I can hear my mother and father talking as I creep out of my bedroom, muted voices drifting up from the kitchen. I guess they're talking about me and how difficult I'm being by simply existing. I'm certain the conversation won't be about making today the special day it should be. I wished really hard last night that I could go downstairs and find a banner and balloons on the front door, that my mother would smile and ask me how many friends I was inviting over for tea. My cheeks burn with humiliation as I recall how the mean girls cornered me in the school playground yesterday. 'Why haven't you invited us to your birthday party, Evie?' Kirsty asked. 'Is it because you don't want to be friends with us?'

I didn't answer, keeping my eyes fixed on my shoes instead, knowing that they were scuffed and two sizes too small, rubbing my feet when I walked. My socks had holes in and everything about me was scruffy, not perfect like her, with her rosy-red cheeks and bouncy blonde hair. She would never be my friend in a million years.

'Is it because you're poor?' she went on, her sharp blue eyes narrowed spitefully. 'Or is it because your mummy doesn't love you?'

I could feel my heart thudding against my chest as I held my breath, trying hard not to cry in front of her, squashing the memory of my mum lying on her bed the day before, pretending to be asleep, pretending I wasn't there. I did cry then, because she knew I was there and I realised she didn't love me; that my dad must hate me to look at me the way he did sometimes. How would cow-bag Kirsty know that, though?

'Why did you lie about having the Furby game, Evie?' she asked, making me wish the playground would open up and swallow me, because I had lied. I'd been caught out when she'd asked me the name of the home the Furbys had to get back to. It was the Furbyland cloud, but of course I didn't know that. 'You told us you had one, but you don't, do—' She stopped suddenly, a look of stunned surprise on her face as she was yanked backwards.

'She does have birthday parties, but bitches aren't invited,' Chloe growled in her ear. I'll never forget the look of fear on Kirsty's face as Chloe wound her curls tightly around her hand and tugged hard. 'Piss off,' she hissed, 'before I pull it out by its roots.'

Miss Grantham marching towards them sent Kirsty and her friends scurrying like the cowards they were, and Chloe wrapped an arm around me. 'Okay, Evie?' she asked, squeezing my shoulders.

'I'm okay,' I assured her, though I actually felt more like crying then.

'I'm sorry about cow-bag Kirsty,' Chloe said.

'Don't be. It's not your fault.' I shrugged and wiped a hand under my nose. 'It's not Jacob's fault either,' I made sure to add. 'He can't help being poorly.'

Seeing the tears roll down my cheeks, Chloe hugged me to her. 'I'm glad to have such a nice person as a friend,' she said. 'Take no notice of those horrible girls. They're just jealous. You might not have lots of toys and posh clothes, but you're much prettier than any of them.'

I knew I wasn't, though. Wouldn't my dad look at me kindly if I was? Chloe was just lying to make me feel better.

Overhearing, Miss Grantham smiled at Chloe, telling her what a kind friend she was. She said Chloe was quite right and that I was a pretty, intelligent young lady and I should hold my head high, but I didn't believe her either. 'I'm not pretty,' I mumbled once she'd gone. 'Not like you and Kirsty.'

'Yes you *are*,' Chloe insisted. 'Kirsty's ugly and she knows it. I hope she wakes up tomorrow with a face full of spots, which will make her even uglier, if that's possible.'

I wished worse. I wished she wouldn't wake up at all.

Arriving at Jacob's bedroom door, I pause to make sure my parents are still talking in the kitchen, meaning it's safe for me to go in. At least they don't argue quite so much now. My dad seems less angry whenever Jacob's ill. He was poorly again last week. Mum went into the nursery to check on him and I could tell by the way she screamed for my dad that something was wrong. His leg was swollen, too, where he'd developed an infection after an antibiotic injection for a chest infection. I listen carefully now whenever he's taken to the hospital. I even make notes, thinking they might be useful. I think I might like to be a doctor who looks after children, and Chloe thinks she would too, since she's been helping me look things up.

The swelling on Jacob's leg won't heal. Liam said he has an abscess and they can't understand why it won't get better.

They've put a drip in him now to make sure he's getting all the antibiotics he needs into his system. Jacob's very brave, though. He cries sometimes, but I manage to coax him to smile. His eyes light up when I tell him the story about the secret upside-down forest where all the animals are magical and there are no bad people allowed. I've promised I'll take him there one day when he's stronger. I know it doesn't exist, but I'm thinking maybe I could take him to the botanical gardens. We went there once on a school trip and it was really magical. Jacob and I could let our imaginations conjure up the animals. They're going to do an evaluation of Jacob soon. I'm not sure what that means, but I've reassured him I'll be there with him.

My dad will be there too, I suppose. I think he really does love Jacob, and I can't help feeling jealous. Chloe said it's because Jacob's a boy. My dad cried the first time he got poorly and told my mum he was sorry. I wasn't sure what he was sorry for – being so angry with her all the time, I guess. It's my mum who seems more angry now. With me anyhow. She doesn't shout much. She just goes silent and I can sense that she's cross even when she doesn't say a word. It's like a saucepan simmering on the cooker ready to spill over. That's worse than the shouting in a way. I keep trying to get things right, be considerate and helpful, keep out of the way when I'm told, but it doesn't seem to make much difference.

Sighing, I push Jacob's door open and tiptoe inside. His bedroom is bright and cheery, decorated with fluffy white clouds and star shapes, a great big Disney Dumbo mural covering the whole of one wall. It says *Dream Big Little One* underneath. I doubt whether Jacob does dream big. How can he when he's spent the first two years of his life in this little bed or a hospital bed?

I wish they'd let me make my room bright and cheery. My mum looked at me as if I'd gone mad when I asked her. 'Do you think I have the energy or the time to decorate? I don't have time to *breathe*, Eve. And where do you think the money would come from?' When I tried to convince her I could do it myself, she laughed and shook her head, as if I didn't know how to use a paintbrush. That hurt. I painted a whole wall at school. Miss Grantham was doing a Christmas frieze across the back wall of the hall. She said I could help her because I was good at painting. She even called me Santa's little helper. My mum didn't see it. Jacob wasn't well, so she didn't come to the school play. Miss Grantham said I should be proud of myself. I tried to be, but I wanted my mum to be proud of me more.

Squashing down my disappointment, which is like a heavy stone inside me, I tiptoe across the room to share my birthday news with my little brother. I don't want to upset him, though I always do, according to my mum, which is why she doesn't like me coming in here on my own. 'I'm ten years old today, Jacob,' I confide quietly. 'Chloe's going to bring me her old Tamagotchi because she has a new one. They're little virtual pets and you have to feed them and look after them, or else...'

Trailing off, I stop at his cot-sided bed, tip my head to one side and study him. He's still sleeping, propped up on his special pillow, the one that helps him to breathe, and I notice his head is lolling awkwardly to one side. Glancing back to the door, I debate for a second, then make my decision. 'Jacob?' I whisper, moving the feed to his drip to one side and gently rousing him. His eyelids flutter. He has really long lashes and I marvel at how pretty he is for a boy. 'Jacob?' I say again, and his wide brown eyes flutter open. 'It's only me,' I reassure him, sliding a hand under his head, easing his pillow from beneath him. He whimpers, and I feel a flutter of panic inside me. 'Nothing scary's going to happen, Jacob,' I promise, lying him flat for a second. 'I'm just going to fix your—'

The words freeze in my throat as the door bursts open. My tummy lurching, I whirl around to see Mum hurtling towards me. 'What are you *doing*?' she cries, her eyes full of accusation as she clutches my arm, pulling me away from the cot.

'I was s-s-straightening his pillow,' I stammer.

My dad has come in close behind her and he's glancing from me to my mum.

'You've lain him straight,' Mum snaps, causing Jacob to jerk out a cry. 'You'll close his airway. What in God's name is *wrong* with you? You stupid—'

'*Lydia*.' My father stops her. 'You'll upset him.' There's a warning in his voice, and I can hear the anger simmering.

Jacob is crying in earnest now. It's not a distressed cry, just bewildered, but still my mum fusses over him.

'He's all right,' I say quickly, desperate to make the anger go away, to put right what I've done wrong. I don't want her to not talk to me, not today. 'He looked really uncomfortable when I came in,' I hurry on. 'I was just trying to help him.'

My mother doesn't answer. Her back is towards me as she bends over Jacob, supporting his head with one hand, easing his pillow back under him with the other, and then making a big point of checking his drip and the needle in the back of his hand.

'Is he okay?' my dad asks.

'He seems to be.' She breathes in sharply, and for an awful second I think she might be about to cry. 'I'm doing my best, David, really I am, but it's so hard sometimes.' She presses a hand under her nose.

'I know,' he says gruffly, and walks across to place a hand on her shoulder. 'You're doing a good job, Lydia.'

My mum looks pleased at that.

'Do you need me to do anything?' my dad offers. I'm not sure why. I don't think he knows how to do anything that would help with Jacob, or around the house.

Mum shakes her head. 'No. I can manage,' she says bravely.

'Just get her out of here.' She doesn't turn around. Doesn't look at me. I wish she would. I wish that one of them would see me.

'Come on.' My dad extends an arm in my direction. He doesn't wrap it around my shoulders like I wish he would, but puts a hand on my back instead to push me towards the door, and I feel my own anger bubbling up. Why can't they thank me? Occasionally praise me?

Why can't they love me?

TWENTY-THREE

I get a panicky feeling in my tummy when my dad offers to drive me to school. I'm old enough to walk now, but remembering what he said on the day my mum's hair ended up in the bathroom sink, I decide not to tell him that, in case he thinks I might talk to boys on the way. Since he's never normally at home when I leave, he probably doesn't know I walk on my own. He probably doesn't know it's my birthday. Best to stay quiet, I decide, which isn't difficult. I'm used to being alone with just the thoughts in my head, and when he switches the car radio on, I guess he doesn't want to talk anyway. He doesn't often speak to me, talking to my mum about me in front of me instead, which makes me feel as invisible as I do when she goes silent on me. He doesn't look at me much either, or else looks at me with such dislike I think that whatever Chloe and Miss Grantham say, I must be really ugly.

As he pulls up outside the school, I reach for the door handle and wonder whether I should say goodbye. I know he'll probably say goodbye back, but he won't wish me a lovely day like some of the mums and dads wish their kids in the playground, and that will make me upset today because it's my birthday. I decide I should say it in the end, and I mumble thank you too as I push the door open.

'Make sure you apply yourself to your studies,' he says as I climb out. I'm surprised, as I didn't realise he knew I was studying hard, but I turn and nod. I'm not sure whether to smile, and decide against it. He won't smile back – I can't remember him ever smiling at me, except that one time at the pub, and look how that ended up.

Hurrying through the school gates, I hope none of the horrible girls will spot me. They usually do, though I try hard to blend in. I don't blend in, though. I know I don't. None of the other girls in my class secretly slip their socks off during assembly and turn them inside out so the dirty marks don't show. I don't suppose I'll ever fit in really. I'm just not like them.

Thankfully, no one calls out snidey remarks to me as I walk across the playground with my gaze fixed downwards to meet Chloe in our usual place behind the temporary terrapin class-room. I'm pondering why it's called a terrapin – it's not turtle-shaped – when I look up and notice that Chloe is in a huddle with Kirsty and her gang. I grind to a halt. My chest feels funny, like my heart is trying to burst out of it, and I'm not sure what to do – run for the cover of the terrapin and hide, or stay where I am for fear of drawing attention. My decision is made for me as Chloe glances over her shoulder, and I feel like I'm fixed like a sad clown in the spotlight.

Turning back to Kirsty, she quickly says something, then twirls around to run towards me. 'Hi. Happy birthday,' she shouts, waving as she approaches, acting as if everything is perfectly normal. But it isn't. It was Chloe who said we should just ignore them, so why is she talking to them? I feel confused and awkward and obvious, sure that everyone is looking at me as my face heats up. 'You're late. I wondered where you were.' She smiles and gives me a hug when she reaches me, just as she always does.

I don't hug her back. I want to, but I can feel the butterflies flapping manically in my tummy, and I know something's not right.

'Are you okay?' She pulls back, her forehead furrowing into a frown.

'Uh-huh.' I glance down and back. 'What were you doing talking to Kirsty?' I ask, searching her eyes, praying she won't lie, because I think I'll be able to tell if she does, and then, with no friends at all, I don't know what I will do.

She shrugs. 'We were just talking,' she says, looking uncomfortable. 'I was explaining about your brother.'

'You told them about Jacob?' I gawk at her, now truly disbelieving.

'Only that he had a bug. I didn't tell them the whole truth. I thought they'd be less horrible to you about your birthday party if they—'

'But I didn't want you to tell them *anything* about him. I *told* you.' My heart sinks. I don't want anyone to know about the way things are at home, about Jacob, about how my mum is with him, about how she is with me. They would use it to taunt me. I told Chloe this. She said she understood, so why has she been talking behind my back? I would never tell her secrets, not ever.

'I'm sorry. I was only trying to help.' There's a flash of annoyance in her eyes, but it soon passes. 'I actually don't think Jacob being poorly should be a secret, Evie,' she goes on with another short shrug. 'Especially after what you told me about your mum. I think you should tell on her.'

Now she looks upset, and I try to forgive her, to believe that she told Kirsty about Jacob to explain why my mum was too busy to organise a party, but I can't quite do it. I feel let down, betrayed by my best friend, more so when Kirsty blinks in pretend sympathy at me as we file out at playtime and says, 'How's your little brother, Evie? It must be so hard for your poor mum looking after a sickly baby all the time as well as a stupid daughter. Chloe's going to join our gang, by the way. Did she tell you? Just Chloe, not *you*.'

She has a horrible gloating look in her eyes as she links arms with her friends and skips away. I just stand there, feeling as stupid as Kirsty said I was. Chloe didn't tell them Jacob had a bug. It's obvious she said a lot more than that. She lied to me. I feel my stomach tighten painfully.

Thoughts whir like demented wasps in my head as I make my way home alone. We usually walk home together, but I didn't wait for Chloe today. I feel so badly let down and I hope she'll realise just how badly when she finds me gone, though I suppose she won't care if she's decided to stop being friends with me.

I don't want to go to school the next day, or the next. I can't bear the thought of sitting behind the terrapin all on my own. That's when I take the tablets out of my mum's bathroom cabinet. I know they make her sleep and that's what I want to do. Go to bed, dream about the upside-down forest where all the animals are magical and there are no bad people allowed, and never wake up again.

TWENTY-FOUR

PRESENT

Eve

'Have you spoken to Chloe yet?' Dom asked as Eve gulped back her coffee before she had to set off for work.

A knot of panic tightened inside her. The truth was, she'd been avoiding Chloe since their shocking conversation the day after her birthday. Chloe had texted a few times over the two weeks since, short messages asking if they could meet up for a chat, but Eve had avoided making a commitment. After the things Chloe had said, the things she'd overheard, she wasn't sure she could trust her any more, which was not only devastating but extremely worrying considering all that Chloe knew. Could she trust Steve? Recalling their conversation outside the house, it was obvious he was devastated too. He'd said he felt used. She could see why he would feel that way, but she had always valued his friendship. Been grateful that he had been there, more than he could know.

She shook her head in answer to Dom's question. 'She

wasn't in when I popped round yesterday,' she lied, playing for time while she tried to think what to do. She hadn't gone round yesterday. She'd also been vague about what had happened when she *had* seen her, telling him that Chloe was upset, that she and Steve had barely been talking, but no more than that. 'I sent her a text,' she said, avoiding eye contact with him as she climbed off her stool, 'but she hasn't got back to me yet.'

'She'll be in touch,' Dom assured her, yawning widely and helping himself to coffee from the jug. 'You two are inseparable.'

Because they'd no choice but to be since that day Eve had tried so hard to forget, as she had tried to forget other dark episodes in her life. What about before then, though? Had Chloe really felt she was a ball and chain around her ankle, that she was clingy and needy? See-sawing between anger and sympathy, Eve tried again to rationalise the hurtful things her friend had said. She'd been lashing out, hurting the person she was closest to. She would probably have regretted it as soon as Eve had left. Eve hoped so, because she had no idea what she would do if Chloe decided their friendship was over.

'I'll see to those,' Dom offered as she went across to the sink to swill Kai's bottles ready for the steriliser. 'You get off or you'll be late.'

Eve nodded and turned to him. 'You will call me if you need to, won't you?' she asked, trying to quieten the perpetual fluttering in her tummy at the thought of what Chloe would say when she did eventually meet with her.

'I'll call you,' Dom promised, reaching to still her hand as she twisted her watch around her wrist, a nervous habit she wasn't aware of until he had pointed it out. 'Now begone.' He smiled. 'I have some bonding to do with my son.'

He was joking, but Eve didn't miss the point. She needed to give him space. To trust him. Nodding again, she took a breath and smoothed down her jacket. 'Do I look okay?' she asked. She realised that she actually was being needy now, seeking reassurance, but she couldn't help it. Despite her together life – what *had* been a together life – her successful career, she suddenly felt like the child who didn't fit in again.

'Sensational. I'm liking the doctor thing you have going on,' Dom said with a mischievous wink.

Eve smiled, despite the heaviness in her chest. 'I'll ring you later,' she said, leaning to brush his lips with hers.

'Might be a good idea not to ring too often. I might be feeding or bathing Kai,' he reminded her. 'I don't want you to worry if I don't answer.'

'Oh, right.' Eve got it. He was asking her to back off. She was trying, but she couldn't shake off her growing sense of dread. 'I'll text you instead then,' she said. 'Just to check everything's okay,' she added quickly.

'And I promise to report back.' Dom smiled indulgently. 'Go on, go. He'll be fine.'

Eve went, though still somewhat reluctantly. *He* will *be fine*, she tried to reassure herself as she pulled off the drive.

She was right to be worried, she realised as she noted her mother's number flash up on her hands-free minutes later. The dread that had settled like ice in the pit of her stomach since Lydia had turned up at the house had only increased since she'd told her to stay away from her family. She'd known that she wouldn't. Lydia hadn't reappeared, causing her world to start teetering, only to fade quietly away again. She was back in her life, and she wouldn't rest until she'd achieved her aim: to *ruin* her life, as she'd imagined that her daughter had ruined hers.

As her mother called for a second time, she braced herself and put the call on speakerphone. 'What do you want?' she asked bluntly.

'Just to see how you are,' Lydia answered cautiously. 'I know things weren't easy for you growing up. There's no way to undo the past and put that right, but I do worry about you.'

Anger burning white hot inside her, Eve said nothing.

'One of your uncles brought me some things from your grandmother's house he thought I might like,' Lydia went on after a pause, during which she'd obviously gathered that Eve didn't intend to engage with her. 'I couldn't bring myself to go through them before now, with so many reminders of your father,' she added, sighing expansively.

Was she expecting sympathy? Eve baulked inwardly.

'There are some photographs of him when he was younger. He was a good-looking man.' Lydia sighed again, almost nostalgically. Eve could hardly believe it. 'I could send you some if you'd like?'

'Don't!' Eve choked the word out. Did she really think she would want them? Did she not realise that the images she had of him, would always have indelibly scorched on her mind, haunted her every single day of her life? Of course she did. How could she not?

'There are some baby clothes, too. I mentioned to your uncle that you'd become a mother and he thought you might be able to use them. They're all pristine, clearly expensive,' Lydia hurried on. 'I can't think why your grandmother wouldn't have let me have them for Jacob. She knew how tight things were for me. But then God forbid she should ever have done anything that might have made my life easier.'

Mention of Jacob hitting her like a thunderbolt, Eve clutched the steering wheel hard.

'I could bring them over if you'd like me to?' Lydia finally got to the crux of her call. 'Or we could perhaps meet up?' she suggested, her tone hopeful.

Unbelievable. What was wrong with her? Why would she imagine that Eve would dress her dear, sweet, innocent baby boy in her father's clothes? 'I don't *want* his fucking clothes!' she spat. 'I don't want to meet up with you. I don't want anything to do with you! Not *ever*! Stay *away* from me!'

'I just want us to talk, Eve,' Lydia said shakily. 'I thought you might need someone to confide in.'

'I don't!' Sweat wetting her forehead, nausea rising hotly inside her, Eve ended the call. She wasn't going to stop, was she? Was she insane? Suffering from early stage dementia? How could she consider for one second that Eve wanted any involvement with her whatsoever? Or was she just downright cruel?

TWENTY-FIVE
PRESENT

Chloe

Chloe had decided enough was enough. Who did Eve think she was, treating Dom as if he were incompetent of looking after his own child, Chloe herself as if she were suddenly indispensable? She'd been extracting herself from Chloe's life for a while, and now she appeared to have shut her out completely, claiming she was too busy with work and family to even go out for a coffee. As if Chloe *wasn't* busy? It was clear that Eve thought Chloe's job, working part-time at a call centre, whilst bringing up *two* children almost single-handedly, left her with bags of time on her hands. It was also clear where Chloe was on her priority list: rock bottom.

Eve obviously thought nothing about her feelings. Chloe still couldn't believe what she'd said when she'd gone to see her about terminating her pregnancy, a decision she'd agonised about. In the end, no matter how hard she tried to tell herself she would cope, she knew she wouldn't. Aware that Steve had been attracted elsewhere, she'd been struggling with two children. There was no way she'd felt able to bring up three. Eve had suggested that if things were that bad between them, maybe they should split up. 'You're emotionally overwrought,' she'd told her, as if Chloe didn't know that. 'You both are.' Was she concerned for her or for Steve? Chloe wondered now. Or was she more concerned for herself? Who knew what Steve might do, the secrets he might spill, after all, if he felt forced to stay in an unhappy marriage?

At first Chloe had regretted telling Eve some long-overdue home truths. She hadn't meant to hurt her feelings, which she obviously had. She couldn't take them back, but she had tried to reach out to her. Eve had snubbed her, despite the many times Chloe had been there for *her*. She'd saved her when things had come to a head with her obnoxious bully of a father, with no thought of the consequences for herself. But when she needed Eve, her so-called friend was nowhere to be seen.

With Steve cheating on her too, Chloe felt lonelier than she'd ever felt in her life. She and Steve had been together forever. They'd finally got together properly when she'd come back from university. That dreadful day with Eve's father had meant they had an inextricable bond anyway, but she'd wanted to be with him. He was her strength, someone she'd felt would support her. He'd wanted to be with her, at least up until recently. When had he grown tired of their marriage?

Was it because of the way she looked? She'd gained weight after her termination. That Eve hadn't seemed to put on a single pound while having Kai hadn't helped Chloe's confidence. She'd had a tweak or two, but still she couldn't seem to keep the interest of the man in her life. She breathed in deeply. Well, if Eve wanted to distance herself, so be it, but it would be Chloe who would do the dumping.

She nodded determinedly, went to her dressing table and selected a lipstick to paint on her smile. The sad fact was that sometimes you simply had to give up on people. Not because you didn't care, but because *they* didn't. Dom would realise it too, in time. She should go and see him while Eve was at work, offer him a shoulder. With everything that was going on – Lydia reappearing, Kai being taken suspiciously poorly – he would undoubtedly need one.

She smoothed down her flattering jeans and checked the mirror. Satisfied that she didn't look too bad, even if Steve didn't think so, she gathered her courage and went across the road to Eve's house.

Dom looked surprised as he pulled the front door open. 'To what do I owe the pleasure?' he asked, his eyes trailing curiously over her as he moved back to let her in.

Hearing the hint of sarcasm in his voice, Chloe tried not to mind. She had behaved pretty abysmally the last time she was here.

'Eve's not home,' he said, shutting the door. 'Did you need something?'

'Just a few words,' she said, following him to the kitchen.

'Problem?' He headed for the bottle warmer. Eve really should be counting her blessings where he was concerned, not shutting the poor man out. 'Kai's due his feed soon, but I can give you a minute.'

Very generous of you, I'm sure. Chloe couldn't help but feel miffed. Another person who apparently had no time for her, yet he devoted his whole life to Eve.

'I know I was a bit tipsy when we came over, but I meant what I said, you know.'

Dom arched an eyebrow in her direction.

'You're an absolute gem,' she went on, deciding it would do no harm to stroke his ego. 'I don't know how Eve would manage without you.'

Looking decidedly unimpressed by her flattery, Dom shook

his head. 'You were more than a bit tipsy, Chloe. You were pissed.'

'It was my birthday,' she said defensively.

'I suppose that's as good an excuse as any.' He smiled.

Scornfully, Chloe noticed, growing more peeved. 'I didn't make a fool of myself, did I?' Burying her annoyance, she arranged her face into an embarrassed smile.

Dom considered. 'You're drinking too much,' he answered bluntly, meaning he thought she had, which was infuriating. Who was he to make judgements about her? He might be good-looking and caring, but he was no saint. Nor was Eve. 'Eve was upset. And concerned about you, obviously,' he added. 'Again.'

Which meant what? Chloe definitely didn't like his tone now. 'We're best friends. We look out for each other,' she pointed out, back to defensive and not sure she should be. He knew nothing about their relationship, why they'd made a vow to always be there for each other. If he did, maybe *he* wouldn't be so defensive of Eve.

'Right.' Again Dom paused, frustratingly. She'd come here for sympathy, not criticism. 'But do you have to be in constant contact to prove your friendship?' he asked. 'It's just that in my opinion, a good friend is someone who's there if you need them but who also respects your boundaries.'

Chloe stared at him, flabbergasted. 'I'm *not* in constant contact,' she refuted. 'Only as often as Eve wants me to be.'

'Really?' Dom smiled wryly. 'It seems to me that you are.'

Chloe bristled. She'd thought he liked her. Now he was looking at her with pity and what seemed like outright dislike. 'What on earth is this all about, Dom?' she asked, feeling more upset than when she'd arrived, if that were possible.

Dom took a second. Then, 'Eve has a life, Chloe,' he pointed out, hurtfully. 'It would be nice if she could live it without you hanging off her shirt tails.'

Chloe felt her chest fill up. 'I see.' She swallowed. 'I, um... I should go.' Breathing deeply to stop the stupid tears falling, she whirled around.

'Chloe, wait.' He stopped her. 'I'm sorry,' he said with a heavy sigh. 'I'm concerned about Eve, that's all.'

'Obviously,' Chloe said flatly. 'Just so you know, I am too.' Taking another breath, she turned to face him. 'So where is she? Please don't tell me she's gone to see Lydia.' It wouldn't hurt, she decided, to plant a little doubt about his perfect wife, who he clearly thought could do no wrong.

'At the surgery.' He looked at her quizzically. 'It's a workday today.'

'Ah, of course.' Chloe nodded. 'I forgot, unsurprisingly, with so much going on in *my* life.' She thought she would make that point, since hers wasn't quite the bed of roses Eve's seemed to be.

Dom scrutinised her carefully. 'Do you think she might go and see Lydia then, despite everything?'

'Not if she's got any sense.' Chloe huffed. 'She should have nothing to do with her, considering how miserable the woman made her and everything that happened with Jacob.' *Careful*, she warned herself. She couldn't reveal too much.

Dom narrowed his eyes. 'What did happen, Chloe?' he asked. 'Exactly how did she make Eve's life miserable?'

Her expression one of reluctance, Chloe glanced away.

'You said at the hospital that Lydia destroyed her children's lives,' he reminded her. 'What did you mean?'

Chloe looked at him warily. 'I don't like talking behind her back, Dom.'

He drew a hand over his neck. 'No, I know. I respect that. I wouldn't ask, but with what happened to Kai...' He stopped, his look anguished. This was torturing him. Could Eve not see that?

Chloe hesitated. 'I understand, Dom, I do, really.' She stepped towards him. 'But to be honest, I don't really know everything, just what Eve told me: that her mother and father seemed to get along better whenever Jacob was ill. She said it never lasted and that her father would eventually go into one of his dark moods again, becoming aggressive and abusive, largely towards her mother, but you can imagine what the effect was on Eve. She used to creep around like a mouse in the end, try to make herself invisible.'

The last was a nice touch, she thought, indicating how much she herself had cared for Eve. And she had, despite what she'd said about her becoming clingy and needy; she had liked being with her, the bond they'd shared, the stories they'd told. She'd enjoyed their time at university together, until it had all gone horribly wrong. And now that Eve seemed to have outgrown her, she couldn't help but feel terribly hurt.

'And Jacob?' Dom asked, looking sick to his soul.

Chloe paused. 'He got worse,' she said, and dropped her gaze, hopefully communicating that she really didn't want to say any more.

'But what happened to him? I still don't...' Dom stopped as the baby monitor on the worktop alerted him to Kai beginning to fret. 'I need to check on him.' He nodded towards the kettle. 'Stay. Grab a coffee.' He left her in the kitchen and went quickly up the stairs.

Debating for a second, since he'd been so horrible when she'd first arrived, Chloe made up her mind and followed him.

He was picking Kai up when she approached the nursery door. The baby quietened immediately. Dom really was a natural with him. Eve must be mad to keep shutting him out in the way she did.

'Hey, little man, what's up? Missing me already?' he asked, nestling Kai in his arms and smiling down at him. It really was a heart-warming scene, this undeniably handsome man looking so lovingly down at his small child.

Chloe drank it in, feeling a familiar little flip in the pit of her tummy. 'Need any help?' she asked, stepping into the room.

'No. I think Kai's got me nicely trained,' Dom assured her, his gaze still on his son.

Chloe sighed longingly. 'He's a lucky boy. I wish Steve had been half as affectionate with our children when they were little. Or now, for that matter.'

Dom glanced at her, a flicker of concern at last in his eyes. 'Are things still no better between you two then?'

'Not really,' she said as he carried Kai across to his bouncer and strapped him in. Straightening up, he looked back at her.

Chloe dropped her gaze, pulling in a shuddery breath and wiping quickly at her cheeks.

'Christ,' Dom uttered. 'Are things really that bad?'

'Worse.' She emitted a sob as he walked across to her. 'He's been so awful to me.'

'Awful how?' Anger in his voice, Dom hesitated, then circled an arm around her.

He was concerned for her. She'd known he would be. That he hadn't meant the dreadful things he'd said to her downstairs. Tears streaming down her cheeks, she lifted her face to him. 'I'd rather not talk about it,' she whispered, and pressed herself closer.

Dom searched her eyes for an excruciatingly long moment, hesitancy and agony in his own, then breathed in sharply. 'I can't do this, Chloe,' he said, his voice hoarse with longing and regret. 'I just can't.'

And Chloe felt another stab of rejection. 'But *why*? Eve will never find out,' she murmured, pressing herself still closer. 'You know I would never do that to her.'

TWENTY-SIX

PRESENT

Eve

Noting the panic in Jasmine's eyes as the little girl's gaze flicked to her mother, Eve's heart ached for her. She felt a surge of relief as the mother smiled at her, albeit stiffly at the prospect of a referral to a healthcare professional, and then reached to give her hand a squeeze. Jasmine's relief was palpable.

'Don't worry, Jasmine, the lady you're going to see is lovely,' Eve assured her, making a quick note on her file and then lacing her hands on the desk and making sure to hold eye contact. Children could sense a lie a mile away, if only adults knew it. Recalling the conversation she'd had with Lydia on the way in, she quashed her anger. Her patients needed her to be fully engaged. 'Her name is Lucy,' she went on, 'and she's really easy to talk to. If there's anything you're not ready to talk about, that's all right too. You can say as much as you want to and go at your own pace, okay?'

Jasmine nodded, a small smile twitching at her mouth,

which Eve considered huge progress. The girl had been as timid as a mouse on her previous visits. Eve had empathised. It could have been her sitting there, too terrified to speak.

She turned to the mum with a reassuring smile. 'I'll get Lucy to contact the surgery as we agreed.' The woman hadn't wanted a letter sent to the house. Eve had guessed it was because she didn't want her husband to open it. 'Ring us here any time meanwhile if you need to. We can always squeeze you in.' It would actually be a struggle, with their horrendous back-log, but Eve was determined not to let Jasmine down. Jenny would take some of the load if she needed her to, she was sure.

'Thanks.' The woman's look was a mixture of wary and grateful.

'No problem.' Eve smiled, and prayed that now she had taken the first difficult step, she would gain enough confidence to find a way out of the nightmare she might be trapped in.

Waiting until the door had closed, she reached for her phone and checked it, smiling as she looked at the video Dom had sent earlier. She'd texted him asking how her two favourite boys were. *Bonding*, he'd replied, then added, *We're doing fine. I think our son finds my efforts at motherhood extremely amusing.* The video he'd attached of Kai waving his arms excitedly and laughing at him was one she would treasure forever.

She'd been hoping he'd answer the text she'd sent before seeing Jasmine. Finding that he hadn't, a niggle of worry began to gnaw away at her. He was probably in the middle of some-thing, might even have dropped off while rocking Kai to sleep, which she often did herself. But what if there was something wrong? What if Kai had been taken ill? Then Dom would have called her, she told herself firmly. Still, she couldn't dismiss the worry that had wormed its way into her head. The thought of not being there if her baby needed her was almost too much to bear.

She was probably being neurotic, but she couldn't just leave it. She was about to call him, even though she'd promised not to, when she remembered the Wi-Fi app. When they'd bought the digital video monitor, she'd moved the old camera to the windowsill in the nursery, which didn't provide a close-up of Kai but did give a good view of the room. Quickly she tapped the app. She'd finally got round to subscribing to the cloud, and after a bit of fiddling, she managed to pull up the stored videos dated this morning. She was hugely relieved at the sight of Dom nestling his son close as he fed him, the same look of wonder on his face that he'd had when he'd first set eyes on him.

She found the latest videos; the first one of Kai alone in the room, his little limbs flailing as he began to fret. Despite knowing that that was what babies did, still her heart caught in her chest. The next clip showed Dom coming through the door and picking him up, talking to him. The audio wasn't good, so she couldn't hear what he was saying, but she noticed that Kai calmed down as soon as Dom smiled at him. He was a good man, a gentle, caring man. A good father. She felt her chest swell with love for him. She had to be careful of pushing him away. If she couldn't share the truth about her past with him, she had to stop this incessant worrying and being overprotective of Kai. She had to allow Dom the freedom to be a proper father to his son or she would ruin everything, even without Lydia's assistance.

Flicking to the next video, she squinted at it, confused, as another figure appeared at the door. Chloe? What was she doing there? Eve's stomach tightened. She must have dropped by, but why would she have done that when she knew Eve was at the surgery today? To speak to Dom? It was possible that she'd gone round to explain to him to why things were fractious between her and Eve and to ask him to intervene, though Eve knew that was highly unlikely. But whatever her reason for calling round, what the bloody hell was she doing upstairs?

Stop. She tried to rein in the graphic scenarios that began to race through her mind, to block out the images of Chloe looking at Dom in open adoration whilst reeling off all the reasons she thought he was wonderful. This was her husband. A man she trusted. She didn't, though, did she, not completely? What was more, she made it obvious to him that she didn't.

This was nonsense. She really was being neurotic now. Chloe had followed him upstairs while he dealt with Kai, that was all. A voice of sanity did battle with the suspicion whispering away in her head.

Chloe was saying something now. *Dammit.* She jabbed at the app, wishing the audio was clearer. Whatever it was, she appeared to be studying Dom intently as he placed Kai in his bouncer. Eve's chest constricted as she saw Chloe wipe a hand across her face and realised she was crying. Why? Had something else happened that Eve was unaware of? Or was it a ploy to get Dom's attention? Because that would certainly do it. A sharp knot clogging her throat, she watched him straighten up, his expression concerned as he walked across to Chloe. The two of them exchanged a few words, then seconds later, Dom circled her with his arm. They seemed to stay like that for an eternity. What was he *thinking*? Would he do this if Eve were there, knowing how it would look?

But it's not how it looks. Eve's blood pumped so fast her head swam as she saw Chloe gaze up at him. *She's upset.* It was quite obvious that she was. He was comforting her, that was all this was. Wasn't it? Nausea rose hotly inside her as her mind crashed back to another time she'd felt utterly betrayed by her friend. But that hadn't been how it had looked either. Chloe had sworn it wasn't, and Eve had believed her best friend when she said she hadn't betrayed her. Now, looking at the screen, she was left wondering if she could trust her at all.

TWENTY-SEVEN

2009

Eve

Desperately in need of some air, we're leaving the end-of-term party when an 'I Wanna Dance with Somebody' remix blasts out from the hall behind us. 'Oh my God, I love this!' Chloe twirls on her heels, grabs hold of Zac's hand and attempts to yank him back inside.

Zac glances at me as I hang onto his other arm, high heels and too much celebrating necessitating the support. 'I think I'll pass, Chlo,' he shouts over the music. 'Bed's calling.'

'Aw, Zac.' Chloe locks her other hand around his wrist and blinks beguilingly. 'I know you're on a promise with the most beautiful girl in med school, but Eve won't mind waiting. You can't let me dance on my own.'

Zac glances amusedly at me as Chloe all but drags him back towards the hall.

'Go on.' I flail a hand. 'I'll follow you in a...' I trail off as he disappears through the doors, a hapless smile on his face. I shake my head in amusement and attempt to steady myself. I still don't think I'm beautiful, with my mad frizzy hair, a nose that's too short and lips that are too full, but Zac definitely is. In my opinion, he's the best-looking boy at uni. Also in Chloe's, if her making orgasmic eyes at him every time he passes by is anything to judge by. He's from a good family too, as in well-to-do. I still can't believe he's dating me.

Feeling slightly queasy, I head for the loos, where, thank goodness, I'm not actually sick, which might dampen his passion a bit. I do feel distinctly wobbly, though. Careful to avoid my mascara, I splash my face with cold water and trickle some down my cleavage to cool myself down, then give myself a minute and make my way back to the hall.

'Rock DJ' booms out as I approach, the low thud of the bass reverberating through my chest, resonating through my entire body and down my spine as I near the dance floor. 'Evie!' Someone grabs my hand and pulls me into a group of girls rocking to the beat. I'm keen to find Zac and Chloe, but also keen to fit in. Thanks to the cliquey girls at school leaving an indelible mark on me, I don't think I'll ever really feel that I do. Soon, with the music thumping, an aphrodisiac heightening my senses, I'm lost in the dance. After a while, I spot Chloe and Zac across the room. They don't notice me, and though I feel a flicker of annoyance that they're both too busy bumping and grinding, Chloe's bum into Zac's pelvis, I try not to mind. Chloe's drunk, having a good time. I don't want to spoil things.

Sticky with sweat after two more dance tunes, I decide I really need to get out of here before I'm embarrassingly ill on the dance floor. I look back to where Chloe and Zac were, but I can't see them. I scour the hall, but there's no sign of them. The strobe lights are rigged to follow the beat of the music, making the mass of gyrating bodies look as if they're all moving in slow motion, and feeling definitely nauseous now, I make my way through the throng to the bar. They're not there. Not anywhere.

A flutter of panic in my stomach, spilled beer and an overabundance of perfumes assailing my senses, I head towards the doors, unsure if I can make it back to my room on my own.

I'm halfway around the campus quadrangle, my shoes in my hand and keeping close to the wall for support, when I stop. I'm stunned for an instant, literally frozen where I stand, and then I'm fighting the urge to eject the contents of my stomach, which are rising fast inside me. I fail, and retch violently as Chloe disengages herself from Zac and looks at me. Her expression is one of alarm. Zac's face is shocked too as he stares past her, and then his finely chiselled features flood with guilt.

Shoes dangling from my hand, I wipe an arm across my mouth and emit a strangled, scornful laugh. I can see why he feels so guilty, with his hands still clutching her arse.

I'm face down on my bed, my pillow over my head, but I can't drown out the sound of Chloe hammering on the door. 'Eve, please let me in,' she pleads through it, yet again. 'I'm worried about you.'

Worried? Ha! Fury and adrenaline pumping though my veins, I scramble from the bed to the door and yank it open. 'Piss off, Chloe,' I hiss, and attempt to slam it closed again.

Her foot prevents me. 'Evie, *please.*' She pushes the door, and though I want to shut her out, out of my room and out of my life forever, I don't have the energy. And anyway, I can't. We're linked by our past forever.

Trailing listlessly back to the bed, I plop myself down. Chloe almost falls into the room, then rights herself and limps across to me, and I realise I've hurt her. Not as much as she's hurt me, though. I'm still trying to process, but my brain simply refuses to compute that my best friend would do this. After all we've been through together, how *could* she?

She stops in front of me. 'You look dreadful,' she murmurs.

I drag my gaze over her, feeling nothing but bitter contempt. I register that she looks possibly worse than I must, with her hair and clothes bedraggled and tears ploughing two ugly black tracks down her face, but she could never feel as bad as I do, not ever.

'It wasn't how it looked, Evie,' she says tearfully.

I sneer at that and peel my eyes away from her. 'Go away, Chloe,' I mutter. 'You two deserve each other.'

'Eve, it *wasn't*.' She drops to her knees and reaches for my hand. I snatch it away. 'He caught me by surprise. I didn't know what to do. He's *strong*, Eve. I tried to push him away. I was about to tell him to fuck off when you—'

'I don't *believe* you!' I jump to my feet, sending her sprawling back on her haunches. 'It's obvious you fancy him. It always has been. I think you're just a jealous cow!'

'Evie, it's the truth!' she cries behind me as I stride to the door. I stop, though, as I reach it. I want to go through it. To run and keep running. But I have nowhere *to* go. No one to go to. No one in my life who cares for me but Chloe. And now... I wrap my arms around myself. The pain in my chest is unbearable. I can't breathe.

'Evie, you *have* to believe me,' Chloe begs, her voice cracking. 'It's the truth, I swear it is. I'm not jealous. I would *never* do that to you. I'll go if you want me to. I'll quit the course and I'll go, but please believe that I would never willingly hurt you. I love you.'

With immense effort, I turn back to her. She's sitting on the floor, sobbing quietly, and I'm torn. I want to scream at her, shake her, but I also want to go to her and tell her everything will be all right.

'He doesn't love you, Eve.' She squeezes the words out, tears streaming down her face. And I know she's not lying. Because the truth is, I'm not worthy of love. I never have been.

TWENTY-EIGHT

PRESENT

Eve

Coming through the front door, Eve dropped her case in the hall and tugged off her coat.

'Dom?' she called, hooking the coat on the pegs. Getting no answer, she stopped and listened, and then went to the stairs, the knot of apprehension in her stomach twisting itself tight as she glanced up them. She trusted Dom implicitly. At least in this regard. She wanted to trust Chloe, but try as she might to ignore the ghosts of her past that were floating painfully back, she couldn't. Her needs as a child had been simple. Apart from to go to school in clean white socks, she hadn't craved material things. She'd just wanted to feel loved. She'd believed Chloe had loved her. She believed Dom did, at least the person she strived to be. Now, though, she wondered: did he?

Her mind shot back to university, when she'd felt as if the ground had been ripped from beneath her. She'd believed

Chloe then, but was that because she'd needed to? Chloe had dropped out of med school a few weeks after that, not because of the thing with Zac; she'd promised Eve it wasn't that. 'I'm just not as clever as you are,' she'd said with a sad shrug as Eve had waited with her at the train station.

'What will you do?' Eve had asked, concerned for her.

'Haunt you.' Chloe had smiled.

'You better had. Together forever, remember?' Eve reminded her, clasping her hand and squeezing it.

Chloe nodded, her smile now sadly reflective.

'I'll call you,' Eve promised, tears welling in her eyes. 'We'll meet up every weekend. I'll miss you.'

'I'll miss you too,' Chloe had whispered, turning to hug her as the train pulled in. 'Love you.'

'Love you more.' Eve had hugged her back hard. She'd seen something in her friend's eyes, though, as she'd eased away: a flash of annoyance, she'd been sure. The same spark of anger she'd seen years before in the school playground, when Eve had been upset with her for sharing things she'd promised to keep secret. Chloe had sworn she hadn't, but Eve had known she had.

Taking a tremulous breath, she started tentatively up the stairs, then jumped, her heart leaping, as Dom appeared at the top of them. 'Shh,' he whispered, pressing a finger to his lips. Nodding towards Kai's room, he came down to meet her as she stepped back down to the hall. 'He's just gone off,' he said, leaning to kiss her cheek and then heading for the kitchen. 'It was a battle of wills, I'm afraid.'

Eve followed him, 'Is he all right?' she asked, her hand travelling to her face in the wake of his kiss, her mind going to the video and the scene she dearly wished she hadn't witnessed. She squeezed her eyes closed and tried hard to blot out the image of her husband and her best friend together, but failed.

The recording had stopped shortly after. What was worrying her, terrifying her, was that there were no further recordings. The screen had gone blank. Why would it have done unless the camera had stopped working, which was highly unlikely, or else been unplugged?

'He's fine,' Dom assured her. 'He was just refusing to give in. I reckon he's inherited his mum's stubborn gene.'

'My clever gene, you mean. He's clearly worked out how to wangle spending more time with his daddy.' She tried to keep her tone light while she agonised about what to do. Should she confront him, or bury her head in the sand? She wasn't sure she could do that, ignore it and pray it would go away.

'Who's undoubtedly worth spending time with.' Dom gave her a mischievous wink over his shoulder, and her heart dropped. She didn't think she could bear this, the wondering, the imagining him with another woman, her best friend. It would kill her. 'Did you have a good day?' he asked, flicking the coffee machine on. He'd already prepared it. Everything seemed normal, nothing amiss – apart from that intimate embrace with Chloe, which she knew now she couldn't ignore. It just wasn't possible.

'Not too bad,' she answered, easing off her shoes and rolling her shoulders. The dull ache in her head had turned into a thud, her ears buzzing, sharp pinpricks of white light forming behind her eyes, which happened often when she was tense.

'Feeling stressed?' Dom asked perceptively, walking across to administer his trusty massage technique. It was one of the many reasons why she loved him, because he was intuitive, because he cared.

'A little,' she admitted. 'That young girl whose communication skills I told you I was concerned about, her mum agreed to meet with a healthcare professional. That's a huge relief, but I can't help worrying about her.'

'She's obviously decided to trust you, though,' Dom pointed out. 'That's progress, right?'

'Yes. Yes, it is.' Eve knew he was right. 'So, how was your day?' she asked, opening the way for him to mention Chloe. 'Good, I take it?'

Dom stopped massaging. 'Definitely,' he said, going back to the coffee machine. 'I didn't realise that parenthood was such hard work, but I love spending time with my son.'

He didn't say any more, and Eve felt the knot in her stomach twist itself tighter. 'I texted you earlier, around lunchtime,' she said casually. 'I was a bit worried when you didn't get back.'

'Oh, right.' He glanced at her, his brow furrowed in apparent confusion. 'Sorry, I think I must have been feeding him,' he said, his gaze back on the coffee.

Eve's heart skittered against her chest. He would have seen the text, though, surely? But then with Chloe being here, he'd been distracted, hadn't he? How distracted?

'Fancy a biscuit?' he asked, going to the cupboard. 'I thought we'd have chicken pasta bake for dinner, but it might take a while.'

'No. Thanks.' Eve's heart plummeted another inch. 'I've overindulged on biscuits already today.' She had no idea what to do. She should just ask him outright, but she didn't know how to without seeming to be accusing him of something. She scanned his face as he walked across with her coffee. He looked preoccupied. Thinking about what?

'The electrician called,' he said, heading back to the fridge. 'About the light fitting we need in the loft. I told him to come round on Thursday while you're at work. I thought you might prefer not to have your days off interrupted.'

'Oh, right. Thanks. That was thoughtful.' Eve watched him carefully as he extracted the ingredients for dinner. Why wasn't he telling her about Chloe? That she'd been here, upstairs, crying? In his *arms*.

'The graphic design company rang earlier too.' She noted the pleased look on his face as he glanced at her again. 'You know I didn't meet the deadline? They still like my ideas, apparently, so it looks as if the offer of the job is still open.'

'Brilliant,' Eve blurted past the constriction in her chest. 'That's fabulous news.'

'It's certainly a relief,' Dom went on, oblivious to the fact that she felt as if she were dying inside. 'My main concern was that I'd end up with a bad reputation. Most of my work comes from word of mouth.'

'Your reputation is intact. Well done,' she said enthusiastically, and swallowed hard. 'I'll just, um, go and get out of my work clothes.' She was dangerously close to tears, but she couldn't cry in front of him because then she would have to tell him why she was upset. What then? Would he lie? Would he accuse her of spying on him? After all, she'd been watching him with Kai. He would be bound to accuse her of not trusting him.

Wiping a hand quickly over her eyes, she hurried to the stairs, confused and horrified as she realised she was about to go and check the bed; that she actually was doubting him. Dom, her husband, the man she'd felt would never deceive her.

What was happening? Once on the landing, she took a slow breath and tried to still her racing heart. She'd tried to convince herself she could have this, a future, a relationship, a family. Now it all seemed to be crashing in on her. She was in danger of losing everything. And all because of bloody, *bloody* Lydia turning up. That was when all this had started. Her mother coming back into her life had kicked off a chain of events, and now things were escalating out of her control. She'd struggled so hard for this, worked so hard to maintain this life she'd built for herself. Why had her mother come back, dragging her past along with her?

She didn't check the bed. She couldn't bring herself to. Dom had made it, changed the sheets. But he would have done that anyway. He was always trying to pull his weight, telling her she did too much around the house and that it wasn't her responsibility.

But why had he changed them today?

Pulling off her work clothes, she tugged on the first things that came to hand, leggings and the top she'd worn yesterday, and went back to the landing. She paused at the nursery door. Dom might think she was checking up on him, but then he knew her well enough to know she had to make sure with her own eyes that Kai was okay. She also needed to see with her own eyes what had happened to the camera.

Opening the door quietly, she crept into the room. Kai was sleeping contentedly, his softly curled eyelashes fluttering. He was beautiful. Perfect.

Praying to God never to let any harm come to him, she glanced towards the windowsill, where the camera she'd watched Dom through should be sitting. He might well be watching her on the monitor downstairs, but she had to know. It was still there. It was also obscured, which would explain the blank screen. She felt a mixture of relief and trepidation as she saw Kai's Jellycat rabbit sitting in front of it. Dom must have placed it there. When? Why? Why had there been no footage at all after the undeniable intimacy between her husband and her best friend?

Blinking hard, she glanced at the ceiling, desperately trying to stem the tears that were now far too close to the surface. She *had* to ask him. He wasn't volunteering the information and she wouldn't rest until she knew. Nausea and nerves twisting inside her, she crept out of the nursery and, taking another fortifying breath, went back down to the kitchen.

Dom glanced knowingly at her as she walked in. 'He's all right, I take it?'

She nodded and braced herself.

'I poured you some wine,' he said, indicating the breakfast bar. 'Oh, and by the way, Chloe came round earlier.' Closing the fridge door after replacing the wine, he turned to her, a troubled look crossing his face. 'She was a bit upset because Steve appears to be being a prick, basically. You might want to talk to her when you get a chance.'

TWENTY-NINE

Eve felt relief crash through her. 'Did she tell you anything more about what happened?' she asked shakily as she went to fetch salad ingredients from the fridge. She hoped that doing something might give her time to compose herself.

'Not much. If Steve really has been messing around, though, he's seriously out of order. Rose is how old?'

'Almost three,' Eve provided distractedly. She'd been wrong. Terribly, horribly wrong.

'Christ, the man's an idiot.' Dom sighed in despair. 'He has a beautiful wife, two gorgeous kids and he's ready to throw it all away? For what?'

Eve glanced at him. His back was towards her as he prepared the pasta bake. He'd told her. He hadn't lied to her, which she'd been dreading he might. Yet she'd hadn't been truthful with him. She longed to confide in him, but how could she? She couldn't expect him to keep the secrets she'd been forced to keep. At first she'd stayed quiet because it was all she knew how to do. Then, as time had gone on, she'd stuffed it all deep down inside, the dark moods, the horrendous silences, the final fatal argument, what had happened to Jacob. She'd tried to forget, to function, to live instead of existing in shadows, to just be normal. She'd thought she'd attained that. She had a nice, normal existence. A child with a man she loved dearly and who loved her – she'd always believed that to be true. A good man, who her instinct had told her Chloe would steal away from her in an instant. She'd ignored that instinct because she hadn't wanted to acknowledge it. She had accused Chloe of being jealous back at university. She'd been right. She was right about this. The way Chloe looked at Dom, held him in adulation right in front of Steve's face. In front of Eve's face. She was in love with him. It was blindingly obvious. To Steve, too.

'Uh oh, I think a certain little man has cottoned on to the fact that his mum's home,' Dom said, nodding towards the monitor as the sounds of Kai waking emerged.

'I'll fetch him.' Eve turned quickly towards the door, in need of some space to get her thoughts straight. 'Only because you're busy,' she added, not wanting to hurt his feelings, as if his feelings wouldn't be crushed if he learned how suspicious she'd been of him, the things she'd been hiding from him.

'Or to avoid making the salad possibly?' Dom narrowed his eyes in amusement.

'Found out,' Eve said, swallowing hard as she disappeared into the hall. What was she going to do? She had to talk to Chloe, warn her off. She just thanked God that Dom was who he was. She'd been mad to think he might have been tempted, that he would risk his family to embark on an affair. She was being paranoid because she knew she didn't deserve him.

'Coming, sweetheart,' she said, fixing a smile on her face for her baby's sake as she reached the landing. 'Are we hungry, hey, gorgeous little—' *Ouch.* She stopped, wincing as something sharp pierced the bare sole of her foot.

Reaching to pick it up, she squinted at it, confused, and

then stared, thunderstruck. It was an earring. A gold bar studded earring. The sort Chloe wore. She hadn't noticed it before. What was it doing here, outside the main bedroom door?

THIRTY

Eve looked up at the woman who was holding her hand. She looked like her mother; her hair was the same, hacked off close to her head. She wore jeans and a white flowy top, yet she was different. 'Where are we going?' Eve asked, her voice a tremulous whisper. The woman didn't answer. She couldn't, Eve knew. With no mouth on her face, she couldn't even if she wanted to. Fear settled like a cold fist inside her as they walked deeper into the forest. The animals here weren't magical any more, but scary, screeching and shrieking in the tall trees, which weren't upside down and green and leafy, but gnarled and ugly. 'I don't like it,' she whimpered, trying to tug her hand from the one that squeezed hers tighter and tighter until her knuckles hurt. 'I want to go home.'

'But you are home,' something hissed to her side. Eve's eyes swivelled towards the skeletal branches, to the curled copper snake slithering between them. Her heart jumped, the butterflies in her tummy swirling like frantic bees as it dropped to hang an inch from her face. 'This is where you belong,' it said, its voice mocking. 'You have to keep our secrets safe, remember?' It smiled, and its eyes were cat's eyes, but red like the devil's and it wore one earring, yet it had no ears. 'Don't be shy, Evie,' it purred. 'I'll be here with you. I'm your best friend. We belong here, together forever.'

'No!' The hand she was holding had turned into a big man's hand that was tugging her down. And then there were two hands, fleshless, bony, pulling harder, and the slimy wet mud where once were fluffy white clouds was sucking her under. She didn't want to be here. She couldn't breathe. She couldn't—

'Hey.'

Eve jolted upright, her heart banging in her chest as she felt a hand on her shoulder.

'Are you okay?' Dom asked, looking worriedly down at her, then lowering himself to sit on the edge of the bed. 'You've been tossing and turning all night.' He reached for her hand.

Eve pulled it away, dragged her hair from her face and nodded quickly. 'A bad dream,' she said, desperately trying to shake away the cobwebs that still clung cloyingly to her mind.

Dom studied her, his expression a mixture of concern and puzzlement. 'Are you feeling any better?' he asked. 'I was concerned when you came up early. You definitely looked off colour.'

Answering with another short nod, Eve dropped her gaze. She couldn't look at him right now. She'd left him downstairs last night, told him that stomach cramps were the reason she'd suddenly lost her appetite.

'I made you some breakfast.' He nodded to the tray he'd placed on her bedside table. 'Just toast and marmalade. You should try to eat something.'

His voice was soft and kind, the same as it always was. Yet everything was different. He'd lied to her. What hurt excruciatingly was that he could sit here on the bed they shared, the bed in which they'd created a beautiful life together, and perpetuate that lie.

'I'll go and get Kai's feed,' he said, still gauging her carefully as he got to his feet.

Did he know? Eve wondered. Had he guessed that she knew something? 'Is he all right?' she asked him, a new kind of panic unfurling inside her as she realised she hadn't checked on him.

'He's fine,' he assured her. 'Still fast asleep. He only woke once in the night.'

And Dom had gone to him, his son, the child whose life he wanted so desperately to be more involved in. Why would he do that? Why pretend he cared about him, about her, when he was about to turn their world upside down?

'Eat something.' He smiled. 'Take your time. There's no rush.'

'Dom.' Nausea and fear churning inside her, she stopped him as he crossed the room.

He turned back.

She took a breath. 'Why didn't you tell me that Chloe had been here? Upstairs, I mean?'

He frowned. 'Why would I? She's often upstairs.'

'Only when I'm here.' She fixed her gaze hard on his.

Dom shook his head. 'I'm not sure I'm hearing you right,' he said.

'I think you are.' Eve's voice was calm. Her gaze didn't waver.

The furrow in Dom's brow deepened. 'You are joking, right?' He scanned her eyes uncertainly, then, 'You're not, are you?' He laughed in astonishment. 'Jesus, Eve, are you seriously accusing me of...'

Eve continued to stare at him, searching for the lie in his eyes.

'I don't bloody believe this.' Raking a hand through his hair, he glanced away, his expression a combination of bewilderment and disappointment. Anger, too. 'I came upstairs because Kai woke up,' he said flatly. 'Chloe followed me. But clearly you know she did. I won't ask how, because that would obviously be accusing *you* of something, wouldn't it, Eve?'

Eve ignored that. It was a classic tactic. She'd lived with it, lived her childhood with people who were masters at deflecting blame to justify their own monstrous behaviour. 'Did she pick him up?' she asked, remarkably calmly considering her world appeared to be disintegrating right before her eyes.

'What?' Now Dom looked confused. 'No. What the hell's going on here, Eve? Why would you even think—'

'So he wouldn't have accidentally pulled her earring out then?' Eve spoke over him, her voice still calm, though inside she was trembling.

'Eve, for God's *sake.*' Dom kneaded his forehead in frustration. 'I have no clue what this is all about. You are really beginning to worry me.'

What was he so frustrated about? she wondered. That she obviously didn't believe him? Or that he'd been caught? 'Her earring, Dom, that's what this is all about,' she provided. 'I found it on the floor, outside our bedroom door. Would you like to tell me how it got there?'

'I'm going to see to Kai.' His jaw visibly clenching, Dom turned away.

'Why were you embracing her?' she asked, throwing the duvet back and almost sending the tray crashing as she jumped to her feet. 'Gazing into her bloody eyes? Holding her *close*, Dom. Tell me that!'

His hand froze on the door handle. 'You *were* watching, weren't you? *Spying* on me.' He turned slowly back to her. 'Why, Eve? In case I neglected my *son*?'

'You haven't answered the question.' Eve worked to keep her voice quiet.

'I don't bloody know *how* to answer it!' Dom's voice rose. 'I told you yesterday, she was upset. I went to her. What did you want me to do, stand there and watch her cry?'

'Why did the camera stop recording?' she demanded.

'I've had enough of this.' Sighing agitatedly, he carried on to the landing.

'Do you expect me to believe it just stopped?' Inhaling hard to stop the tears, she went after him.

He ground to a halt and turned back to her. 'No.' His face taut, he answered shortly. 'I expect you to believe that when I lifted Kai out of his bouncer, it came up with him and caught the plug. I pushed it back in at some point.'

'And stood one of his soft toys in front of the camera.' Eve folded her arms across her chest. 'Why did you bring me breakfast in bed?'

Dom sucked in a breath. 'Meaning why am I making an effort unless I have something to feel guilty about?'

She said nothing, but still she held his gaze.

'Ironic, isn't it?' He emitted a scornful laugh. 'So many times I've willed you to look at me, Eve. So many times you wouldn't. Because you didn't trust me, I thought, and you didn't want me to see it in your eyes. And now, when you think you have proof that you *can't* trust me, here you are looking right at me. Just so you know, I'm getting the message, loud and clear. In answer to your accusation, I brought you breakfast because I happen to care about you. But clearly that doesn't count for much, does it?'

He stopped, glancing towards the nursery as Kai began to whimper. 'Someone needs to see to our son,' he said more quietly. 'I'll just assume you don't want me to do that since I'm so bloody incompetent, shall I?' Dragging disillusioned eyes over her, he turned to the stairs.

Eve felt a confusion of conflicting emotion. She was angry, but who should she be angry with? *Had* she seen what she thought she had? Chloe had come here after she'd left. She had been upset, that had been evident, but had it been a ploy to get Dom's attention? She clearly wanted it. Recalling the spiteful things her friend had said, she realised that Chloe actually *was* jealous, that she had been for a long time. Was it possible that she was engineering the situation so that Eve would do exactly what she was doing right now: destroying her own marriage? 'Dom, *wait*,' she called after him.

He faltered.

'I wasn't spying on you. I looked at the video because you didn't text me back,' she explained. 'I thought it was strange. I was worried and I—'

'I'll tell you what's strange, Eve.' Dom spun around. 'The way you're behaving. The way you've been behaving since your bloody mother turned up. I've begged you to tell me what's going on, but do you know something? I'm not sure I want to know any more.' Eyeing her furiously, he carried on down the stairs, grabbed his jacket from the pegs and his car keys from the hall table, then yanked the front door open and walked out, slamming it behind him.

THIRTY-ONE

PRESENT

Lydia

She'd loved her house when they'd first moved into it. A red-brick thirties semi, it was all she'd dreamed of after living in a tiny flat over a fish and chip shop where everything smelled of grease and she was constantly having to keep Eve quiet for fear of upsetting the landlord downstairs. The house was so spacious, with chimney breasts and alcoves creating a sense of depth and character. Then there were the curved bay windows, which softened the rooms and lent themselves to window seats and reading nooks. She'd been planning the decoration before they moved in. It had been her dream come true, until it had turned into the worst kind of nightmare, one she'd found it impossible to escape from. The bay windows looked dark and uninviting now, the rooms soulless. Perhaps it was just the rain making everything grey and gloomy, or else the way she was feeling.

Hearing it spatter unrelentingly against the glass, she recalled how Eve had stood forlornly in the window when she was small, watching the raindrops trickle down it like tears. She'd been a sad little thing, never quite knowing what mood her father would be in, but things had been manageable. Or perhaps they hadn't been. Perhaps Lydia had just been fooling herself rather than face the prospect of leaving him, starting all over again in a dingy little flat with paper-thin walls, assuming she could find a way to rent any kind of property. Then, when Jacob had come along, she'd been stuck, trapped like a dog, fed scraps of affection, too frightened to try to escape the man who'd said he would find her wherever she went. Her mental health had suffered. Eve's had. Poor little Jacob had suffered most of all.

Her thoughts were on him, the things she'd done so terribly wrong, when she caught a movement outside, a man hurrying from a car parked on the opposite side of the road. She didn't recognise him until he stepped onto the path. Dominic, she realised. She steeled herself and went to the hall as he knocked on the front door.

She hesitated, then opened the door tentatively.

'Hi,' he said, looking as wary as she felt. 'I'm sorry to call unannounced. Do you mind if I come in?'

'Has something happened?' Eyeing him worriedly, Lydia moved back from the door. 'It's not Kai, is it?'

'No, it's nothing like that,' he said quickly, his eyes travelling over the austere white walls of the hall Lydia hadn't had the heart to do anything with. 'I hoped we might have a chat about Eve. I'm worried about her.'

'Oh. I see.' Lydia's heart skipped a beat. 'Why?' she asked, her chest tightening as she considered what he might be worried about, what Eve might have disclosed to him.

He took a breath. 'I'm not sure exactly. It might just be me she has a problem with, but she doesn't seem to be able to trust me. She insists on caring for Kai herself. She won't talk about her past and...' He paused, shrugging uncertainly, then, 'I love her, Lydia,' he said, his eyes – such expressive eyes, Lydia thought – filled with confusion. 'I just want to help her if I can. To do that, I feel I need to know more about her, do you see?'

Again Lydia hesitated. She hadn't wanted anything from Eve. She'd simply wanted to be able to talk to her. Might Dominic be the conduit between them?

'What happened between the two of you, Lydia?' He held her gaze, desperation now obvious in his eyes. 'What went on in her childhood that she's so reluctant to talk about?'

Lydia nodded slowly. She would need to be careful, but he clearly needed answers. Since he was here, she couldn't avoid talking to him. 'You'd better come through,' she said, and turned to lead the way to the lounge. 'Can I get you some tea or coffee?'

'No thanks. I'm good,' he replied, following her through.

She gestured him to the sofa and he took a seat. He didn't sit back, she noticed, leaning forward and lacing his hands in front of him instead, a man definitely on edge. 'Will you talk to me, Lydia?' he asked her.

She walked across to the armchair, trying to quell the nerves that were making her heart beat too fast as she lowered herself into it. 'She wasn't an easy child,' she said at length. Meeting his gaze briefly, she fell silent, plucking idly at a strand of cotton at the edge of her cuff as she waited for him to comment. It would be safer, she decided, to be led by his questions rather than offer up information that might open doors that needed to stay closed.

'How so?' he asked inevitably.

Lydia looked up. 'She was withdrawn, uncommunicative. She seemed to be in a world of her own sometimes.' It was a version of the truth.

Dominic nodded, but he didn't look surprised, confirming

that Eve still had similar traits, perhaps out of necessity – there were certain things she would never be able to talk about. Lydia so wished she would talk to *her*. Who else did she have, after all? Chloe wasn't to be trusted. She never had been, if only Eve would realise it. She wouldn't let Lydia anywhere near her, though. And definitely nowhere near Kai. She'd made that abundantly clear. Lydia understood why. Shutting her out, though, was unwise. And cruel. Didn't she have a right to see the child? He was her flesh and blood, after all.

'I told you her brother was sick.' She searched his face, unsure how much Eve had discussed with him.

Dominic nodded tightly.

Lydia's gaze drifted down. 'I assume you know he had epilepsy? Also asthma.'

Again Dominic nodded. 'That must have been stressful to deal with,' he said sympathetically.

'It was.' Lydia closed her eyes, recalling the last time Jacob was in hospital, the medical staff wary of her, constantly watching her. She quashed a spark of sudden anger inside her. 'More so because the doctors refused to listen to me. They thought they knew better, of course, but no one knows a child as well as their own mother.'

'I know that,' Dominic responded, his expression one of concern. Lydia breathed in, relieved. At least he didn't appear to be judging her. 'It's instinctive.' He smiled contemplatively. 'It certainly is with Eve.'

Lydia didn't comment, turning her gaze away again to look at nothing in particular on the wall to her side. 'Eve became disruptive,' she continued, once she'd given herself a minute to formulate her thoughts. 'Whenever Jacob was ill, she seemed worse. I admit I struggled to cope. Her father wasn't the most tolerant of men, you see, which made life terribly difficult.'

'I gathered.' There was an angry edge to Dominic's voice.

Lydia snapped her gaze back to his. 'She told you about him?'

He studied her thoughtfully. 'That he was controlling, yes.'

She sighed regretfully. 'He tended to take it out on Eve. Not physically,' she added quickly. 'But his verbal tirades were no less damaging. I begged her to behave, but in the end, I found the only way to calm her down was to ignore her.'

'You stopped speaking to her.' It was a statement rather than a question, telling Lydia he knew that much too.

She nodded. 'In retrospect, that was probably a mistake. She was obviously seeking attention, but I didn't know what else to do. She became more withdrawn,' she continued, although resurrecting the past was painful. 'Depressed, I suppose you would call it now. I took her to see our GP. Eventually he referred her to a psychiatrist.'

'A psychiatrist?' Dominic looked at her, bewildered.

Lydia studied her hands. 'It was Eve who found Jacob after he...'

'She found him *dead*?' Dominic's look was one of palpable shock.

Lydia nodded sadly. 'Chloe was with her at the time. I thought she needed help to process her feelings. I'm not sure it did help. She began to harm herself,' she whispered.

She heard his sharp intake of breath. 'Jesus,' he hissed. 'How?'

'Bruising mostly,' she murmured, knotting and unknotting her fingers. 'Self-inflicted. The odd cut.' She looked up to see him staring at her in incomprehension. Glancing away again, she searched her sleeve for a tissue. She found one and pressed it under her nose. 'I tried to tell the doctors what was happening, to get her to talk to me, but she wouldn't. She became secretive, keeping things to herself. The only person she ever confided in was Chloe.'

'I didn't know any of this.' Dominic sounded choked.

'You should, for Eve's sake. She also took tablets,' Lydia went on, feeling obliged to tell him that too. 'Just once. Though she wouldn't admit it, I believe that was something to do with her friendship with Chloe. The two had a falling-out, I think. Eve was obviously badly affected by it.'

Dominic didn't speak for a long moment. Then, 'And did Chloe know about this?' he asked, clearly stunned.

Lydia nodded. 'They spoke on the phone. Chloe came to see her afterwards, looking very sheepish. They were extremely close. Even when Chloe struck up a friendship with Steven, she and Eve were inseparable.'

'Steven?' Dominic furrowed his brow in confusion. 'As in her husband, Steve?'

Lydia paused. Would revealing what she was about to cause truths she didn't want to surface to spill out? She thought not. But should certain things come to the fore, that might be no bad thing. As far as she could see, Chloe and Steve living so close to Eve was almost like a threat hanging over her. 'He and Chloe have been together a very long time,' she confided. 'I'm not sure whether you know, though, that he and Eve also have a brief history.'

Clearly he didn't. He looked utterly stunned.

'Nothing too serious. They went out once or twice, that was all. I'm not sure Chloe was ever aware of it. The girls were attending different universities back then.' She paused thoughtfully. 'I do wonder, though, why they would choose to live quite so close to you. Was that Chloe's decision, do you know?'

Dominic blew out a breath. 'I've no idea,' he said. His face was pale as he got to his feet. 'I think I should go.' He was obviously shaken, as Lydia had guessed he would be.

'Will you give her my love?' she asked as she walked him to the front door.

He emitted a strangled laugh, then shook his head. 'Do you

think I could use the bathroom?' he asked, looking paler by the second.

Lydia glanced to the stairs. She didn't like people going up there, but with no downstairs toilet, and him looking definitely queasy now, she guessed she didn't have a choice. 'It's at the end of the landing. The door facing you.'

She went to the kitchen, listening for sounds of running water, the toilet being flushed. The creak of the floorboards told her he'd left the bathroom. Her gaze on the ceiling, she waited. His footsteps overhead told her he was doing what she'd hoped he wouldn't, taking the opportunity to look around. He had no right to do that. She felt a mixture of panic and anger tighten her stomach, and tugged in a breath. It stopped short of the pain in her chest.

He was in the nursery when she found him. 'I couldn't bear to disturb things,' she said quietly, her gaze travelling past where he stood at the door to the fluffy white clouds and the huge Disney Dumbo on the opposite wall.

Dominic's gaze was shocked as he turned to her, his face now seeming to have no colour at all. 'I should leave,' he said, his eyes almost horrified as he moved towards her.

Lydia stood aside to let him pass. She heard him stumble on the stairs, spit out a curse, and swallowed guiltily. She should have done something about that loose rod on the carpet. David had said he would. He hadn't, of course, and then had fallen victim to his own laziness around the house. She was sure he would have regretted leaving everything to her if he'd been able to.

She did understand why Dominic had been so shocked. Walking across to the cot-sided bed, she paused to adjust the IV drip stand that stood next to it, then reached to stroke the soft silicone cheek of the reborn baby boy toddler doll that looked lovingly up at her. He really was so lifelike, she almost expected him to speak to her.

'Come on, little one,' she whispered, picking him up gently and carrying him to the window. Opening it as her visitor stumbled back to his car, she called out to him. 'Oh, Dominic.'

Turning to look up at her, he took a step backwards.

'About Chloe. Don't believe everything she might tell you,' she warned him. 'She doesn't have Eve's best interests at heart. I'd be wary of Steve too, if I were you.'

THIRTY-TWO

2000

Eve

The butterflies in my stomach are more frantic than ever as we wait in the reception area of the Oak Development Centre, thoughts buzzing manically around my head. What questions will she ask me? If she asks me to tell her about Jacob, about my father, what will I say? I'm sure I won't have the right answers. My mum hasn't spoken since we got here, other than to say, 'Stop fidgeting, Eve.' She placed a hand over mine to stop me twirling my watch around my arm, and I was startled and sad at the same time because I realised she doesn't actually touch me very often. We don't hug or anything. We used to, I think, years ago.

The butterflies go into a frenzy as the doctor comes out of her office to meet us. I'm surprised she does that, but I suppose that's how they do things here to put people at their ease. 'Hello, Eve,' she says, extending her hand as she approaches. 'I'm Georgia. I'm hoping we can have a chat about a few things. It's nothing to worry about. Just an opportunity for us to get to know each other. What do you think?'

Suspecting I shouldn't say what I think, which is that I'd rather not be here, I nod uncertainly, my eyes travelling to her name tag. It reads *Dr Georgia Sutherland*, and I guess she wants me to call her by her first name to make me feel more comfortable.

'That's fine, isn't it, Evie?' my mum says, getting to her feet, but Dr Sutherland stops her.

'I thought it might be a good idea for just the two of us to have a chat initially, Mrs Lockhart,' she says, looking at her kindly. 'If that's okay with you?'

'Oh.' My mum's eyes skitter to me and back to the doctor. 'Yes, of course.' She smiles, the same brittle smile she wears when she gets annoyed with the doctors at the hospital. She was annoyed the last time Jacob was taken in. The doctor who'd been doing his checks asked if he could have a word with her in the corridor. I heard him say they were going to transfer him to the paediatric intensive care unit so they could monitor him more closely, and then something about the injury to his head and also something about the IV drip they'd put into his arm when he came in. It wasn't working properly apparently. I couldn't make out much of what he was saying, even though I moved close to the door, keeping myself flat against the wall so they didn't see me. I heard my mum's reply, though. 'I've never heard anything so ridiculous in my life,' she snapped. 'Do you honestly think Jacob's injury could have been caused by anything other than an accident? I've *told* you, there's a loose rod on the stairs. I fell. Jacob was in my arms. As for the drip, I doubt very much whether Eve or I could possibly have trapped the tube without realising. Quite obviously one of your nursing staff is incompetent.'

I asked Liam about it afterwards. He said not to worry about it, that sometimes the equipment was dodgy, but he looked at my mum oddly. I think maybe he was thinking the same as the doctor.

Mum sits back down, and I can see she's nervous now. She's weaving her fingers in and out of each other like she sometimes does, and I actually feel quite sorry for her. I glance back at her as I follow Georgia across the reception, giving her a small smile to try to reassure her. She doesn't smile back.

Once I'm sitting in her office, Georgia offers me a drink. 'We have tea or coffee, or fresh orange juice if you'd prefer?'

'No thank you.' I decline with a shake of my head and sit on my hands to keep them still. 'I had a Coke on the way here.'

'I have to admit, that's my favourite tipple. I'll get some in next time,' she says, sounding quite friendly, and I relax a little.

She pours herself some water and comes to sit in the chair opposite me. 'So, Eve,' she places her glass on the coffee table, 'tell me a little bit about yourself.'

I frown, because I have no idea what she wants to know.

'How's school?' she asks with a smile. 'I hear you're quite clever.'

I feel my cheeks heat up. Miss Grantham at my junior school said I was, but she only ever said it to me. I think she knew I didn't want the other kids to know.

'What's your favourite subject?' Georgia waits expectantly.

I know I have to answer, and I guess it's safe to. 'I like art,' I tell her. 'I like maths and science too, but we don't do much science.'

'Do you think you'll choose science as one of your subjects?'

I smile and nod. I will. It's important for my studies.

She steeples her hands under her chin. 'And how do you get along with the other children, Eve?'

I glance down and then quickly back, because I don't want to look like my mum, as if I'm too nervous to hold eye contact with anyone. I'm really having to fight the urge to pull my hands from under my thighs, though. I find that sliding my watch around my wrist makes me feel less anxious. I'm not sure why. Possibly because it distracts me from whatever I'm feeling on the inside. 'I get on okay.' I shrug. I actually don't talk much to the other children at this school. I worry that if they get to know about me they won't like me. Chloe's in my class, though. We're still there for each other, together forever. I absolutely don't want to discuss the girls at junior school and why they didn't like me. I'm not even sure why they didn't, apart from what Chloe told me: that they were jealous. I still don't think that's the reason, though. I think it was the fact that I didn't look like them. I just didn't fit in. I'm not sure I will at this school either, but I'm trying.

Georgia pauses for a while, and I glance towards the window. There's a fat grey pigeon on the ledge outside. He's cooing, looking for a mate probably, and I can't help thinking that he's lonely too.

'Can you tell me a little bit about how you're feeling, Eve?' she asks as I look back at her. 'About the accident, and what happened to Jacob afterwards?'

I glance down again. I promised myself I wouldn't cry, but I can feel the tears welling in my eyes. 'Sad,' I mumble, and shift in my seat. My chest is heavy suddenly, like there's a stone wedged in the middle of it, and my throat is tight.

'You're bound to feel like that,' she says kindly. 'And it's okay to talk about it.'

I chew on the inside of my cheek. I'm not sure it is. My mum doesn't talk about what happened. Just drifts around the house like a sad, silent ghost. 'I think he's better off now, though,' I add, because after what Miss Grantham told me about God taking little children so he can look after them and love and cherish them, I honestly think Jacob *is* better off.

'Why do you think that, Eve?' Georgia asks. Her voice is soft, sympathetic, but I know it's a serious question.

'Because he wasn't happy,' I answer honestly.

She nods and pauses again. 'Sure I can't get you a drink?'

I shake my head. 'No thanks. I'm fine,' I assure her, though my throat feels like sandpaper.

'Why do you think he wasn't happy?' she goes on after a second.

I struggle for a way to explain. 'Because my mum stifled him,' I say eventually. It's true, I think.

She nods thoughtfully. 'Can you tell me what you mean by stifled, Eve?' she asks, her eyes troubled as they search mine, like my mum's sometimes are.

Again I struggle for the right words. 'He couldn't breathe,' I say, glancing back to the window. 'He never felt the sun on his face,' I add, freeing one of my hands to wipe at my nose.

Georgia pulls a tissue from the box on the coffee table and passes it to me. 'Okay?' she asks, once I've blown.

I take a huge breath and nod determinedly.

She furrows her brow – in concern, I realise, not anger. 'Are you all right to continue, Eve?' she asks. 'We have a few more minutes, but we can stop whenever you want to.'

'I'm good.' I dredge up a smile, even though I can feel the tears bursting to get out. They won't. I'm an expert at damming them.

'This might be a difficult question,' she says, her face sympathetic. 'If you'd prefer not to tell me, that's absolutely fine, I promise.'

Again I nod and brace myself.

'How did you feel when Jacob was being stifled? What were your thoughts, can you tell me?'

I shrug, feeling more nervous now, because I think she'll think I was a horrible sister. 'I didn't have any really,' I answer honestly.

She looks puzzled, and I know I need to explain, but I'm not sure how. 'I don't think about it,' I tell her hesitantly. 'I go some-place else.'

'Such as?' She nods encouragingly.

'An upside-down forest.' I feel embarrassed as I say it. 'The animals are magical, kind and friendly and there are no bad people allowed.'

She smiles. 'It does sound magical,' she says. 'Why is it upside-down, though?'

I frown. 'I'm not sure. Because we prefer to walk on the clouds, I think, so our feet won't hurt.' I'm acutely aware of my shoes digging into the backs of my heels as I answer, but I don't say anything.

'And do you remember what's been happening in the real world when you come back from the forest?'

I shake my head. I wouldn't want to remember even if I could.

'So do you think your mind blocks it out?' she asks, looking at me thoughtfully.

I consider it and then nod. 'I think so,' I reply hesitantly.

'Don't look so worried.' She smiles kindly again and it makes me feel a bit better. 'That can happen sometimes. Think of it as a kind of cut-off mechanism, something our mind does involuntarily to dissociate from something like a perceived threat or to prevent bad memories being relived. Do you understand?'

I nod, and try to smile back, but the worry I had before when I saw the GP is worming its way into my head. 'So does that mean I'm evil or mad?' I ask. It's bad enough now, but the thought of being taunted all over again at high school terrifies me.

'Your emotional reaction causes a physical effect,' Georgia explains gently. 'Your mind can't cope with how upsetting experiences make you feel. It's an unconscious reaction, Eve. You have no control over it. It doesn't mean you're evil or mad.'

I try to process as she continues to explain that the cause of such events is often a traumatic incident: a major accident or illness in the family, severe emotional upset, a difficult or abusive relationship, being bullied. I guess I tick all those boxes and I'm not sure whether I'm relieved or even more worried. 'Your memories may always remain hidden,' she tells me. 'You may never remember.'

I do remember, though, certain things. I tune out sometimes, pretend I don't see or hear what's happening, but there are some things I remember. I want to tell her, but I don't. My mum would be furious.

'Do you mind if ask you something else?' Georgia says, and I nod, not wanting to appear unhelpful. 'Your father,' she begins, and I feel the butterflies whirling, 'are you sad that he left?'

A wasp buzzes a warning in my head and I shake it away. 'I'm glad he's gone,' I tell her honestly. 'It's his fault. All of it.'

She pauses. 'What's his fault, Eve? Can you tell me?'

I tuck my hands back under my thighs. 'The sadness. His dark moods, they caused it.'

'And the bruises, did he cause those?' she asks gently. 'Did he cause you to take the tablets? There's no shame in talking about it, Eve,' she adds when I don't answer.

But I think there is, because my dad told me I should be ashamed of myself when my mum had already got so much to worry about. He slapped my face and called me a selfish bitch, and my mum didn't say a single word. If I tell her all that, though, I know I'm going to be in terrible trouble. I look at her. I know she's trying to help, that she cares, but I just can't.

'I fell,' I say, and glance away.

THIRTY-THREE

2000

Lydia

Her chest pumping with shock and anger, Lydia stared at the woman, horrified. 'I don't believe Eve said those things,' she said shakily. 'Why would she have?'

Georgia Sutherland simply looked at her, a guarded look, one Lydia had seen many times before whenever she tried to tell people, quite calmly in her estimation, despite being out of her mind with worry, that her baby boy was ill. Clearly she was assessing her. Was she even qualified to? She looked far too young to be a doctor.

Lydia should never have agreed to this. She really couldn't see how all this psychobabble could help anyone. From what she could see, in fact, the aim of the so-called child development centre seemed to be to tear families apart. Eve was all she had left. Only Lydia and her daughter knew how things had been at home, what had happened on the day of Jacob's accident. They'd agreed never to talk of it, for the sake of Eve's future, for her own future, and for Chloe's, although that girl's constant influence over Eve had helped no one. And now these people were trying to extract information from a girl who, at twelve years of age, couldn't possibly realise that anything she might say could be taken out of context. It *had* been an accident, Eve would never have said anything to the contrary. What had happened before and afterwards was a secret she could never tell. Eve was an intelligent child. She would know it would impact on all of their lives forever.

'Eve wasn't coerced into saying anything, Mrs Lockhart,' Dr Sutherland assured her, her voice full of false sympathy. Lydia had experienced that before, too. 'This is a safe space for children to talk about their emotions in order to be able to deal with them,' she went on. 'Eve simply talked about how she felt.'

Lydia looked away. Her expression must be murderous, and the woman would see it, but she couldn't help it. Fixing her attention on her wedding ring, she twisted it around her finger. She'd thought it had been given with love. That the vows David had made had meant something to him. They'd actually meant nothing, just as *she'd* meant nothing.

'Your husband left suddenly, didn't he?' Dr Sutherland asked.

Lydia looked up and away. She couldn't hold eye contact with the woman while she was sitting in judgement of her. 'Shortly after we lost Jacob, yes,' she confirmed tightly. 'We argued. He left.'

'What did you argue about?'

'The fact that he was too busy with the trollop he was seeing to care about his own son.' Lydia's voice was filled with bitterness, though that wasn't what they'd argued about. She was aware that he saw other women, for sex, no doubt – she couldn't imagine that a man who was incapable of empathising with another human being would have become emotionally involved with anyone – but she'd never dared confront him about it. The truth about what had happened on the day of Jacob's accident, though, the timing around when David had disappeared from their lives, could never come out. Eve *knew* this.

'Has he been in contact at all since he left?' the woman asked.

Lydia felt as if she were under interrogation. The picture that thought evoked chilled her to the bone. 'I haven't heard a word from him,' she answered, her voice laced with contempt. 'He hasn't been in touch with Eve either. As I said, he doesn't care. He never did.'

'I see.' The doctor nodded and made another note on her pad. She paused for a moment, and Lydia could hear the clock on the wall ticking, like the slow drip of a tap, fraying her already fraught nerves. 'I've spoken to my colleagues,' the woman continued after an interminably long silence. 'We'd like to refer you for a psychiatric evaluation, if you're amenable?'

'What?' Lydia's stunned gaze snapped back to her. 'Why?'

Dr Sutherland avoided the question. 'We would have preferred to see both you and Mr Lockhart, together and separately,' she said instead, 'but if he can't be immediately contacted...' She let it hang, like a guillotine.

Lydia simply stared at her. 'But *why?*' she repeated shakily.

Dr Sutherland drew in a breath. 'Lydia,' she said, using her Christian name, an attempt to bond with her, Lydia guessed, 'have you ever heard of something called fabricated or induced illness?'

Lydia felt a cold chill of apprehension prickle her skin. She didn't answer. Couldn't.

'It used to be known as Munchausen syndrome by proxy and covers a wide range of behaviours, usually involving parents, relatives or carers seeking healthcare for a child that is found to be unnecessary.'

Lydia laughed in bewilderment. 'Are you suggesting that I would have deliberately hurt my *child*?'

'We're not suggesting anything, Lydia. We'd just like to do an initial—'

'It's utterly preposterous. Outrageous. I came here because my daughter needs *help*, and you accuse me of... I wasn't even in the room when he had his first attack. Nor was I with him at the hospital when he died, because they wouldn't let me *see* him.' Tears sprang to her eyes and she stood up.

'Lydia, wait.' The woman got to her feet too. 'Please let me continue.' She placed a hand on her arm. 'I mentioned that it covers a wide range of behaviours. This varies from making a child ill to exaggerating or inventing symptoms to gain attention. Is it possible that you or someone else might have been trying to—'

Lydia snatched her arm away. 'I did want to draw attention, yes,' she fumed. 'To the fact that Jacob was ill. And now he's dead, which I think rather proves the point, making all of this point*less*. I'm leaving.'

THIRTY-FOUR

PRESENT

Eve

Eve's heart leapt into her throat as she heard his key in the front door. He was back. She closed her eyes, relief crashing through her. She'd texted him and rung him. He hadn't answered. After admitting that she'd spied on him, as good as accused him of cheating on her, she'd convinced herself she'd driven him away. Quickly she checked the baby monitor in the kitchen, and then went to the hall, dread pooling in the pit of her stomach at what she might see in his eyes. She couldn't bear it if it was the same anger bordering on hostility she'd seen this morning. That wasn't Dom. She'd never known him to lose his temper. Not once.

'I'm sorry,' she said as soon as he walked in. 'About the ridiculous things I said, being so suspicious when I know there's no reason to be. It's not you, it's me, my insecurities. Anyway, I'm sorry.' She shrugged apologetically.

Dom drew in a breath, placed his car keys on the hall table.

For an excruciatingly long moment he didn't look at her, and Eve felt a new wave of panic unfurl inside her.

'Dom, please talk to me,' she said tremulously.

At last he brought his gaze up, a mixture of confusion and sympathy in his eyes. 'Why do you feel so insecure, Eve?' he asked her. 'With me, I mean. Knowing as much as I do, I understand to a degree, but I've never given you cause, have I?'

'No.' Eve dropped her gaze. 'I just don't feel I deserve you,' she admitted. 'This. Security. Family.' She looked back at him. 'I keep waiting for someone to take it away from me.'

'And you thought Chloe might?' he asked, clearly worried about her. He was right to. She was beginning to worry about herself. That she was dreaming about magical forests, having nightmares about ghosts from her past *was* worrying. Back then, she'd successfully blocked things out, dissociative seizures eventually being her diagnosis and, actually, her ally, allowing her to escape her waking nightmares if only for a short while. The fact was, though, she'd come to with bumps and bruises and she'd had no idea how she'd got them. She didn't want to go back there. Or to be dragged back there by her mother, for whatever selfish, warped reason the woman had. She wanted to keep moving forward. She had a responsible job, a beautiful child, a good marriage she was in danger of jeopardising. She had to stop this now.

She didn't want to dredge up things that had happened between her and Chloe in the past either, but after their confrontation the day after Chloe's party, and unable to rid herself of the feeling that Chloe was going after Dom, she wouldn't have much to do with her in future. She also owed Dom an explanation if he was going to understand why she was all too ready to judge him.

'We had a falling-out once over a boy I was going out with. It was silly, a long time ago when we were at university,' she said, careful to keep it low key. She had no wish to go into it in depth.

'You mean Steve?' Dom asked, knocking her sideways.

He knows. How? Not from Steve, she was sure of that. She'd asked Steve specifically about that very thing when they'd last spoken. Unless he'd told Chloe since then, which she doubted. Why would he have? 'No, I...' she faltered. 'I mean, I did go out with him a couple of times, but—'

'Hold on.' Dom stopped her, eyeing her quizzically. 'You mean you went out with him even though he was seeing Chloe?'

'She wasn't with him then, not officially,' she explained quickly, feeling as if she was now the one under scrutiny. Also feeling very uncomfortable. 'He wanted to be, though. And Chloe wanted to be with him, so it never came to anything between us.'

Dom nodded slowly.

'And now she wants to be with you,' she added, bringing his attention swiftly back to the subject in hand.

'Come again?' Now he looked perplexed.

'You have to admit, it's pretty obvious she fancies you.'

'Does she?' His expression changed to one of thoughtful surprise. Then, 'She clearly has good taste,' he said.

She arched her eyebrows in amusement. 'What happened to Mr Modesty?' she asked.

'Gone missing,' Dom said. 'I've obviously turned into a lady-killer. Just so you know, though, I don't fancy *her*.' He walked towards her. 'It's you I fancy, Dr Howell.' Circling her with his arms, he gave a mock scowl, then brushed her lips softly with his. 'Could you please remember that when you're next consumed with self-doubt?'

'I will.' Immensely relieved, despite the niggling question as to how he had come to know something that definitely hadn't come from her, or Chloe, who'd never been privy to the fact that she and Steve had had the odd date, Eve hugged him back hard. Dom had been her anchor, grounding her when she'd still felt emotionally adrift despite having completed her postgrad course and secured a position at the surgery. Outwardly she'd been confident, but inside she'd suffered badly from imposter syndrome. It was still there, under the surface, crippling sometimes whenever she felt vulnerable.

'Coffee?' Dom suggested after a moment. 'With extra chocolate sprinkles for energy. Remind me to have breakfast before I strop off in a sulk next time.'

Eve laughed. 'I'll pack you a sandwich,' she said, giving his rather pleasingly toned hindquarters a cheeky squeeze. 'Where did you go?' she asked, working to sound only casually interested as she headed for the coffee machine.

'Nowhere in particular. I just walked around for a while,' Dom answered. Going to the baby monitor to check on Kai, he studied it for a second, then turned towards her. 'Actually, that's a lie,' he said, and paused, causing a prickle of apprehension to run the length of her spine. 'I went to see Lydia.'

Eve's stomach clenched. Now it made sense. 'Why?' She shook her head in confusion.

He surveyed her carefully. 'I needed to know what was going on, and you clearly weren't going to talk to me. I'm sorry I went behind your back.'

She swallowed back the stone in her throat. 'And?'

'We talked,' he said. 'She told me some things about your upbringing, why things are the way they are between you.'

'Painting herself as a picture of innocence, no doubt,' Eve muttered, turning away.

Dom was quiet for a moment, watching her as she stuffed a filter into the machine, spilling the coffee as she spooned it in. *Slow down*, she cautioned herself, her nerves tightening like a slip knot inside her. *Listen to what he has to say.*

'She didn't, actually,' he went on eventually. 'She seemed upset. She clearly found it difficult to talk about.'

Ha! Eve managed to suppress a cynical laugh. She'd never known a time when Lydia wasn't upset, mostly with her.

'I get the sense she thought she'd failed you,' he continued. 'If it helps, I think she did,' he added.

Eve concentrated on the coffee, tried to stop her hands shaking. He didn't know the half of it. Or rather, he only knew as much as her mother had told him.

'She mentioned that you'd been referred to a psychiatrist,' he said guardedly.

She reeled inwardly, her chest constricting as she tried to work out what Lydia's agenda was. She was clearly attempting to poison his mind. Chloe had been right about that.

'Why didn't you feel you could tell me?' he asked quietly. 'About the bruises? The tablets? I care about you, Eve. You know I do. You must know I would never have judged you.'

'Why didn't I trust you, do you mean? Would you trust me if I went scuttling off to *your* mother with our marital concerns?' Eve heard the anger in her voice and hated herself for it. This wasn't his fault.

'That's unfair, Eve.' He sighed heavily. 'I didn't want to have to talk to your mother, for God's sake, but the way you were behaving left me no choice. I was concerned, for *you*, for Kai. Can you really blame me for trying to find out more about your brother's history, what happened to him?'

Eve's heart skidded against her ribcage. 'She told you about him?' she said disbelievingly.

Dom nodded and ran a hand over his neck. 'I saw the nursery,' he said, a mixture of sadness and wariness in his eyes. 'When I went upstairs to the bathroom, I looked into the bedrooms. Did you know she's kept it intact, everything just as it must have been when he died? She has a doll in the cot, one of those lifelike dolls. I almost had a heart attack when I saw it. I

couldn't help thinking that maybe it's your mother who needs
the psychiatric help.'

Eve latched onto that. 'She *does*,' she agreed emphatically.
'What did she tell you?'

He eyed her curiously. 'What his symptoms were. That you
were there when he died. That must have been beyond devastating for you.'

Eve's mouth ran dry. He was waiting for her to say something. What? She warned herself to be careful. 'It was,' she
stammered. 'I didn't realise at first. What was happening, I
mean. I had my earphones on, in my bedroom, and...' She
trailed off as Dom narrowed his eyes. He was suspicious – of
her. What had her bloody mother told him? Asked outright, she
would have lied – she would have to have done to save herself –
but how could Eve know what she'd said?

'Chloe wasn't with you?' he went on cautiously.

'No. Yes, I...' She groped for the right answer. 'She had
been, just before. She'd gone home for her tea, I think. I don't
really remember.'

'You didn't find him, then?' He scrutinised her for a long,
blood-freezing moment.

Eve shook her head, swallowed hard. 'Did she say anything
else?' She squeezed the words out, panic rising so fast she
thought it might choke her.

'Not much.' Dom was still studying her intently. 'I left
shortly afterwards. I tripped on the stairs, unfortunately.
Almost broke my neck on the way down.'

She told him. Eve's heart froze, icy coldness spreading
through her as her mind flew back there. She was twelve years
old again, petrified, dry-eyed with shock and fear as she
watched the body bounce off every step of the stairs. So much
blood as he'd landed, flowering into the cream carpet beneath
him like an ink stain. But *how much* had she told him?

THIRTY-FIVE

She could feel Dom's eyes on her as she turned to the worktop. 'You can talk to me about it, you know, Eve,' he said quietly as she studied the image of her little boy softly sleeping, sweetly dreaming. 'That is, if you want to.'

She felt her heart constrict. Oh, how she wanted to. More than anything, she wanted to blurt it all out, right here, right now, but there was simply no way to. There would be consequences. There would have to be. She couldn't just burden him with the knowledge and expect he would do nothing about it. Steve had been young, brave and stupidly naïve; a hero in Chloe's eyes and in hers. He would never say anything. She'd worried he might with his marriage breaking down, but in reality he couldn't. Dom, though, would be obliged to.

'I know. And I do, it's just...'

'Too painful,' he finished. 'I understand. But you know what they say about a trouble shared?'

She wished that could be true, that he could help her carry the weight of her secret. He couldn't. It would drag him down. It would hurt Kai, too, and she didn't think she could bear that.

'Eve?' he said, right behind her. 'Please talk to me.' He

reached for her.

She moved away. 'I will,' she said, pulling the overhead cupboard open and reaching for a tumbler. 'I just... *Dammit.*' She sucked in a breath as the tumbler slipped like butter through her fingers, crashing to the floor to shoot a thousand slivers of glass across the ceramic tiles. 'Shit.' She clenched her teeth, tried to bite back the tears that were close to spilling over.

'It doesn't matter.' Dom squeezed her arm and locked his gaze on hers, his expression one of deep concern, peppered with uncertainty. 'I'll clean it up. No harm done.'

But there was. She watched him crouch quickly to the floor to retrieve the larger pieces. The glass smashing was symbolic. She could feel it. Her marriage would be broken, too, shattered into a million pieces. There would be no way to fix it.

Nausea churned in her stomach. The ache in her head went from a dull thud to a deafening din. She couldn't think. She couldn't do this. Do this to *him.*

'Eve?' Dom said behind her as, pressing a hand to her mouth, she stumbled past him.

'I have to go to the bathroom.' She squeezed the words out, then, with Dom close behind her, flew up the stairs, closing and locking the bathroom door quickly behind her.

'Eve?' Dom reached it seconds later. '*Eve.*' He knocked and tried the handle.

Cold fear swirling inside her, she pressed her back to the door.

'Eve!' He rattled the handle. 'Please don't lock yourself in there. Whatever it is that's worrying you, we'll talk it through.'

'What else did she tell you?' she asked, her voice tremulous.

He went quiet for a second. 'Let's not talk through the door, Eve. Come out. Please.'

She *had* told him then: about that day with her father that would haunt her forever, about all of her past probably. Why else would he not simply put her mind at rest? 'It's all lies, you know that, don't you?' she murmured, swallowing back the acrid taste in the back of her throat. '*All* of it. She's not right, Dom. Not well. You know she's not.'

'Okay,' he answered, after another interminably long pause. 'Okay. Please just come out and we'll sit down and talk.'

Eve tugged in a long breath and held it. He would think *she* was mad, but he had to know how she felt, her deepest fear. What she believed with every part of herself to be her mother's heartless agenda. 'She's trying to steal my baby, Dom.' She exhaled shakily. 'She's trying to take Kai away from me.'

He didn't answer.

'Dom?' Eve's heart turned over. He didn't believe her.

'I'm here,' he said at last, his voice hoarse. 'I'm right here, Eve.'

She closed her eyes. She needed him to be there. She needed *him*. 'She's insane, Dom,' she went on, desperate for him to understand. 'She spent time in a psychiatric ward after Jacob died because of what she'd done. She suffered from depression and delusions. She was on all sorts of tablets, antipsychotics and antidepressants. She wasn't well then. She's *still* not. You have to believe me.'

Again Dom took a second, and Eve's heart almost stopped beating. 'I believe you,' he said. 'I saw the evidence of it with my own eyes, remember? Please come out, Eve.'

'Chloe's lying too,' she added quickly, realising that, given the latest twist in their relationship, Chloe might have confided to him more than she should. 'If she's said anything to you, it's not true, Dom, do you hear me?'

'I hear you,' Dom said after another stomach-churning silence. 'But you need to make me understand. Why would Chloe lie to me?'

Eve emitted a strangled laugh. 'You don't get it, do you?' she asked him, incredulous. 'She wants you. She's made that abundantly obvious. She's trying to take you away from me.'

'I see,' Dom said softly. 'Sounds like a conspiracy,' he joked
– and Eve felt her world sliding from beneath her. He *did* think
she was mad.

'Kai's awake,' he said, alerting her to her son crying in the
nursery along the landing. Her urge was to yank the door open
and go to him, clutch her baby tight to her, flee through the
front door and keep going. But how could she? She had to find
out just what her mother had hoped to gain by doing this.

'I'll see to him,' Dom said as she stayed where she was,
trusting him, finally, where she felt she couldn't trust herself.
Not now, not in this moment. Kai would sense she was upset,
and he would be upset in turn. She would never allow that.
Never allow her mother to get her claws into him. Even the
thought of it caused bile to rise in her throat. As for Chloe, if her
aim was to take Dom away from her, she should know that Eve
would fight her with every weapon she had.

'It's okay, little guy, Daddy's here.' She heard his voice, calm
and reassuring, drifting back from the nursery. He loved his son,
unequivocally. He loved *her*. She felt safe in that knowledge.

Why was this happening? Her mother hadn't made any
great effort to contact her over the years. And now, when she
finally had a life worth living, the woman had made it her
mission to take it away. She'd silenced her as a child, silenced
her as a teenager. As an adult, Eve had stayed silent. And now
Lydia was revealing things to her husband, dropping information like pebbles into water. The ripples would grow wider and
wider, and no matter how hard Eve tried to keep breathing, the
weight of the secrets she carried would drag her down.

What should she do? Stifling a sob, she turned to the sink,
clutching the rim and trying to contain the nausea swirling
inside her. She blinked hard at what she saw there. Her mind,
which she'd worked so hard to keep focused, was now playing
tricks on her, dragging her back to another house, another bathroom, her nightmare in which coiled copper snakes writhed and

hissed and threatened to rise up and bite her. She squeezed her eyes tight, tried to block out the sound of her brother's whimpers echoing hauntingly around the tiled walls. Jacob had clung to her on that day she'd tried to obliterate from her mind. As she'd teetered on the stairs, too petrified of the raging monster that was their father to go up or down, he had held tight to her, the person who should have stopped it all, who should have saved him.

She knew why Lydia had come back into her life. Dom might not believe her, but she knew why she'd kept Jacob's room exactly as it was. Eve would never let her have access to her child, not *ever*.

Kai's cries were quieting. Dom was carrying him down for his feed. She snapped her eyes open, saw her reflection in the mirror and knew she could never escape the fear and the pain as long as her mother had a hold over her.

A shudder shook through her. She had to get out, find some space in her head to think. She couldn't face Dom now. She couldn't breathe. Turning to the door, she listened for sounds. Hearing Dom in the kitchen, she pressed down the handle and headed quietly along the landing and down the stairs.

Careful not to jangle them, she picked up her car keys from the hall table, then glanced back towards the kitchen. Dom was talking softly to Kai. He would change him, warm his feed for him, make sure there were enough bottles in the fridge. She knew he would do that, that he knew how to. That he would always be the best father a man could be to his son. That he would protect him. She had to put her trust in him. Right now, she didn't think she was capable of caring for Kai as he should be cared for. She really did feel as if she were going mad, icy fingers clutching at her heart and her mind. She couldn't go back there. She had to find the strength to do what she'd done once before and make it stop.

THIRTY-SIX

PRESENT

Chloe

Well, that's ruined the mood a bit. Hearing someone at the front door, Chloe sighed and submerged herself deeper in her scented bathwater. If she ignored it, hopefully whoever it was would go away. With the children having been hyper and fractious since Steve had dropped them home, having no doubt spoiled them, she considered she'd earned some time to herself. She was aiming to have a pamper evening. After a nice hot bath, she was going to do her nails and then curl up in front of the TV with one of the films she'd been meaning to watch. Realising they were mostly romantic films, which was why Steve hadn't wanted to watch them – with her, anyway – her heart sank. Maybe she'd check the apps and look for a good drama instead. Hopefully there would be one where the husband ended up being murdered.

Closing her eyes, she tried to relax; then, realising the person at the door wasn't going to go away, she cursed and heaved herself up. Who on earth was it? Stepping out of the bath as the knocking grew more urgent, she snatched up her glass of wine from the corner, had a quick glug, then grabbed her fluffy towel and padded to the landing.

Tightening the towel around herself, she peered over the stair rail, then stepped sharply back as she saw a tall, dark silhouette through the opaque glass in the front door. She almost jumped out of her skin as Thomas appeared behind her. 'Mum, there's someone at the door,' he informed her, kneading his eyes sleepily as he stepped onto the landing.

'I know.' Chloe turned to usher him back to his room. 'It's fine. Go back to bed, sweetheart.'

'Aren't you going to answer it?' Thomas asked in confusion as she reached to close his door.

'When I have my bathrobe on,' she assured him, and turned quickly to her own room to grab the robe from the hook. Also her phone from where she'd left it on the dressing table. Whoever was down there was unlikely to be a sales caller at this time in the evening. It could be anyone, a mad axe murderer for all she knew, and here she was on her own half naked with two children in the house, thanks to her shit of a husband.

Whipping off her towel and quickly tugging the bathrobe on, she selected Dom's number as she made her way back to the landing. Whatever the situation between them, he wouldn't leave her alone and vulnerable with a lunatic outside her house. With her nerves tying themselves in knots, she approached the stairs, then stopped as she realised that his phone was ringing right outside her front door.

A thrill of excitement running through her, she hurried down to open it. There must be some kind of crisis. He needed her, quite obviously. Composing herself, she took a breath, arranged her face into a smile and reached for the handle.

'Is Eve here?' Dom asked immediately.

'No.' Noting the alarmed look on his face, Chloe stepped back to let him in. 'I was in the bath. Why? What's happened?'

'Has she called or texted?' There was a hint of desperation in his eyes.

She felt a ripple of apprehension. 'No. At least I don't think so. My phone's been on silent. Hold on.' Quickly she checked it, then shook her head. 'No, nothing.'

Seeing how concerned he was, she began to grow worried, even though she was furious with Eve for sidelining her. For threatening her when she'd said she wasn't sure she could carry on the way things were. She'd had enough – of her claustrophobic relationship with Eve, and of Steve. She hadn't been that sure about marrying him in the first place, but Eve had convinced her he worshipped her, that he would do anything for her – apart from stay faithful, obviously. She'd been caught up in her friend's excitement for her. She'd thought he loved her. She'd thought Eve did. She'd stayed by her side because she believed she needed her. But Steve didn't love her, and neither did Eve. Chloe needed to stop thinking of others now and live her life for herself. She was ready to go after what she wanted, just as Eve had. She still cared about Eve, but didn't she deserve a little happiness too? As for Lydia, she had no real hold over either of them, if only Eve would realise it. She couldn't say anything without incriminating herself.

'What's going on, Dom?' she asked him. 'There's clearly a problem.' A thought occurred, and Chloe felt a flutter of guilt at the seed she was about to plant, despite the hurt Eve had caused her. 'She hasn't done anything stupid, has she?' she asked, gauging him carefully.

'Like what?' Dom's expression darkened.

Chloe dropped her gaze. 'Nothing. I just... She's more fragile than she seems sometimes, that's all.'

He breathed in sharply. 'I have to get back.' He turned to leave. 'I've left Kai on his own.'

'Dom, wait.' Chloe caught hold of his arm. 'You need to tell me what's going on. I've been worried to death. Eve's been acting so strangely, and I—'

'You knew, didn't you?' Dom narrowed his eyes. 'That she once attempted something "stupid", as you call it; that it was possible she might again.'

'No.' Chloe shook her head, glanced quickly down and back. 'Yes, but—'

'So why the *hell* didn't you tell me?' Dom's expression was now thunderous, and Chloe was not happy about that at all. How was it always *her* who ended up being in the wrong? Steve had accused her of driving him to cheat on her because she'd said she liked Dom. Eve was treating her abysmally, and now Dom was turning on her. It was all so *unfair*.

'I didn't tell you because Eve wouldn't have *wanted* me to,' she answered, feeling peeved and tearful. 'There are quite a few things Eve wouldn't want me to tell you actually,' she added pointedly. 'As I'm pretty sure there are things *you* wouldn't want me to tell *her*.'

'I gathered.' He eyed her coldly, and Chloe's heart plummeted, then froze when he added, 'Lydia told me.'

Her stomach turned over. 'What did she tell you?'

'Enough,' he said shortly. 'I need to go.'

'Wait.' Panic tightening her chest, she skirted around him. 'Whatever that woman told you, it's all lies,' she said forcefully. 'You have to believe me.'

'So Eve said.' He moved to get past her.

'Dom, don't, please.' Chloe moved closer. 'Don't go like this, looking as if you hate me. I can't bear it. All I've ever done is try to protect Eve. To be there for her. I love her.'

'Really? You have a strange way of showing it.' Dom shook his head, and this time she couldn't mistake the look in his eyes, one of scorn.

'And you don't?' she retorted, and then, anger and impulse

driving her, she slid her arms around him and pressed her mouth hard to his.

He caught hold of her, gripping her arms hard and pushing her away. 'For fuck's sake, Chloe, what the *hell* are you doing?'

Chloe watched, staggered, as he wiped the back of his hand across his mouth, wiping *her* off. 'Picking up where we left off!' she spat furiously.

'*Jesus*. Are you serious?' He looked at her as if she were mad. 'There's nothing *to* pick up.'

'That's a lie, Dom.' She matched his look with one of contempt. 'You *know* it is.'

He sucked in a breath. 'I was drunk. We both were. Whatever you're imagining might happen between us, Chloe, it's not going to. End of,' he said, his tone flat.

She looked him over stonily. 'You bastard.'

'Probably. Undoubtedly, in fact. For what it's worth, I'm sorry. You should go back inside. Your kids need you,' he added, looking past her to where Thomas had appeared on the stairs.

Chloe glanced up at her son. 'Go back to bed, Thomas. I'll be up in a minute.' Thomas hesitated. 'Go,' she repeated. She turned back to Dom to find him heading out of the front door. 'Where are you going?' she demanded.

He didn't look back. 'To find my wife.'

'And when you do, will you shatter her illusions and tell her what a total shit you are?' she seethed behind him. 'Or shall I? I mean, what kind of friend would I be if I didn't open her eyes to the fact?'

Dom kept walking.

Oh no. No. No. No! He didn't get to do this. He didn't get to walk away from her too. Not after leading her on, ruining her marriage. And he had. Steve had been right. She had thought Dominic Howell was perfect, doing the right thing, marrying the woman who was carrying his child. The spark had been there, though, right from the outset. It *had* been. He'd married

Eve, but he'd wanted *her*. Or she'd thought he did. Her hands strayed to her lips in the wake of his humiliating rebuff, which hurt possibly more than anything had in her life.

She loved him. He knew it. He *did*. He'd been using her. They were all bloody well using her. Fury settled like a cold stone inside her. This was Lydia's fault. All of it. If she hadn't reappeared, none of this would have happened. Eve wouldn't have turned on her. Dom wouldn't have rejected her, riddled with guilt because Eve, who worked at being competent and calm, was clearly acting irrationally.

Fuming, she whirled around, heading for the kitchen. Yanking the fridge open, she pulled out the open bottle of wine and poured an extremely large glass, which she badly needed. Enough was enough. She had to do something about this. But what could she do that wouldn't rebound on her? She'd been a child, she reminded herself. It had ultimately been Lydia who'd been responsible for what had happened all those years ago. Lydia who'd engineered what had happened afterwards, terrifying them into keeping the secret that had blighted her life. Lydia who would be blamed if Chloe could just get Eve back onside and make sure they got their stories straight.

THIRTY-SEVEN
PRESENT

Eve

Hot tears streaming down her face, Eve sat where she was, too stunned to move. She couldn't believe it. How could he? She gulped back the jagged stone in her throat as she watched Dom walking back to their house, glancing at his phone as he went, no doubt checking the app, making sure their son was all right after leaving him alone to do *this* to her.

He'd moved the soft toy from in front of the camera, smiling at her as he did. 'You have a very vivid imagination,' he'd said in that easy-going way he had, despite what she'd accused him of.

Not vivid enough, plainly. She squeezed her eyes closed, desperate to erase the image of her husband and her best friend kissing intimately, openly, right in front of her. Obviously they hadn't realised she was there, parked just a few yards away. She dragged a hand across her cheeks, emitted a half-hysterical laugh. Or maybe they had. Chloe at least. It was possible she knew she was watching, her aim to push home the knife she'd plunged into Eve's back.

Pressing her hands over her face, she stifled a moan that came from her soul. Sucked air into her lungs and tried to do the simplest thing of all and just breathe. What should she do? She couldn't just sit here like a frightened deer caught in the headlights. She had to face him, confront him with this. She reached for the door handle, then wavered. And what then? He might try to lie to her, but she thought not. He couldn't, could he, faced with the evidence of her own eyes? There would be no going back then. No way to go forward. All her life she'd strived to do that, to make a life worth living. And now the two people who were supposed to love her were taking it away.

They'd argued on the doorstep. She couldn't hear what they'd been saying, but the words had been heated. Dom's agitated body language had told her that much. Why would that be? Chloe had said something that had angered him, that had been obvious. But what? Eve wondered. She placed herself in Chloe's shoes, a woman who knew her own husband had cheated, who seemed not to want to fight for him. Plainly that was because she was in love with a man who belonged to someone else, her best friend.

Had she issued Dom with an ultimatum? Threatened to reveal their sordid little affair in the hope that he would choose between them? That he would choose *her*? Anger ripped through Eve's chest, the pain of betrayal like an icicle through her heart.

If that were the case, then Chloe should know that Eve already knew. That she would kill before she would allow that to happen.

THIRTY-EIGHT

PRESENT

Chloe

A sharp pain scissoring through her stomach, Chloe tipped her wine back. What had happened? She should never have been the one who'd faded into the shadows. She'd shone bright at school, her timid, mousy little friend bathing in her aura. She couldn't place when the natural order of things had been flipped on its head and she'd become the one who went unnoticed. Now it was time for the tide to turn back again. She topped up her glass, took another long swig. Karma was catching up with them. And *she* would be the one to swim.

Determined, she went out into the hallway, then spun around as she caught something flitting past the window in her peripheral vision. Her breath stalled in her chest and she inched towards the window. *Shit.* She started, her heart lurching violently at a sudden unearthly screeching, then almost wilted with relief as she realised it wasn't some ghostly night creature but the neighbours' cats fighting.

Feeling spooked nevertheless, she hurried on towards the stairs. She needed to reassure her children. And then she needed to get dressed. Eve would be back, of that much she was certain. She wouldn't leave Kai in Dom's care for long. And when she did turn up, Chloe would be there for her, as she'd always been, picking up the pieces, lending her a shoulder. Dom wouldn't dare to stop her. She had to talk to her, mend fences between them and make her see that there was only one way forward where Lydia was concerned.

She was halfway up the stairs when she heard another noise, one that sounded suspiciously like the back door quietly opening. Fear tickling the length of her spine, she froze, and listened. Hearing nothing but complete silence, she allowed herself to breathe out. She was imagining things, definitely spooked by those cats, and Dom upsetting her hadn't helped. She'd turned the key in the door, she was sure.

She hadn't realised there was someone mounting the stairs behind her until it was too late. The grip on her ankle as she tried to flee was like a vice, a hand with the strength of ten men. Panic sliced through her twofold as she heard Thomas emerge from his room mumbling sleepily, 'Mum?'

'Thomas, don't come down!' she screamed, desperate for him not to see. 'Get your sister, go to the bathroom and lock the door, and don't come out until I tell you—'

Her breasts hit the stairs first. A sharp yank, then a thump... thump, thump, thump as she was dragged backwards, her chin striking each step on the way down.

The air was forced from her lungs as she landed face down on the tiles in the hall, jarring every bone in her body. Disorientated, she blinked hard and tried to lever herself up, to crawl away and call out, but all that spewed from her mouth was a spray of rich red blood, spattering her newly decorated white walls stark crimson. Unable to articulate, she spluttered and coughed, and finally spat out something hard – one of her teeth, she realised, nausea rising like hot bile inside her. Now the feral screeching was hers, a half-muted animal wail deep in her throat.

Primal fear, all-encompassing, engulfed her. She wanted to say she was sorry. And she was, truly. She tried to formulate the words, but her attempt was inaudible, nothing but a bloody gurgle. She was at the foot of the stairs, unable to speak, at the mercy of whoever it was behind her. Terror pierced her heart like an icicle as she realised that karma really had caught up with her.

THIRTY-NINE

PRESENT

Eve

Eve pressed her foot down on the accelerator. With no idea where she was going, she was driving too fast, breaking the speed limit. *Slow down*, she urged herself, her heart wrenching as she pictured her beautiful, innocent baby boy. The thought of leaving him, of hurting him, allowing anyone else to, brought her sharply to her senses and she eased her foot up. She couldn't allow that to happen. She *wouldn't* allow that to happen. She had to stop it, stop Lydia, because if the secrets came out, she would have no choice but to leave him. She had to be strong, face her demons, slay them, all of them. It was that simple.

She hadn't realised her destination until she arrived there. The company still traded under her father's family name, one of his brothers having taken over the running of it. *Lockhart Construction. Your Future Safe in Our Hands.* She read the signage over the entrance of the building as she approached and emitted a bitter laugh.

Walking past the building, a converted warehouse, she took the towpath down to the canal that ran at the back of the trading estate behind it. It was prettier now than she remembered, flower tubs and benches placed along it. She'd spent many an evening here with Chloe after her father had gone, staring down into the inky depths of the water. The canal had originally been used to transport coal, ore and limestone to the local industrial regions. Now it was used mainly by holiday hire boats. They'd made up dark fairy stories rather than magical ones, speculating at the murky secrets it held and the tales it could tell should it ever be dredged. Eve doubted that would happen. Waiting as a child for her mother to finish work, she'd spoken often to canal workers cutting back vegetation or overhanging trees that impeded navigation. She'd learned there was no practical way the huge volume of water could ever be drained. The canal would keep its secrets forever, one man had told her, looking out across its surface.

Lydia needed to keep her secrets. She needed to disappear from her life. Eve had to make sure that happened.

Going back to her car, she pulled out her phone, braced herself and called Dom. She wouldn't confront him with what she'd witnessed between him and Chloe, she'd decided, not yet. The pain of his betrayal had fractured her heart into a million pieces, each one piercing her chest like a knife. For the moment, though, she needed him to be the man she'd thought he was, someone she knew she could trust with her son.

'Eve?' He answered immediately. 'Where the hell are you?'

'I've been driving around. I needed some space,' she answered vaguely. 'Where's Kai?'

'Here, with me. I'm in my car. I've been trying to find you.' He paused. 'What in God's name is going on, Eve? What did you mean when you said Lydia had received psychiatric care because of what she'd done?'

Debating how much she should tell him, Eve didn't answer.

'Eve, talk to me. What did she do?' Dom's tone was a combination of frustration and anger.

Eve took a second, then, 'I thought you might have gathered from what happened to Kai,' she said, and let it hang.

'You mean... *Lydia?*' He almost choked the word out. 'Are you telling me that *she* was responsible for what happened to him? That she almost fucking *killed* him?'

Eve could feel the fury emanating from him, even over the phone. 'I'll be home soon. I have something to do first, but you're right, we do need to talk – about Chloe.'

'Chloe?' There was a new inflection in his voice; guilt or fear, Eve couldn't tell which.

'She's not all she appears to be. She's dangerous, Dom. You need to be wary of her too,' she said, and hung up.

FORTY

Lydia

Lydia was getting ready for bed, humming 'Amazing Grace' while thinking of Jacob, when she heard something downstairs. Her heart fluttering, she hurried from the bedroom. She was heading along the landing when she heard it again, a distinct creak on the first step of the stairs. She froze, ears straining against a silence suddenly so profound she was sure she could hear her blood whooshing through her veins. 'Hello?' she called tremulously. 'Is someone there?'

Nothing. She cursed her overactive imagination. It was her paranoia at play. She would often hear David creeping around, usually in the dead of night when she lay somewhere between sleeping and waking. She'd thought when he'd gone that she would at last be free of him, of the fear she'd lived with, his violent mood swings. She knew now that she would never be, not truly. His presence would always be with her. It was karma, she supposed. She'd tried, but she hadn't been a good wife, not in the end.

She was making her way back to the bedroom when she heard it again, higher up this time, the step in the middle of the stairs. She knew the sounds the house made. This wasn't wood settling. Another creak, louder, and she whirled around, goose-bumps prickling the entire surface of her skin as she realised it was the third step from the top. The loose rod was two steps before it. Clearly whoever was here – and now she was sure that someone was – knew that the stairs could be lethal, a death trap. They'd stepped over it.

She swallowed a ragged knot in her throat as her mind flew back to the day that had been the beginning of the end of her baby boy's life. She could see it as if it were yesterday, hear it, the cacophonous noise from the television, David's furious voice booming above it, Eve sobbing, Chloe screaming. A body bouncing off each step of the stairs. The look of startled surprise on his face as he'd landed. The final nauseating thud that made sure he never got up again. Still the smell permeated her senses, metallic, sickly sweet and coppery.

Eve had been frozen with shock, too stunned to move. Visibly trembling, Chloe had stared down at the bloodied poker. Jacob's sobs as she'd lifted him free of his father's lifeless arms were what had haunted Lydia's nights since. Raucous, heart-wrenching sobs that had racked his small body until he'd grown weak with the effort of crying. Or so she'd thought. She hadn't realised until she placed him in his bath that some of the blood he'd been soaked in was his own.

Her heart jolted as the light through the window from the street lamp outside cast a dark shadow on the landing wall. 'Who's there?' she whispered, her voice harsh against the stillness.

There was no answer, nothing but the sound of someone breathing. 'Eve?' she said, foreboding settling like ice in the pit of her stomach as she took a tentative step towards the stairs. Was it her? Eve had often found her way back into the house through the kitchen window after fleeing her father's temper. The window catch was still loose. Lydia had never got around to fixing that either.

Still whoever was there didn't speak, and Lydia felt a sharp pain pierce her chest. 'What do you want?' she asked, blinking as the silhouette on the wall seemed to grow longer, swaying and undulating before her. She wondered whether she might be hallucinating as the light flickered, growing dimmer. She blinked hard again, panic rising swiftly. 'Please, who are you? What you do want?' she croaked, her words incoherent as they came out, her tongue feeling too thick for her mouth.

'It's a simple request, Lydia.' The response was flat, unemotional. 'I want you to stop.'

'I don't...' *Understand*, Lydia wanted to say, but the sentence seemed beyond her ability to formulate. Feeling desperately nauseous, a sudden blinding pain shooting through her head, she found herself stumbling towards her bedroom, one leg dragging stubbornly behind her.

'*Lydia*.' A command, a hand clutching her arm; she felt it for a second, then nothing, no feeling at all. Numbness. Her arm useless. 'I know what you're trying to do.' A hissed whisper. 'I won't let you.'

Lydia. Was that her name? she wondered, as the floor shifted and she felt herself falling, nothing beneath her but all-encompassing deep, impenetrable darkness.

FORTY-ONE

PRESENT

Eve

As Eve came through the front door, Dom emerged from the lounge with Kai in his arms. She had no idea what to say, how to be with him. Before tonight, with her emotions screaming, she would have been desperate for him to hold her, to feel the reassuring solidity of his body close to hers. Without him her life would be unbearable, but she had to keep living and breathing whatever the future held. She had to stay strong for her child, though she felt as if the foundations of her world were crumbling beneath her.

Dom had been her hero, a man she could depend on to be there for her, never to hurt her. And now? She had no idea who he was any more. Time would tell, she supposed. His response would, once she faced him with what she'd witnessed. There was no way he could deny the intimacy she, and possibly all the neighbours, had seen between him and Chloe. If he tried to, if he did lie to her, then she would have her answer. For now, she would stay quiet. It would kill her, but she would hold her tongue and her tears back; she was an expert at that. She needed him. She had her son's future to consider. However betrayed she felt, she had to stay calm until she knew the course of her own future.

He smiled as she dropped her car keys on the hall table, clearly trying to act as if everything were normal, as if anything could ever be normal again. How could he do that? Why had he done *this*? Destroyed them so blithely? He loved Kai, she had no doubt of that, but had he ever truly loved her? Cared about her at all? A wave of grief crashed through her, so ferocious she felt herself reel.

She gave herself a second, attempting to compose her emotions. Something broke inside her, though, as she watched him smiling down at his son, widening his eyes in surprise as Kai reached out excitedly to him, emitting a sound that sounded remarkably like the beginning of the word 'Daddy'.

He said it again as Dom carried him through to the kitchen, the whole word this time, 'Dada', and Eve felt another piece of her heart splinter.

'At your service,' Dom laughed, clearly delighted. 'Do you reckon that was his first word?' he asked, glancing at Eve.

'I think it might have been.' She felt her throat close.

'Well done, little guy.' Looking mightily proud of his son, Dom pressed a kiss to his forehead and handed him gently to her.

'There's blood on your shirt.' Eve frowned as she noted a dark crimson fleck below his collar. 'Are you bleeding?' Her gaze shot to her son. 'Is Kai?'

'What?' Dom glanced at the stain and back to her. 'It's nothing,' he assured her quickly. 'I cut my hand picking up the broken glass from the tumbler you dropped, that's all. Are you okay?' he asked, his face flooding with concern as he looked her over.

She lowered her gaze, kissing Kai's cheek, breathing him in and holding him close. She couldn't look directly at Dom. Couldn't bear to see what might be in his eyes. She'd thought she could read his every emotion there. Could she really have been so wrong about him?

'You scared me half to death, running out like that.' She could feel him studying her, hear the uncertainty in his voice. 'I've been worried out of my mind.'

So worried that your first instinct was to go across to see Chloe? Eve's gaze flickered over him and then back to Kai. 'Why?' she asked.

Dom frowned in confusion. 'Because you were upset,' he reminded her, a disbelieving edge to his voice. 'After what you said about your mother, about Chloe, and then racing off the way you did, you must have realised I would be concerned.'

Eve turned away, heading for the fridge. The tears were way too close to the surface. She couldn't give into them, risk everything spilling out. Not now.

'You were in no fit state to be driving, Eve,' Dom pointed out unnecessarily. 'Where the hell were you going?'

'Nowhere in particular.' Eve tried to keep her voice on an even keel. 'I just drove around, trying to calm myself down.' Extracting Kai's bottle from the fridge, she placed it in the warmer and turned her attention to him. 'Have you been a good little boy for your daddy, sweetheart?' she asked him, feeling her throat catch as she looked into eyes, which were crystal clear with the innocence of childhood. What would all of this do to him? She was supposed to protect him. She'd sworn she would the second she'd given birth to him. But now she'd let him down. In allowing Lydia into his life, she'd opened a Pandora's box, and now all the ghosts of her past were tumbling out. And though she'd tried, there seemed no way to stop them. *Please God, don't let my sins ever hurt him*, she prayed silently.

'Do you want me to do that while you get his feed?' Dom

asked as, resting Kai in the crook of one arm, she set about unbuttoning his coat with her free hand. He was wearing the fleece baby bear jacket that Chloe had bought him, she realised. It had *Good Things Happen* embroidered on the back. She felt another sharp stab of grief as she thought of her friend and the enormity of what she'd done. The one and only good thing to have happened in Eve's life was Kai. She would give that life for him in an instant. Love was a fickle beast, wasn't it, transient and painful, twisted, possessive. It could drive people to all sorts of madness, even murder. Eve had sworn she would kill anyone who might seek to harm her child. She would without question.

'I can manage,' she said. 'Has he been all right?'

'Fine,' he answered with a sigh. 'We drove around looking for you for a while, but...'

She glanced at him. He'd been distracted by a sudden deluge of rain lashing at the kitchen window. She felt a chill reach right down to the core of her. It sounded like fingernails tapping against the glass. She caught her breath as a petrifying stark image of someone standing outside looking in flashed through her mind.

Quickly she shook herself, and took the bottle Dom had fetched from the bottle warmer. 'Thanks,' she said with the ghost of a smile.

'You look exhausted,' he said, his expression still troubled. 'Why don't you let me see to Kai while you have a soak in the bath? I could bring you a glass of wine once he's settled.'

Eve shook her head, grieving now the imminent loss of the simplistic ritual between them that had meant so much, making it almost possible to forget her former life, at least for brief periods. She could feel his fingers massaging her neck, his hands gliding gently over her back. It was possibly the only time she'd ever relaxed.

'I've missed him,' she said, smiling down at Kai as he caught hold of a tendril of her hair, his eyes wide with wonder as he tugged it and watched it bounce springily back. 'I should take him up.' She half turned, then turned back. 'Oh, is Chloe okay, by the way?' she asked, needing now to see his reaction, even though she'd promised herself she wouldn't go there tonight.

Dom furrowed his brow. 'I don't know,' he answered, scanning her eyes carefully as she finally looked at him full on. 'Should I?'

'Not really. I drove off a bit erratically. I thought she might have noticed and come over to speak to you, that's all.'

'No. I, er...'

And so it begins. Swallowing back the stone lodged painfully in her chest, Eve lifted Kai higher in her arms and headed for the hall.

'What did you mean when you said I should be wary of her?' Dom asked behind her.

'I'm not talking about it now, Dom. I need to see to Kai.'

'Eve,' he stopped her as she mounted the stairs, 'about Chloe. There's something I need to tell you.'

Dread pooling like ice in the pit of her tummy, Eve squeezed Kai closer as she turned to look back at her husband.

'You were right. What you said earlier.' Dom drew in a tight breath. 'She has this idea that we... Had this idea that...' Trailing off, he looked at the ceiling and blew out a sigh.

'What?' Eve squeezed the word past the parched lump in her throat.

He hesitated. 'It was my fault,' he went on awkwardly. 'We kissed. Just once,' he added quickly. 'At the New Year's Eve party we all went to.'

She stared at him, staggered. So was he saying there was nothing between them? After what she'd just seen with her own eyes? 'Have you had sex with her?' she asked bluntly.

He closed his eyes.

'Have you had *sex* with her?' she demanded, causing Kai to start in her arms.

'No!' Dom refuted outright. 'For Christ's sake, Eve, surely you know me better than that?'

He was turning it around, trying to make *her* feel guilty. Eve's blood pumped, a jolt of pure rage shooting through her. She'd thought he was different, that he didn't have a manipulative bone in his body. 'I clearly *don't* know you, though, do I?' she seethed, her tears exploding with hurt and confusion.

'Don't, Eve.' His voice agonised, he moved towards her. 'Please don't cry. I didn't plan it. I'm not even sure how it happened. She was upset about Steve not paying her any attention. One minute we were talking and the next...' He trailed off helplessly.

Eve remembered the party well. Heavily pregnant, she'd been in the loo for ages, feeling hot and exhausted. She hadn't wanted to leave early. She hadn't wanted to spoil it for Dom. For Chloe. Her stomach roiled. It was history repeating itself, the exact same thing that had happened at university, except this time the man Chloe had been trying to steal was her husband. What lies would she have told her? The same lies as before? That Dom had pursued *her*? That he'd taken advantage of her? *Liars!* Everyone who had access to her did nothing but hurt her. *Why?* She choked back a sob.

'Eve, please.' Panic flooding his features, Dom reached for her.

'Don't.' She recoiled.

'I was drunk.' He fumbled for an explanation, his voice desperate. 'We both were. She thought I was interested. I tried to tell her I wasn't, but... I should have told you. I'm sorry, Eve. I should have said something, but *how*, without ruining your friendship? Please believe I would never do anything to—'

The phone ringing on the hall table cut him short. He left it, pushing his fingers through his hair as he waited for the answerphone to pick up. When it did, they both listened to the voice that spoke. 'This is the Royal Hospital with a message for Mrs

Eve Howell in regard to her mother, Lydia Lockhart. Please could Mrs Howell—'

Dom turned to snatch it up. 'This is Dominic Howell, Eve's husband,' he said. He turned to face her as he listened. Eve watched his face grow pale, registered the shock in his eyes as he locked them on hers. 'Okay.' He nodded tightly. 'Okay. We'll be there as soon as possible.'

Ending the call, he dropped his gaze briefly. When he looked back at her, his eyes were filled with trepidation, and she felt her stomach turn over. 'She's had a stroke,' he said throatily. 'She's not good, apparently. They're...'

He was by her side in an instant as she felt the strength drain from her body. Taking Kai carefully from her, he hitched him against his shoulder, threading his other arm around her. 'I'm here, Eve,' he said softly. 'Just take a breath and—'

He broke off as someone rapped hard on the front door. His gaze shot towards the door and then back to her. 'Come on, you need to sit down,' he said, trying to encourage her down the few steps she'd climbed.

Eve's legs, though, refused to budge. She couldn't speak. Couldn't move. Couldn't *feel*. Anything.

'It's all right. Just stay there a minute. I'll put Kai in his bouncer and... For Christ's sake, I'm *coming*,' he yelled as whoever it was rapped harder, causing Kai to emit a raucous cry.

He went to the door and yanked it open. 'What?' he said tersely.

'Mr Howell?' the man standing outside asked. 'Dominic Howell?'

'That's right.' Dom's voice was less strident.

'DS Mike Atkins,' the man said. 'And this is PC Alina Cho. We'd like to ask you a few questions about Chloe Adams.'

Her heart faltering, Eve stepped shakily down.

Dom didn't speak for a second, then, 'Chloe?' He stared at the man, shocked.

'She was attacked tonight,' the detective went on, his face impassive. 'We have witnesses who place you at her property at the time of the attack, so if you wouldn't mind...'

FORTY-TWO

'So let me get this right.' Detective Atkins eyed Dom sceptically. 'You're saying you didn't visit Mrs Adams this evening?'

Dom drew in a breath. 'I'm saying I didn't see Chloe this evening. I didn't say I didn't go to the house.'

'She didn't come to the door then?' the man asked.

'That's right,' Dom answered. Lying. He was *lying. Tell the truth!* Eve wanted to scream it out loud, but how could she without revealing the fact that he was lying? *Why* was he? But she knew. He didn't want to admit he'd seen Chloe – the intimate exchange between them, the obvious argument between them – in front of her. That's what this was. *All* it was. He hadn't done the horrendous thing they clearly imagined him capable of. He *couldn't* have.

'And you're quite certain Mrs Adams didn't answer her door to you?' the detective pressed.

Dom nodded stiffly. 'I guessed she was upstairs. In the bathroom, maybe. I waited a minute and then left.'

'Right.' The detective studied him intently. 'It's just that we have more than one witness statement, you see. Both of which confirm that Mrs Adams did, in fact, open her door to you.'

Dom's stunned gaze shot to his. 'I...' he started, and stopped, clearly groping for an explanation.

'Is that your blood, Mr Howell?' Atkins asked, his gaze travelling to his shirt and then back to him.

Dom squeezed his eyes closed. 'Yes,' he said, his voice hoarse. 'I cut myself. Earlier. I—'

'Dominic Howell, I am legally obliged to inform you that I am arresting you on suspicion of causing grievous bodily harm with intent to do grievous bodily harm.' The detective spoke over him.

Dom's stunned gaze shot to Eve's – and Eve's heart stopped beating.

'You do not have to say anything but it may harm your defence if you don't mention when questioned something which you later rely on in court,' Detective Atkins went impassively on. 'Anything you do say may be given in evidence. Do you understand, Mr Howell?'

'Yes,' Dom answered gruffly, his gaze fixed on hers, the look in his eyes one of sheer terror. 'I didn't do this, Eve,' he said, his voice cracking as the officer took hold of his arm, urging him towards the door. 'Please believe me. I went there, I spoke to her, but I didn't do this.'

Holding Kai close, her tears wetting his head, Eve watched, stunned, as her husband was led to the waiting police car. 'Dom?' she murmured weakly. She felt the ground shifting beneath her as he glanced desperately at her before burying his face in his hands as the car pulled away. *He didn't do it!* A sharp sob escaped her, and she tried to process what had just happened. A jumble of thoughts fought for space in her head and she couldn't make sense of anything. What should she do?

She was alone with her child on her doorstep, her husband just arrested and her neighbours standing gawping and gossiping. She glanced across to Chloe's house. Her friend was unconscious. Unable to tell them what had happened. *Her jaw's badly broken*, the policewoman had said, the look she'd given Dom as she'd spoken one of pure venom.

Eve felt sick to the bottom of her soul. Whirling around, she stumbled back into the house, shoving the door closed behind her. She needed to feed her baby, change him, reassure him. His sobs were bewildered, reminding her so much of Jacob she felt her heart break. *A solicitor*. She needed to call one. Grabbing her phone, she turned to the stairs to retrieve Kai's bottle from where she'd left it, then went to the kitchen. Whatever Dom had done, he hadn't done this. She knew it with absolute certainty. She should have said so, told him she believed him as they'd taken him, but the words had wedged in her throat.

Her stomach lurched as an image of Chloe lying bleeding and broken crashed into her head. She had to see her. Softly reassuring Kai, though her tears almost choked her, she managed to get him to take half his feed. She changed him quickly, then nursed him in her arms while she called the hospital back to establish how Lydia was.

'Are you a relative?' the nurse who came to the phone asked her when she finally got through to the ward.

'Her daughter, Eve Howell. You rang me.'

'Ah, good,' the nurse said. 'You know your mum's had a stroke?' she asked cautiously.

'Yes.' Eve took a breath. 'I'm actually a GP, so I am aware of what the prognosis might be. Could you tell me what kind of stroke she's had and how she is at the moment?'

'Oh, right. Well, she's comfortable,' the woman said. 'It was an ischaemic stroke. She's had a scan, and the vascular neurologist has seen her. We have her on thrombolysis medication; you would need to talk to the doctor more about ongoing treatment. He'll be popping back to see her in the morning.'

Despite all that had happened, past and present, Eve felt for her mother. 'And by comfortable, you mean...?'

The nurse hesitated. 'She does have some paralysis, I'm

afraid. She's not very coherent and she's obviously having problems understanding what's being said to her. You'll probably do better to speak to one of the doctors regarding her recovery.'

But she wasn't going to recover, was she, not fully? The concern was what level of dependency she would be left with. 'I see,' Eve said, and fell silent while she attempted to process her emotions. She had loved Lydia once. As a child, she'd wanted nothing more than for her mother to love her back, to see her and talk to her. Even after *he'd* gone, the monster she'd known as her father, they'd never really spoken about anything of consequence. But then that hadn't been possible when the three of them had agreed there were things they would *never* talk about. Eve couldn't wait to get out of the house that had become a mausoleum. She'd rarely gone back after leaving for university. She could barely contemplate the thought of going back there now, but realised she might have to.

'Was there anything else?' the nurse asked, clearly wondering if she was still there.

'Sorry,' Eve said. 'It's come as a shock, as you can imagine.'

'Of course,' the woman said understandingly. 'You can come and see her any time,' she added.

'I have an emergency here right now. A close friend who's been attacked. I have to liaise with the police,' Eve bent the truth a little, 'but I'll be there as soon as I can.'

'Oh no,' the nurse gasped. 'You really have had a time of it, haven't you?'

'Definitely.' Eve swallowed. 'Could you give her my love? I know she might not understand, but...'

'Absolutely. And please try not to worry. She's in good hands.'

'Thank you.' Eve wiped away a tear she was surprised to find spilling down her face. 'There's just one more thing,' she said. 'Sorry to take up your time, but do you know who called the ambulance?'

'We don't, I'm afraid. The call was made from your mother's landline, according to one of the police officers who forced an entry. Whoever it was didn't speak and the phone was left connected, apparently. It was all a bit odd. Lydia was found on the landing, you see, and with the phone being downstairs in the hall, it's doubtful she would have been able to make the call herself.'

FORTY-THREE

Once Eve had managed to talk to a solicitor early the next morning, she placed Kai carefully in his carrier. He'd fallen asleep in her arms, and she thanked God for small mercies. She had to take him with her. She had no one she could leave him with. Chloe had been the only person she would trust with him. She had to go to her, even if only to see with her own eyes how she was – assuming the hospital would let her. She picked up the carrier and grabbed her coat and car keys, then pulled the front door open – and froze.

'I heard what happened with Dom,' Steve said, looking haggard as he stood on her doorstep.

Feeling wretched for him, and with no idea what to say, Eve stood back a little. 'Do you want to come in?' she asked, though he was the last person she wanted to see. She probably shouldn't even be talking to him under the circumstances.

'No thanks. The kids are in the car.'

Eve glanced past him to the road, her heart aching for him and the children both. She wanted to ask him when he'd collected them, since the police had said they hadn't been there when Chloe had been attacked, but she guessed he might not want to answer questions right now.

'I just came to ask you to give your husband a message for me, assuming you'll be seeing him.'

Answering with a small nod, Eve braced herself. She couldn't think of anything good Steve would want to say to him.

'Tell him I hope he gets put away. And that I hope he's banged up with blokes who like to mete out their own justice to the kind of scum who would attack a defenceless woman. I hope the bastard rots in hell.'

Eve reeled at the vitriol in his words. 'You surely can't believe it was him. You know him. He would never do something as dreadful as this.'

Steve paused, seeming to debate for a second. 'Actually, I *don't* know him that well. He hasn't been around that long after all, has he, and he certainly doesn't go out of his way to have anything to do with me.' He narrowed his eyes. 'It strikes me that you don't know him that well either, Eve. It's bloody obvious he did it. He was right there, for Christ's sake, kissing her on the doorstep, according to the neighbours.'

Eve felt her stomach lurch. 'So why would he have attacked her?' she asked. 'For kicks?'

'Probably,' Steve answered, his eyes filled with disdain. 'He's so perfect on the outside, it makes you wonder what goes on inside, doesn't it?'

He was angry. He was bound to be, but should he really be judging Dom? 'You're not perfect either, are you, Steve?' she said, holding his gaze.

He smiled wryly. 'And you are, of course: caring mother, loving wife, competent career woman. You would never do anything to jeopardise your relationship with Chloe or with Dom, would you, Eve?'

Noticing the challenge in his eyes, she looked away. 'I have to go. I have things I need to do,' she mumbled, flustered, and made to close the door.

Placing his hand against it, he stopped her. 'I made a mistake, Eve. We all do, don't we, as *you* would know very well, but nothing excuses what that bastard husband of yours has done. He's been having his cake and eating it. You *know* it. You've just been so dazzled by his perfect image, you couldn't see it. I've no idea why he attacked her. Maybe Chloe tried to break it off with him, I don't know. I can't know anything for sure yet, if ever, because my wife has just been put into an induced *coma*.'

What? Eve felt herself reel.

'One thing I *do* know is that if I see him again, I'll break his fucking neck.' He turned away, then glanced back at her. 'By the way, if you're thinking of going to see her, don't. It wouldn't be smart while the police are holding your husband. And frankly, Chloe's better off without people like you in her life.'

FORTY-FOUR

With Kai in his baby sling, his head nestled to her breast, Eve paused outside the children's ward as she passed by on the way to the stroke unit. It had hardly changed, the same brightly coloured creatures adorning the walls that were here when Jacob was, which was often. She recalled the hide-and-seek game she would play with him whenever he was wheeled to one of his many procedures. The creatures, indefinable monsters with cartoon eyes and huge smiles, could be found all along the corridor from the foyer as well as on the ward, peeping out from door frames and corners. The idea was to distract small patients from frightening situations. Jacob had been soothed by them. Confined to his bed most of his short life, he'd never learned to articulate well, but he would smile when Eve whispered stories of the adventures the creatures would have while everyone was sleeping. They'd named one Blobcat. A big blue blob of a creature with cat's ears and a long floaty tail. Eve remembered thinking it looked like a ghost cat, but she hadn't wanted to tell Jacob that.

He must have been so confused, so terrified sometimes, and so terribly lonely. Eve held her breath, her chest physically aching at the recollection. She would have given her life after he'd gone to bring him back. She'd prayed at night, even written a letter to God and placed it under her pillow, begging him to take her instead of her baby brother. It had done no good; wishes simply didn't come true.

'Are you here to see someone?' a cheerful voice asked, jarring her from her thoughts.

She looked around to see a male nurse behind her, and déjà vu swept through her, leaving her weak in its wake. He was older, possibly near retirement age, but he was unmistakably Liam, his twinkly, slightly mischievous eyes radiating kindness and warmth.

His brow knitting, he studied her intently for a second, and then his eyes widened. 'Eve?' he said. Somehow she wasn't surprised that he'd remembered her. He'd always made sure to be there for her whenever Jacob was brought in during his shift, always gone out of his way to take her under his wing. 'How are you?' he asked, looking thrilled to see her.

Eve managed a smile. 'Okay,' she said. 'I qualified as a doctor. I'm a general practitioner now, mostly thanks to you.'

'Wow!' he said. 'Well done, Eve.' Making sure to be careful of her baby sling, he gave her a congratulatory hug. 'I knew you could do it, despite everything. Good things happen, hey?'

Eve's mind shot to Chloe, and her throat tightened. She'd called the hospital she'd been taken to, but they wouldn't disclose any information. She wasn't a relative. Yet they'd been as close as two people could be. At least Eve had thought they had. She had to see her, learn her side of the story.

'You're not here for the little one, are you?' Liam asked, sweeping a worried gaze over Kai. Realising he was genuinely concerned, that he cared, Eve felt suddenly like bursting into tears.

'No.' She shook her head and gulped back her tears. 'My mother.'

'Oh.' Liam's eyes hardened at the mention of Lydia. 'She's poorly, I take it?'

'A stroke,' Eve confirmed.

He nodded, his expression one of muted sympathy. 'I'm sorry, Eve. For her too, obviously.' Eve sensed there was a 'but' he was too kind to voice. 'How's your father? Is he here?' he asked, the same scorn in his eyes Eve had detected years ago.

'He left,' she said, dropping her gaze. 'Shortly before Jacob...' She couldn't finish the sentence.

Liam reached to squeeze her arm. 'And good riddance,' he muttered, clearly unable to hide his disdain.

Eve understood why. Her father hadn't hurt Jacob, not physically anyway, but she couldn't blame Liam for thinking he had.

Liam had been here the day Jacob had died, held her while she'd sobbed, inconsolable with grief. He'd watched in disbelief as her mother had walked away from the trolley where Jacob's small body lay, dry-eyed and seemingly emotionless. He had made assumptions, the same assumptions Eve's psychiatrist had made. It had never been proven. During her psychotherapeutic process, her mother had never admitted to fabricating or inducing Jacob's illness.

FORTY-FIVE

2000

Eve

I can't take my eyes off my little brother. I know it's serious because of Dr Kelman's tense expression, the curse he utters as he races into the room. 'What did the CT scan show?' he asks, skirting around my mother, who stands transfixed amid the flurry of activity and the pinging alarm bells, which seem to resonate in my chest.

'Skull fracture and subdural haematoma,' Liam answers tightly, his gaze pivoting between the doctor and my mother, and the anxious knot in my stomach twists itself tighter.

Jacob's head is jerking, and I know the doctors and nurses know what they're doing, but still I feel compelled to tell them. 'He's having a seizure,' I murmur.

Dr Kelman's gaze flicks towards me. His brow furrows briefly and then he turns back to Jacob. '*Dammit.*' He spits out another curse as he examines his eyes. 'Pupils are fixed and dilated. We need to alleviate the intercranial pressure. Tell PICU to alert the neurosurgeon. *Now!*'

My heart bangs so hard I'm sure it's about to burst through my chest as they begin frantically manoeuvring the trolley. I don't know how it happened. There was so much noise, the TV booming from the lounge, my mum screaming, my dad bellowing and swearing. I tried to hold onto Jacob, but I just wasn't strong enough. And then the carpet shifted and the stairs shook beneath me and my dad stopped yelling, grunting instead as his body bounced and rolled down the steps. I don't remember much after that, apart from the brief silence that followed, silence so complete I was sure I could hear the beat of butterflies' wings. I remember the blood, the salty, sickly sweet taste of it on my lips.

'When was he brought in?' Dr Kelman asks. 'Do we know what happened?'

My eyes swivel to my mum's, panic rising inside me as I wonder whether I should answer. She fixes me with a look and I know she doesn't want me to.

'His mother slipped on the stairs,' Liam provides with another loaded glance at my mum. 'The details and presenting symptoms are in the file.'

'Bring it with you,' Dr Kelman says. 'We need to move him.'

I step back as two more nurses join them and they trundle Jacob's trolley towards the door, Dr Kelman stooped over him, trying to revive him, I realise. Jacob's body is convulsing and I want to scream at them to help him.

'He has epilepsy,' my mum says, following the trolley, her expression tight. It's her coping face, the one she wears whenever she's recounting Jacob's symptoms. 'He has seizures every single day,' she tells them. 'I told that young junior doctor when he first came in. I warned him this would happen. Why aren't you doing more tests? Why aren't you trying to *help* him?'

Jacob's had loads of tests, EEGs, MRIs, injections and tubes stuck into him. Mum has always agreed to them, no matter how painful. I wondered sometimes why she didn't scream at them to stop.

'I'm afraid this is a little more serious than we first thought, Mrs Lockhart.' One of the other nurses goes to her, wrapping an arm around her shoulders. 'Why don't we go and wait in the family room and give the doctors some space to do their job?'

My mother glances after Jacob as the trolley is raced at breakneck speed along the corridor. For a second there's fear in her eyes, but other than that her body language is stiff, as if she's trying to hold herself still. I can tell she doesn't want the nurse's arm around her. She never wants my arms around her either. 'I told them he has epilepsy.' Her voice quavers. 'My father has it. It's hereditary.'

The nurse hesitates before answering. When she does, it's as if she's trying to reassure her. 'It's possible that Jacob may be at higher risk than normal,' she says, 'but the chances of passing epilepsy on to your child are usually low, Mrs Lockhart.'

'Slightly higher than two out of every hundred,' I provide, and the nurse looks at me in surprise.

'I've been studying.' I feel my cheeks burn, and my eyes skid to the safety of the floor. 'To be a doctor. Liam said I could be if—'

'For goodness' sake, Eve!' my mother cuts in sharply. 'Will you just *stop* with your facts and figures? What possible use are they?'

The nurse looks at me sympathetically and then back at my mother. 'Is Mr Lockhart here?' she asks. 'Would you like us to contact him?'

I hear my mum draw in a sharp breath. 'No.' She shakes her head. 'There's no need.'

'He's at work,' I blurt, feeling panicky.

Mum moves swiftly across to me. 'We've already spoken to him.' Smiling tightly, she takes hold of my hand and squeezes it so hard I'm sure she'll break my bones. 'Haven't we, sweetheart?'

Realising what she wants from me, I bite back my tears and nod fervently.

'I'll just go and check the family room is free.' The nurse squints oddly at me as she turns away.

'Keep *quiet*,' my mother hisses behind her, squeezing harder, and I struggle to fight back a whimper.

FORTY-SIX

PRESENT

Eve

Arriving at the stroke unit, Eve hesitated before going in, her feelings equal amounts sadness and rage. Part of her wanted to cry for the woman she'd once loved despite everything. Part of her wanted to go in there and shake her, scream at her to tell her why she'd stayed with a man who'd ruined their lives, why she'd made Eve and Chloe complicit in the lies to explain away his sudden departure. Lying hadn't helped. It had dogged them ever since, blighting their futures. And now Chloe was lying in a coma, seriously injured, her life broken, Dom detained for attacking her.

Lydia's reappearance had precipitated all of this. Eve hated her. Yet somewhere deep down, she still craved her approval, the natural love and affection a mother should have for her child.

She had to go in and see her, find out what her level of understanding was. And then? She had no idea. From what she'd been told on the phone, it was probable that Lydia might never recover fully. That she might have long-term disabilities. Depending on her progress, she would need help with rehabilitation and the transition from hospital to home. The worst-case scenario was that she might never be able to manage on her own. Eve didn't want to go in there. No one but Chloe would understand that she wanted to run, and keep running. But she couldn't. For years she'd put as much distance as she could between herself and Lydia. Now it seemed she had to stay right by her side.

Steeling herself, she pressed the buzzer and pushed through the double doors into the unit. 'Hi.' She smiled as she approached the nurses' station, though her facial muscles felt frozen. 'Eve Howell. I've come to see my mother, Lydia Lockhart.'

'Ah, yes.' The woman smiled back. 'She's in room fourteen, my lovely, straight down the corridor, second from the end on the left.'

Eve nodded her thanks, feeling the familiar flutter of butterflies taking off in her stomach as she set off along the corridor.

Lydia was in a room on her own. Eve was shocked as her gaze fell on the thin frame occupying the bed, her body hooked up to a cardiac monitor. She wavered by the door and then forced herself to step in and approach her. She looked small, emaciated almost, her face pale against the stark white of the sheets. It was obvious immediately that her left eye had drooped, along with her mouth under the oxygen mask, meaning there would be weakness or paralysis on one side of her body.

As Eve looked down at her, Lydia opened her good eye. For an instant the fear that crushed Eve's chest was reflected there, then it gave way to disorientation. Eve couldn't help but feel some compassion for her. How ironic that she had woken to find herself trapped in her body, forced into silence this time rather than choosing to stay silent. Reminded of those times she'd been desperate for her mother to talk to her, her heart hardened.

Lydia's right hand fluttered feebly towards her oxygen mask, and Eve reached to loosen it for her. She watched her mouth move. She was trying to say something, but her speech was slurred and garbled, nothing coherent emerging. In time she might find a way to communicate, either verbally or with pen and paper. With no real idea yet what her progress might be, Eve would have to cross each bridge as she reached it.

As her mother's hand came to rest on her chest, she took hold of it and squeezed it. 'I'm sorry this happened to you,' she said, looking sympathetically down at her. She saw a flicker of confusion and wondered whether Lydia might have problems understanding what she was saying to her.

She thought not, though, for when she added, 'I'm here for you, Mum. Don't worry, I'll care for you just as you cared for me,' her mother's look was alarmed, briefly, and then fatalistic.

Chloe

She could hear them talking as she sat all alone on the canal bank, voices around her yet there was no one there. It was just the wind, she tried to convince herself, whispering her name as it rustled through the leaves on the upside-down trees. She was cold, lashing rain biting through her flimsy T-shirt right down to her bones. She shuddered, wrapped her arms tightly around herself. Why hadn't she brought a coat?

'Because you didn't have time,' Lydia answered. 'We had to drop the poker into the water.'

Chloe frowned, remembering. It had sunk easily. Lydia had tried to reassure them it would never be found. Eve, though, just kept staring at the water, mumbling something about the ripples growing wider and wider. 'We'll never escape it,' she'd whispered.

Where was she? A sound jarred, a clang, metallic, like the mooring chains attached to the sidings. She could still hear the distant voices, a male voice, a female voice, and she twisted around, squinting up and down the towpath and behind her at the overgrown foliage. Still there was no one there. No Steve, who'd promised to help, telling them they couldn't manage the weight on their own. No Eve. No Dominic. But Dominic shouldn't be here. Eve was too young to have his baby, and anyway, Chloe saw him first.

She heard it again, the metallic sound, and now there was the sound of a man spluttering and coughing, coughing, coughing, coughing, grating against her skull, and the wind kept whispering her name: *Chloe, Chloe, come with me. It's quiet down here.*

It wasn't coming from the trees. Icy fingers trailed over her skin and she realised it was coming from the water. She tried to scream, but there was something clogging her windpipe, and she gagged and clawed at her throat.

'Chloe.' An urgent voice permeated the panic crashing through her. 'Chloe, it's all right.' Hands caught hold of hers, forcing them still. 'You're in hospital, sweetheart. You're safe.'

Get it out. Please get it out. Chloe's eyes snapped open to see a nurse looking worriedly down at her.

'You're safe, Chloe,' she repeated, her eyes kind. 'You have a breathing tube in, my lovely. It's just temporary, don't worry. We'll be removing it soon.'

Feeling her panic subside a little, Chloe stopped fighting, gazed pleadingly at the concerned eyes looking into hers. *What happened?*

Seeming to understand her unasked question, the nurse spoke carefully. 'Do you remember that someone attacked you, Chloe?'

Her mind flew back, panic rising afresh as she recalled the vice-like grip on her ankle, her chin hitting the stairs and finally the unforgiving tiles on the hall floor. Nothing more, apart from the long, silent scream building up inside her that she couldn't let out. She answered with a slow, defeated blink.

'Your jaw is broken and you received a hairline skull fracture, but you're going to be fine,' the nurse said, squeezing her hands. 'You'll need some help from a speech and language therapist, but the doctor is confident you'll make a full recovery. And just so you know, there is some swelling and bruising at the moment, but there won't be any permanent visible damage. The orthodontist will be popping in later to see about getting you fixed up with a partial temporary denture. You'll be back to smiling in no time, don't worry.'

Her tooth. She'd spat it out. Nausea swilled inside her, and she gagged painfully again.

'We'll get this tube out as soon as possible,' the nurse said, smoothing away the hair that was tickling her face. 'And then we'll pop a tiny tube through your nose and get some sustenance into you. As soon as you're a little bit stronger, I'll bring you a pen and paper. The police will want to have a word when you're ready. If you know who did this to you, I wouldn't hesitate to tell them, if I were you.'

Closing her eyes, Chloe felt tears squeeze from under the lids. She knew exactly who'd done this, but she just couldn't believe it.

FORTY-EIGHT

PRESENT

Eve

Coming through the front door with Kai in his carrier, Eve almost had heart failure as she heard footsteps in the kitchen and realised someone was in the house. With her son's safety her first priority, she whirled around and was halfway back to her car when someone caught hold of her arm.

'Let go of me!' She struggled to wrench herself from the firm grasp that held her.

'Eve! For Christ's sake, it's *me*,' Dom said as she turned, ready to fight and kick and claw to protect her baby. 'It's just me,' he repeated, looking as shaken as she was.

She felt relief flood every cell in her body, until she remembered that this was the man who was sleeping with her best friend. A man she'd trusted implicitly not to hurt her. 'What are you doing here?' she asked, stepping away from him.

He sighed heavily. 'I live here, Eve. I tried to call you, but you didn't pick up.' Because her phone had been off while she'd been at the hospital.

'They let you go?' she asked, surprised.

'I suppose you thought they'd charge me?' There was a sad, cynical edge to his voice.

'No,' she lied, her emotions in turmoil. 'I don't know.' She looked away from him. She had thought the police might have investigated further, given his involvement with Chloe.

'They didn't,' he said with a defeated smile. 'Thanks to the solicitor you contacted, I've been released under investigation. I suppose I should be grateful you thought enough of me to do that.'

Eve squinted at him, a hard kernel of anger unfurling inside her. 'What the *hell's* that supposed to mean? What was I meant to think, Dom?'

'I'm sorry. I didn't mean...' Running his fingers through his hair, he trailed off. 'Do you mind if we take the discussion inside?' he asked, glancing across the road. 'I think I've probably already provided the neighbours with enough entertainment.'

She followed his gaze to where curtains and blinds were twitching. Two neighbours had actually emerged to stand on doorsteps, arms folded, eyes sliding in their direction.

'Unless you'd rather not be on you own with me, of course?' He scanned her eyes as she looked back at him. His own were full of nervous uncertainty.

Swallowing back a lump of sympathy she wasn't sure she should be feeling, she nodded and walked back to the house.

He didn't reach for Kai's carrier as he normally would, and when she placed it on the table, he stayed on the other side of the kitchen. He pressed a thumb and finger hard against his eyes, and Eve's heart lurched as she realised he was trying to hold back tears. She wanted to go to him, try somehow to reassure him, but how could she?

'I didn't do it, Eve,' he said, his voice strangled. 'I swear I didn't.'

She battled with the riot of emotions running through her. 'But you kissed her on New Year's Eve,' she stated flatly. 'Just a kiss, no more than that?' She waited, hardly daring to breathe.

Glancing down, Dom hesitated, and then, shamefaced, nodded. 'I'm sorry, Eve. I didn't mean to hurt you. I don't know what else to say apart from I love you.'

'Ha!' That was manipulation if ever she'd heard it. 'So much so you went back for a repeat performance. The same night she was *attacked*.' His gaze snapped to hers. 'I saw you.' She glared at him. 'I was there, Dom, yards away in my car. I saw it all.'

'Jesus.' He glanced at the ceiling, then back to her. 'You didn't see everything, Eve. I promise you it wasn't how it looked.'

He had to be joking. 'It never bloody well is!' she retaliated angrily. 'Do you honestly expect me to believe they were just two random kisses with nothing going on in between?'

'Yes!' Dom replied, growing agitated. 'You clearly don't believe me, but I haven't been seeing her. There's no affair. Nothing happened between us apart from what I've told you. I didn't hurt her, Eve. I swear to God.'

Eve didn't answer. She wasn't going to argue with him, certainly not in front of her child, who was awake and crying now. She turned to unbuckle him, rather than look at a man who she couldn't believe wasn't feeding her lie after lie, no matter how hard she tried.

'Eve, *please*. You have to listen to me,' Dom begged. 'The kids were there when I went over. Whatever else happened, can you really imagine I would have done something like that in front of her children?'

Eve lifted Kai from his carrier, held him close. So when had Steve picked Rose and Thomas up exactly? She was sure the police had said they hadn't been there when Chloe had been attacked.

'I couldn't have done it,' Dom went on desperately. 'I was there barely two minutes. Chloe was upset when I left because I'd told her categorically I wasn't interested, but she was fine. I wasn't *there* when it happened, Eve. I was somewhere else. Or at least on my way there. I couldn't have—'

Eve stopped him. 'Where?' she asked, realising that it might be crucial information should the police be intending to charge him.

He was reluctant to answer, and a chill of apprehension ran the length of her spine. Then, 'At Lydia's house,' he admitted eventually, and pressed his hands to his face. '*Christ*, I wish I hadn't been.'

FORTY-NINE
PRESENT

Dom

'But *why?*' Eve finally asked. 'I've just come from the hospital. She's had a *stroke*, Dom. What in God's name happened?'

'I have no idea,' Dom answered gruffly. 'I was trying to talk to her and—'

'But why were you *there?*' She shook her head in bewilderment. 'I don't understand, why would you have gone without talking to me?'

'You weren't *here*,' Dom pointed out, trying hard to contain his frustration. 'You ran from the house. I had no idea where you were or what you might do considering the state you were in. Before that, you'd locked yourself in the bathroom, refusing to come out. You wouldn't tell me what was going on between you and your mother. And then you tell me that she was responsible for what happened to my son, and you expect me *not* to try to establish what the hell's going on? I was scared, Eve. For you, for Kai. I thought you might even have been at her house. I couldn't just sit here and do nothing.'

Eve's face paled. She held Kai close, and Dom had to suppress an urge to take him from her, take him away from here to somewhere he would be safe. Because right now, he felt his son was at risk, and that was what scared him above all else.

'*Was* she responsible for what happened to Kai?' he asked, watching her carefully.

She answered with the smallest of nods. 'I think so.'

He felt his gut tighten. 'And Jacob?' he asked, not sure he wanted to hear the answer. 'His illnesses, his endless hospital stays, was that down to Lydia?'

Eve said nothing. Wouldn't look at him.

'I saw the nursery, Eve,' he reminded her. 'I saw the doll. It's so lifelike it could be human. She still has the IV drip stand, for Christ's sake. Was she struggling with mental issues before he died?' He waited, his frustration growing as Eve seemed determined not to answer. 'Eve, *talk* to me!' he shouted, causing her to jump and Kai to start in her arms. 'Look at me, will you?' Cold fear twisted inside him. 'Please?'

Pressing her cheek close to Kai's, Eve jiggled him and shushed him, then, slowly, she brought her gaze to Dom's.

'Was she responsible for Jacob's death?' he asked, needing to know, not wanting to. 'Please tell me. I know I've given you reason not to trust me, but please let me in.'

Eve took a deep breath. Then she nodded, more decisively this time.

'Jesus Christ.' Dom reeled inwardly. It was obvious now why she hadn't wanted to tell him any of this, why she hadn't wanted her mother involved in her life. Why she'd been so petrified when she had turned up. He rued the day he'd ever allowed the woman through the front door. 'Eve, I'm so sorry.' He moved towards her. 'I understand now why you kept things from me, but none of what happened is your fault. I wish you hadn't felt you needed to.'

'But you felt you needed to keep things from *me*, didn't you, Dom?' Eve's look was a mixture of disappointment and heart-wrenching sadness.

'Eve...' He took another step towards her.

'I have to go and change Kai,' she said, her eyes averted as she hurried past him to the hall.

Dom sighed tiredly. 'I'll get his feed ready,' he offered behind her. She would have questions about what had happened to Lydia. He wasn't sure what he would tell her.

Minutes later, he went upstairs with Kai's bottle. 'Thanks,' Eve said, lifting the little boy from his changing mat. She wasn't looking at Dom. He wanted to go to her, try to reassure her, to see Kai – he'd missed him so much. He guessed, though, that Eve wouldn't find anything he said or did very reassuring right now.

Backing out, he went to the bathroom. Splashed his face with cold water and tried to get his head around how this had all happened. It had started with Lydia, and with the latest developments it wasn't going to stop, was it? If the police got wind of the fact that he'd been at her house when she'd had that stroke, that he'd inadvertently broken a pane of glass gaining access through the kitchen window, he really didn't fancy his chances. They were already looking at him like the worst piece of scum after what had happened to Chloe. How sick was Lydia? He needed to know. Would she be coherent enough to confirm he'd been there? More pressingly, he needed to know how Chloe was.

He'd felt sick to his gut when he'd learned how bad her injuries were. He'd suggested she might have fallen. The detective who'd been questioning him had openly sneered. 'She was dragged down the stairs and then into the kitchen,' he'd said, his arms folded across his chest as he'd looked Dom over contemptuously. 'There's considerable bruising to her face. Also clear finger marks on her ankle. More's the pity we haven't been able to lift any prints, apart from those you left on the door frame, of course, along with particles of clothing you left on the victim.' Dom hadn't known whether he was bluffing, trying to scare him into admitting something, but he did know he'd made up his mind that he was guilty. He'd told Eve they hadn't charged him, but the truth was, they were an inch away from doing just that.

He was scared. More scared than he'd ever been in his life.

Looking at himself in the bathroom mirror, he breathed in hard. He needed to shower. To eat something. But that would have to wait. Going back past the nursery, he heard Eve softly singing 'Amazing Grace' and felt his heart plummet. She loved Kai, he was her world, but love alone wasn't enough to keep him safe. He had to make her see that.

He was in the kitchen making coffee, the only thing he felt able to stomach, when Eve came in behind him.

'Did you get to talk to her?' she asked. 'Lydia. Did you actually speak to her before she had her stroke?'

He turned to face her. 'No.' He shook his head. 'I couldn't make her hear the front door, so I went around the back, found the kitchen window wasn't closed properly and climbed in, not carefully enough, unfortunately. I managed to dislodge a pane of glass. She was on the landing. By the time I reached her...' He stopped, realising how this looked. The fact was, though, his concern for his son had driven him. He'd needed to see just how mentally unstable she might be.

'Is that how you cut yourself?' she asked, her gaze straying to his hand.

He nodded. 'They tested the blood on my shirt. Realised it was mine.'

'Why didn't you stay?' Eve was studying him cautiously, probably wondering what kind of unfeeling monster he was.

Sighing, he kneaded his forehead. 'I should have done. After what you told me about Kai, though... I honestly don't know what my thinking was. I was angry, I know that. I dialled 999. It was the best I could do.'

Eve nodded. 'She's in a bad way,' she said. 'Paralysis down one side of her body, struggling to communicate. I'm not sure how much she understands of what's being said to her.'

Dom glanced down. 'I'm sorry,' he said.

'She'll need help. When she leaves hospital, she'll need some help with rehabilitation. I'm going to have to be there for her.'

He looked at her curiously. He'd thought she would struggle to care about what happened to the woman who'd undoubtedly abused her. Yet astonishingly, she seemed to. 'But what about Kai?' he asked. He didn't want his son anywhere near the woman, stroke or no stroke.

Eve was quiet for a moment. 'Assuming they don't charge you, you can look after him,' she said, knocking him sideways. He'd expected her to show him the door. Instead, she was showing him she *did* trust him. That she had some faith in him.

'And if they do?' he asked, his chest constricting as he considered again that that was a real possibility, that he might not see his son at all.

'We'll cross that bridge when we get there.' Her eyes flicked to his and then away. 'I'm going to stay at her house. Take some compassionate leave and be her full-time carer. I'm well qualified, after all.'

FIFTY

PRESENT

Lydia

Lydia wished they would do something about the blinding overhead light. She'd tried to ask one of the nurses about it, but she hadn't been able to make herself understood. She knew what she wanted to say but found it impossible to articulate. She understood what was being said to her. She'd understood Eve, her implicit meaning. She'd felt the fear she'd seen in her daughter's eyes. It had been there the day Jacob had died. She should have allowed Eve to take Jacob to Chloe's parents' house that day. She hadn't known what her daughter's thinking was. She'd clearly thought he would be safer there. Clearly, also, she hadn't known where the danger truly lay.

Exhausted with the effort of thinking, Lydia closed her eyes, but still she could see it, the look of startled surprise in David's eyes as he'd landed at the foot of the stairs. Shock, for the briefest of seconds, before the first impact. His skull had cracked like an eggshell. Four times Eve had wielded the poker. Nausea roiled inside her as she recalled each sickening blow. They might have been able to explain away one heavy trauma impact, claiming his head had hit the wall on the way down, but four? Her instinct had been to protect her daughter, and she'd done what she'd had to do.

Afterwards, once she'd buried her dear baby boy, she'd tried to talk to her. Eve, though, had thwarted her every attempt, turning instead to Chloe. Chloe had helped Eve on that terrible day, enlisting Steve's help too, but Lydia had always been wary of her, the way she'd treated Eve almost like a pet. She had been there for her, undoubtedly. Lydia had wondered, though, why she would be.

'Afternoon, Lydia,' someone trilled cheerily to her side, snatching her from her thoughts. 'And how are we today?'

Eve guessed who it was, the young nurse whose name escaped her and whose insistence on talking to her like she would a child annoyed her immensely. Did she expect her to answer her? She wouldn't. The inane noise that came from her mouth was far too embarrassing.

'Ooh, Lydia, is that a small smile I see?' the nurse asked, blinking eyes that were far too made up for a hospital ward.

Lydia sighed inside. Could the woman not see that she wasn't smiling? Her face was lopsided. Lydia might not have completed her nurse's training, but it didn't need someone with a degree to work out that the stroke had affected her facial muscles, causing her mouth to droop on one side. She wondered what medical knowledge the hospital staff actually had. But then she had wondered that for some time, ever since Jacob's frequent hospital visits, when she'd been sure they would eventually find there was nothing physically wrong with him.

'You'll have all the doctors after you, you will,' the well-meaning but irritating girl went on as she fussed around checking her catheter and straightening her sheets. Lydia would have rolled her eyes if she could, but she couldn't, of course.

Eve would have loved all this jolly chit-chat as a girl, revelling in the attention, being in the company of people who liked her, particularly that young nurse, Liam, who'd realised how clever she was.

'Ooh, look,' the girl said, as if Lydia could easily look anywhere other than at the blessed blinding white light. 'Your daughter's here. That's a nice surprise, isn't it? She's such a lovely person, always happy to stop for a quick chat,' she went on, picking up the glass of water from the over-bed table, easing Lydia's head up and attempting to feed the liquid – which Lydia didn't want – to her through a straw.

Feeling it dribble down her chin, wetting the top of her nightie, Lydia would have screamed at the girl to shut up for two minutes, if only she could.

'She's been having a word about how she can help with your rehabilitation once you're discharged,' the nurse warbled on, oblivious. 'She's an absolute angel. If only all the patients had sons or daughters who cared enough for their parents to want to look after them at home. She's having your bedroom redecorated for you. How thoughtful is that?' She widened her eyes, impressed, as she mopped up the spillage. 'I know it's difficult right now, Lydia, but I'd count my blessings if I were you.'

Lydia would have liked to be able to. She would have liked to feel relieved as Eve came across to her, giving the nurse a bright smile and calling her by her name – Lucy, that was it – as she thanked her, but she didn't. They'd come full circle. Eve was now the carer, the mother to all intents and purposes, and Lydia was the child. It was clear she had no choice in the matter, though. Her daughter had certainly won the staff over.

Once the nurse finally left, Eve stepped forward. 'How are you?' she asked, bending to kiss Lydia's cheek. She was still smiling, but her eyes... It was the look in David's eyes after he'd drawn his last breath that Lydia remembered above all. Even in death, they'd been angry. She hadn't realised until now how like her father's Eve's eyes were: beautiful, thick-lashed, and so dark they were almost black.

FIFTY-ONE
PRESENT

Eve

As she stepped inside the arched porchway, Eve felt as if she were passing through a portal into the past. Panic climbed her chest as she fumbled her mother's key into the front door lock, and she faltered. She'd sworn once she'd left that she would never come back here, to the house of her childhood – the house of horrors, she and Chloe had called it after the day Eve tried hard to forget. Still it had come back to haunt her, broken memories, stark images with jagged edges plaguing her dreams and her waking nightmares. Little Jacob's face looking up at her, openly trusting of everyone. It was the sickening dull thud that jarred her awake in the small hours, nausea swirling hotly inside her, sweat wetting her body. The expression in her father's eyes as he'd looked up at her from the hall floor had at first been one of shock, and then palpable contempt. Eve had felt it, breathed it; it had permeated every pore in her body. She hadn't known how many blows she'd rained down. She didn't remember actually doing it; she'd just wanted it to stop, the feeling of worth-lessness inside, the emptiness, the fear and the loneliness.

Steeling herself, she pushed on inside, her aim to search through Lydia's things for anything that might be incriminating, and was immediately transported back to her formative years. The house hadn't been redecorated from that day to this, the austere white walls of the hall still as cold and soulless as they were then, as if the house hadn't got a heart. Shaking off an involuntary shudder, she collected up the junk mail from the hall floor and went quickly to the lounge. That was exactly as she remembered it too, dated peach-coloured paint on the walls, a flowered border around the top and matching curtains hanging at the bay window. It was clean, spotless – her mother had always cleaned diligently, no doubt as therapy – but it had never felt like a home, a place people lived and laughed in. Eve had tried so hard to make her own house bright and cheery, a place where only good memories were made, and now she'd come full circle. She would be back here with her mother. Lydia would be silent. Even if she recovered her ability to speak, which she might in time with therapy, it wouldn't be Eve she would want to communicate with, which left her no choice but to become her carer.

Dropping her bag on the sofa, she glanced at her father's armchair, where she was sure his ghost sat, dark eyes watching her, pinpricks of pure hatred. She recalled what she'd seen in his eyes that day her mother had emerged from the bathroom, her hair shorn, that same warning look drilling into her that Eve had seen so many times. *It won't be long before blokes come sniffing around and her belly's filling out too.* She could hear the deep disdain in his voice as he'd summed up his feelings for her, the young girl growing into womanhood whom he'd never loved as a father should love a daughter. She would never be free of him. Never truly be able to close the door and leave this house and all the hurt and fear behind her.

Shaking off the shudder that ran through her, she went to the long sideboard that dominated one wall. A G Plan piece made of teak, it had been Lydia's pride and joy. She was always endlessly polishing it. Eve was sure that was why her father made sure to rest his cups and glasses on it, never once using the coasters her mother provided. Opening the drawers, she extracted various bits of paperwork regarding the house and Lydia's finances, which were limited, she realised, flicking through the bank statements she found there. She'd obviously been living a frugal existence, surviving on a small wage from a part-time secretarial job. Eve found herself feeling sympathy for her, glad that she'd had at least some company in her otherwise lonely life.

If she'd felt anything other than anger towards her, though, it soon disappeared as she looked through the photograph albums she pulled out of one of the cupboards. She had had birthday celebrations, she realised, complete with fairy cakes and balloons. There were photos capturing every year up until Jacob was born. After that, nothing. There weren't many photographs of her at all, in fact. No happy family snaps that included her after the age of about nine. Why was that? she wondered.

A cold hollowness seeping through her, she shoved the albums away and headed back to the hall. She was halfway up the stairs when she heard it, the child's cry that came to her often in the night. 'Jacob,' she whispered, closing her eyes and gripping the handrail hard. 'I'm so sorry, sweetheart.' *So, so sorry.*

She stayed where she was for a moment, breathing slowly, trying to find the courage she would need to go up. When she pushed the nursery door open and stepped tentatively inside, her heart froze inside her. The room was exactly as Dom had described it, exactly as it had been when Jacob had occupied it, decorated with fluffy white clouds and star shapes, the Disney

Dumbo mural covering the whole of one wall. The occupant of
the cot-sided bed, though, was a gross silicone imitation of her
brother.

Goosebumps rising over her skin, she walked across to the
bed and reached out to the doll with trembling fingers. It was so
lifelike to look at, to touch, she felt Jacob's small ghost walk over
her grave. Anger welled up inside her. Did Lydia believe that it
really *was* Jacob, pretend to herself it was him? Had she imagined when Kai came along that she could play some part in his
life? In Eve's? That he could take Jacob's place? That once the
authorities had been alerted to what had happened to Eve's
father, she could step in and take her baby away from her? If
that was the case, she'd been badly mistaken.

A wave of grief crashed through her so ferociously it forced
the air from her body. She shoved the drip stand away from the
cot and turned away. She should set fire to the place, burn it to
the ground along with everything in it.

Clenching her jaw determinedly, she ignored the soft
chuckle she heard behind her as she went to the room that had
once been hers. The room she'd spent endless hours alone in,
where she'd tried to drown out the alternating arguments and
silence with endless music on the MiniDisc player Chloe had
given her. The decoration in here was a repeat of the hall, the
walls, white, clinical, no colour at all, apart from the fairy lights
Eve had strung around her headboard and an old Take That
poster on the wall.

Do you think I have the energy or the time to decorate? Her
mother's voice reverberated around the room, filled with the
despair that was always there when she spoke to her. *I don't
have time to* breathe, *Eve. And where do you think the money
would come from?* Eve hadn't pursued it. She'd lived with the
sterile walls until she'd felt she was slipping into madness.

She heard him again, the plaintive cry that would follow her
along the landing after she'd gone. The chuckle whenever she'd

paused outside his door, as if he were beckoning her in. It had stopped when she'd escaped, for a short while, but since Lydia had come back into her life, she'd heard him every night, every day. Now, his cries were more urgent, his child's laughter heart-wrenching. He was trying to warn her. She knew he was. She had to make it stop, allow Jacob to rest untroubled in death as he never had in life.

Going across to the dressing table, she saw that there were still a few bits and pieces there that indicated this might have been a teenage girl's bedroom: a hair scrunchie, odd stud earrings, a Madonna-style jewelled cross necklace she'd saved up her pocket money for. Her Andrex stuffed puppy sitting in the corner looking as lonely as she'd felt. Tears she hadn't known she was crying wetting her cheeks, she picked it up and cuddled it close.

After a last glance around the room, she closed the door behind her and went to the main bedroom. The decoration in there was much like the lounge, the walls painted a flat, sickly mauve colour. The whole place felt neglected, as starved of love as Eve had been. It was time it was freshened up, this room at least, ready for Lydia to come home. Eve hoped she would like the colour scheme she'd selected. She'd put a lot of thought into it, and chosen white in the end, fittingly, she'd thought.

FIFTY-TWO

Chloe

Chloe could see where they were going with this. She might not be able to speak thanks to the braces holding her jaw together, but she wasn't stupid. Despite the nurse they'd spoken to when they arrived telling them she was still fragile, the police were bombarding her with questions she couldn't easily answer with nothing but a pen and paper.

'And had you been involved with Dominic Howell for long, Mrs Adams?' asked the detective, a moody-looking man with judgemental eyes, once she'd confirmed that Dom had been there on the night of the attack.

Chloe looked away towards the window, where the sky outside was as heavy as she felt inside. They were obviously drawing conclusions from the witness statements they'd taken from the neighbours. Let them. After the way Dom had treated her, the way Eve had, she didn't feel she owed either of them anything. Hadn't she already given her whole life over to Eve, always there for her whenever she'd needed her to be? Even moving house so she and Steve could stay close, as Eve had suggested. And where was Eve now? Conspicuous by her bloody absence, that was where. Chloe felt a pang of guilt as she considered why that was. Eve would obviously know by now about her and Dom. But then why should she be feeling guilty? Eve had taken him right from under her nose, and Dom clearly wasn't as perfect as he would have everyone believe. Chloe loved him – she did, and it hurt – but no man was worth throwing their friendship away for. The fact that she was the one who'd been planning to do just that didn't escape her, but she didn't want to think about it. She was lying here on her own, having to rely on Steve, another man who didn't give a damn about her, to look after her children. She had no idea what she'd done to deserve any of this. Absolutely none.

Seeing the sky grow darker, rain spattering against the window, her heart plummeted into the pit of her stomach. She didn't want to be all alone when she went home. She didn't think she could bear that.

'Mrs Adams?' the detective pressed her. 'We were talking about Dominic Howell?'

You mean you were. Chloe swiped at a tear spilling from her eye.

'Did he leave directly after your... liaison outside your house?' he asked.

Chloe almost smiled at his attempt at diplomacy. She didn't answer. What did he want her to say? The neighbours had obviously filled him in. There was nothing she could add.

'I think DS Atkins is trying to establish whether he might have come back?' The female officer, who hadn't yet uttered a word, intervened. She hadn't been struck dumb then.

Chloe couldn't help but feel bitter. Who wouldn't, stuck here being questioned about her personal life with no way to adequately answer? Sighing inwardly, she shook her head in reply to the question, and then shrugged – to the detective's frustration, if the audible sigh he blew out was any indication.

'You're separated from your husband,' he continued after a second. 'Because of your infatuation with Mr Howell, we're led to believe.'

Believe what you like, Chloe thought, anger swelling inside her. They obviously did. They believed Steve's version of events. That he was the injured party, the poor broken-hearted husband whose slutty wife was cheating on him.

'Was your husband ever aggressive towards you, Mrs Howell?' the detective added.

Chloe hesitated, glanced warily at him, then shook her head.

'You're positive?' He pursued it, clearly keen to get the case done and dusted and move on. 'He wasn't short-tempered? No sudden outbursts of violence or attempts at psychological manipulation?'

Again Chloe hesitated. Steve had lied through his teeth about cheating and then tried to put the blame on her. Did that amount to psychological manipulation? she wondered. She took a breath, then answered with another small shake of her head.

DS Atkins fell silent. Chloe prayed they were finished and would leave her alone.

Then, 'The thing is,' he said, 'we found no DNA other than that of Dominic Howell and your husband, so we're keen to eliminate one or the other.'

Chloe closed her eyes. *Please just go*, she willed him.

'Did Dominic Howell attack you, Chloe?' he asked bluntly. 'Did you try to end it with him and he wasn't prepared to leave without a fight? Was that what happened?'

She felt her throat closing. The tears she was trying hard to hold back rising.

'Did he try to force himself on you?' the man badgered her,

clearly not about to let it drop. 'Was that why you were trying to get away from him?'

Chloe didn't reply, choking back a sob instead. And then the floodgates opened. Though she tried, she couldn't stop the tears. It was all too much. Too painful. She couldn't bear it. She *couldn't*.

FIFTY-THREE

PRESENT

Eve

Eve was with the two police officers when she heard Dom come through the front door. Trepidation tightened her stomach as the man, a DS Atkins, who'd been questioning her about the state of her marriage, got to his feet.

'Mr Howell.' He nodded shortly in Dom's direction. 'Been getting some fresh air, I gather?'

Dom exchanged a wary glance with Eve. Clearly he'd gleaned the man's not so subtle hint that he should while he could. 'I took my son to the park, yes,' he answered, gazing coldly at the man as Eve went across to help him with the baby sling and take Kai from him.

Atkins nodded again, languidly. 'Bit young for football, though, isn't he?' he commented. 'Be a real shame to miss out on his early years.'

Dom looked away, his jaw tightening. 'I don't intend to.' His eyes were steely as he looked back at the detective, but also tinged with fear, Eve noted.

'You might not have a lot of choice, Mr Howell.' Atkins held his gaze. His expression was hard and unflinching, and Eve's heart stuttered. What had Chloe told the police? They'd gone to see her at the hospital regarding her 'relationship' with Dom – Atkins had said as much, but no more, deliberately leaving Eve wondering. She had noted the man gauging her carefully, looking for her reaction. She'd made sure to give none, asking only how Chloe was. However she felt about her husband's relationship with her friend – and she still didn't know the full extent of it – she was sure Dom hadn't been responsible for what had happened to her. It was impossible.

'Are you here to arrest me?' Dom asked. Eve saw him swallow, but his gaze didn't falter. She was glad. Quite plainly Atkins was trying to intimidate him. The man was of a certain ilk. Thanks to her own experiences at the hands of a bully, she could spot his kind a mile away. Had he manipulated Chloe into telling him what he wanted to hear? Or had Chloe decided on some spiteful revenge out of jealousy because Dom had told her he wasn't interested?

'Not yet, no.' Atkins glanced away. 'But I wouldn't book any trips abroad if I were you.'

Running his fingers through his hair, Dom nodded, his relief palpable. 'So was Chloe able to give you any information that might help with your enquiries?' he asked.

The detective's expression was one of disdain. 'Not as such, no,' he said with a terse intake of breath. 'The fact that she broke down when I asked her if she thought it was you who attacked her, though... Let's just say it confirmed our thinking.'

'Right.' Dom considered. 'But without actual corroboration or any proof, you decided to pay me a visit anyway. Do you mind me asking to what end? Apart from to upset my wife?'

'I'd say you'd managed that all by yourself,' the detective

answered drily. 'I can't see many wives not being considerably upset at finding their husband cheating on them with their best friend, can you?'

Dom breathed in hard. 'I need you to leave,' he said, coming across to Eve to take Kai, who was stretching his arms towards him.

The detective stayed put. 'And I need your watch,' he stated flatly.

'What?' Gathering his son to him, Dom frowned at Atkins.

'The officer in charge of bagging up your clothes failed to ask you for it, apparently, which was remiss of her.' He shot the female officer with him an unimpressed glance. 'I noticed you were wearing one, however. I also notice you're not wearing it now. Did you spot something on it? A speck of blood, perhaps, that might have belonged to the victim?'

'*Christ.*' Dom's gaze flicked to Eve, and this time she could feel his fear. Because they might find something, he was thinking. As was she. Even a minuscule particle might be enough for them to pursue him as a suspect. They were wrong, but clearly this idiotic man was determined.

'This is ridiculous,' she snapped, heading for the door. 'I'll fetch it.'

Atkins stopped her. 'I'd prefer PC Cho to retrieve it, if it's all the same to you, Mrs Howell. We'll need to put it in an evidence bag, you see. Don't want to run the risk of contaminating evidence, do we?'

Bastard, Eve thought. She held on to her patience and her temper while the woman went up to the bedroom to retrieve the watch.

She waited until she was seeing the despicable man out before saying what she needed to. 'You're barking up the wrong tree, Detective,' she informed him.

'Oh?' Atkins eyed her half interestedly.

'Ask Chloe if the children were there when she was

attacked. You said they weren't. Dom said they were there when he was at the house. Steve said he'd collected them. You might want to establish when he could have done that. Meanwhile, if you have any further reason to enter my property, and more specifically, remove items from it, I trust you'll obtain a warrant.'

Leaving him with a puzzled expression on his face, no doubt pondering whether he had cocked up while diligently detecting, she went back to the house. She was diverting attention to Steve and didn't feel good about it, but the fact was, Dom had not done this. There was simply no way he could have.

FIFTY-FOUR

Trying not to meet her father's accusing eyes looking back at her in the mirror, Eve scrubbed her mother's bathroom until it was so clean she could have performed a surgical procedure in there. Then, making sure that everything was in place in the bedroom, and that the Alexa speaker she'd set up on Lydia's bedside table was working properly, she went to check the stairlift she'd had installed. Dom had asked her whether it was a wise investment. Eve had pointed out that for practicality's sake, it was a necessity. Plus the amount involved would be offset against the eventual sale of the house.

Finding everything in working order, she went down to the kitchen to ensure she had all the ingredients she needed to produce balanced meals consisting of lean meats, poultry and fish with plenty of vegetables, salad and fruit. The speech therapist would be coming to the house, along with the physical and occupational therapists, to help her mother relearn her coordination skills, and it was important to Eve to be seen to be getting this right. She didn't want Lydia suffering any more than she had to. There was nothing to be gained by that.

Minutes later, she heard the sound of a vehicle pulling up outside. Bracing herself, she went to the front door and pulled it open, watching as the patient transport staff fussed around her mother.

'Welcome home,' she said, bending to kiss Lydia's cheek once her wheelchair was safely on the pavement. Lydia eyed her with deep mistrust. Eve moved closer. 'Don't worry, Mum,' she whispered, close to her ear. 'I'm used to silence, remember? I won't be devastated by it.'

Lydia flinched. Clearly she understood exactly what Eve was saying.

Going to the back of the wheelchair to steer her towards the house, Eve chatted on cheerily. 'I can't wait for you to see the new decor in your room. I'm sure you're going to love it.'

'Lucky you, hey, Lydia?' one of the staff said over her shoulder as she went ahead with the various bits of equipment supplied by the hospital: adapted cutlery and basic bathroom aids. 'Looks like you're going to be well looked after, my lovely.'

'I bet you're relieved to be out of that noisy hospital ward,' added the man who was carrying Lydia's bag.

Lydia didn't look particularly relieved. She was gripping the arm of the wheelchair with her good hand, Eve noticed. 'Here we go.' Tipping the chair back, she managed to get it up the step, through the small porch and on through the front door. 'Home sweet home.'

Lydia didn't answer. Obviously Eve didn't expect her to. In another world, where they'd had a normal relationship, she might have been upset that her mother couldn't speak. The sad fact, though, as she'd just reminded her, was that Eve had grown so used to the silence in years past, she thought she would hardly notice it.

'Liking the mod cons, Lydia,' the chirpy male medic said, nodding towards the stairlift. 'You'll be living in the lap of luxury.' He smiled at her. Lydia didn't acknowledge it other than with a glower, though Eve knew she could smile if she wanted to. Her facial muscles might be weak, but they weren't frozen. But then she supposed she hadn't got that much to smile about.

The man shrugged cheerfully. 'She'll be a bit tired, I expect. Do you want this upstairs?' he asked, holding up the bag.

'Thanks.' Eve gave him a grateful smile. 'First room on the left. I've left the door open. Could you make sure the rollator is in position on the landing while you're there?' Aware that Lydia could manage a few short steps, Eve had bought her a light-weight four-wheeled walking aid, which should make life easier.

'No problem,' he assured her. 'I'm Tom, by the way, the pretty one.'

'Which makes me what?' the female medic asked, emerging from the kitchen, where she'd deposited the bags she'd been carrying.

'Jealous,' Tom said with a smirk, and bounded upwards.

Eve was sure she could manage, but she smiled apprecia-tively as the two medics helped her manoeuvre Lydia onto the lift and then followed it up to make sure she was safely on her way to the bedroom.

'Don't you misbehave now, Lydia,' Tom joked as they headed back down. 'No loud music on that Alexa speaker of yours.'

Eve laughed. 'Mood music only, Tom,' she replied. 'Hey, Mum?'

She couldn't help but breathe a sigh of relief as the pair shouted goodbye and she heard the front door close. 'Alone at last. Just the two of us,' she said, a step behind Lydia as she negotiated her way slowly to the bedroom. 'The decorator's done a good job,' she added, stepping around her to make sure the door was wide open. 'I do hope you love the colour as much as I did.'

Lydia's look was horrified as she took in the new decor.

'Oh.' Eve furrowed her brow. 'Clearly you don't. That's a shame,' she sighed expansively again, 'since you're going to be spending so much time here.'

FIFTY-FIVE

PRESENT

Chloe

Chloe woke with a jerk, her heart catapulting against her chest as she recognised the face of the man staring down at her. Noting the look in his eyes, dark and intense, her blood ran cold. Why was he here? Why would he risk coming here? Her mind ticked feverishly. The police would know he'd come. He must know she would tell them he had. Unless... Was he here to make sure she stayed silent?

A jolt of fear shot through her as she considered the possibility that he hadn't been overcome by a temporary fit of rage, but that he might actually be some kind of psychopath. She'd fallen in love with him – he was the kind of man women couldn't help but fall in love with, kind, caring, perfect on the outside – but how well did she really know him? *It makes you wonder what goes on inside doesn't it?* Steve's words came jarringly back to her and she attempted to lever herself up, her eyes swivelling frantically around for her buzzer.

'Chloe, don't.' He raised his hands, palms outwards, as if trying to reassure her he meant her no harm. 'It's okay,' he whispered, moving to take hold of her shoulders.

She shrank away from him.

'I'm not here to hurt you,' he said, his voice a mixture of disbelief and desperation. 'You can't think that I...' He stopped, his forehead creasing in deep consternation as he studied her. 'You do, don't you?'

She stared at him, her heart now banging so frantically against her chest she felt it might burst.

'You think it was me who attacked you?' He dropped his hands, his face registering shock as he stepped back. 'Jesus, Chloe.' He shook his head in bewilderment. 'I would never do anything like that. I would *never* hurt you. I was angry, upset, confused. Christ, I was definitely that, but I would never lay a finger on you.'

She continued to stare at him. He seemed so sincere, heartbroken. But he was *always* sincere, she reminded herself. His mesmerising good looks together with his sincerity and his caring nature was a fatal combination. When they'd made love, he'd been caring, even though it had been urgent and rushed. It hadn't been planned. She still wasn't sure how their New Year's Eve kiss had deepened into the kind of kiss that definitely shouldn't be exchanged between a woman and her best friend's husband. 'We shouldn't be doing this,' he'd said throatily as they'd pulled hurriedly apart.

'I know.' She'd tried to resist the undeniable bolt of electricity that had shot between them, but failed, her lips drawn back to his, her hands all over his body, his on hers.

'Not here,' he'd murmured, breathing heavily, his dark eyes burning into hers as they'd come up for air.

She'd taken hold of his hand and led him towards the baby changing room in the foyer of the hotel. Locking the door hurriedly behind them, he'd turned to scan her face. Then,

finding what he needed there, he'd crushed his mouth back over
hers, kissing her with such potency it left her breathless. 'Your
husband must be insane to have strayed,' he'd whispered.
'You're an extremely desirable woman.'

He'd trailed his lips along her shoulder, peeling one flimsy
strap of her evening dress away as he went. 'And you're doing
terrible things to me,' he'd grated, pulling her towards him, one
hand pressed to the small of her back, hitching her hard to him,
the other sliding the flimsy material of her gown up her thighs.
She'd tried to tell herself no. It had been impossible, irresistible.
As he'd thrust deeply into her, his tongue simultaneously
probing her mouth, she'd come not once, but twice, the second
time at the exact same moment he had. That had never
happened to her before. She'd never felt so wanton and desired,
not ever.

'Sorry, I, er...' He'd struggled for something to say afterwards. 'We shouldn't have. I...' Again he'd stopped, and then,
clearly noting her expression as she felt an immediate sense of
dread that he might regret what had happened, stepped quickly
towards her to help her rearrange her clothes.

He'd lifted her chin to press his lips tenderly to hers before
they left.

That small gesture had meant a lot to Chloe. Her fingers
had strayed to her mouth in the wake of his kiss. She'd felt
disorientated, drunk, with lust rather than alcohol, sick with
guilt, but she'd had no regrets. He'd made her feel attractive
again when her ego had been beyond crushed.

'I'm sorry,' he apologised now as she studied him, apprehension churning inside her. 'I shouldn't have come. I just wanted
to check you were... I'm sorry.'

As she watched him turn away, a confusion of emotions
assailed her. *Had* it been him? Had she actually seen him? Her
recollection was hazy, fragmented. Could she really swear it

was? Quickly she swung herself out of the bed and stumbled after him.

As she caught hold of his arm, he stopped, hesitated, and then turned slowly back to face her, the look in his eyes that of a haunted, frightened man.

Chloe dropped her gaze, embarrassed and ashamed. She didn't want him to see her like this, bruised and swollen and ugly. But then she must appear ugly to him however she looked. She'd managed to accuse him without uttering a word. She hadn't confirmed to the police that he was her attacker, but she'd truly thought he was. Assumed that after her threat to shatter Eve's illusions about him, something had snapped inside him. The fact was, though, it could have been anybody. She'd been standing on the doorstep in her bathrobe. Anyone passing might have seen her, someone whose view of women was warped and who was intent on assaulting her. The blood when she'd landed – she shuddered inwardly as she recalled it spewing from her mouth to spatter the walls – would have been enough to make all but the most twisted of psychopaths flee the scene. They'd dragged her into the kitchen before they'd fled, presumably so she couldn't be seen from the front door, so they must have known how serious her injury was, how badly she was bleeding.

Dom wasn't that person. She didn't need the tortured incomprehension she'd just seen in his eyes to tell her that. It was true she didn't know all of him. She hadn't lived with him. But Eve had. Once she'd met him, she'd held onto him like grim death. After all she'd suffered, she would never have done that if she hadn't believed he was exactly who he appeared to be: a gentle, good man. Chloe had been wrong. Horribly, judgementally wrong.

Tears streaming down her cheeks, she lifted her gaze to his. She hoped he could see in her eyes what she couldn't convey any other way: that she was sorry too. *So* sorry. If he hadn't hated her before, he would have every right to now.

He looked at her, uncertain for a second, and then sympathy flooded his features. 'Jesus, Chloe.' His voice cracked, and he circled her with his arms, drawing her gently to him. 'What did that sick bastard do to you?'

Chloe allowed him to hold her, the tenderness in his voice, the warmth of his body driving the chill of fear that had settled inside her from her bones.

He stroked her hair as she rested her head on his shoulder. It was enough. Even if she didn't like herself very much, Dom didn't hate her. She'd had no incentive to do anything while she'd been in here, but now she did. She had to be there for her children. For Dom. She had to convey to that awful detective that he wasn't guilty. She couldn't lose him too.

FIFTY-SIX

'Here you go.' The nurse who'd offered to help Chloe passed her the new notepad she'd fetched her from the hospital shop.

'Thanks,' Chloe mouthed. With the help of the therapist, she was learning how to articulate around her injury, but her speech was still clumsy. She could manage a few sentences with effort, but she certainly couldn't cope with a whole telephone conversation. Certainly not with DS Atkins, who was like a dog with a bone where Dom was concerned and would be bound to take the opportunity to pepper her with more probing questions.

'No probs.' The girl smiled brightly. 'I bet you're looking forward to going home later. I know I would be.'

Chloe nodded and smiled back. The nurse was right. She'd gone from absolute hopelessness to positive since Dom's visit. And now she couldn't wait to get out. More so now that he had offered to pick her up. He really was one of the good guys, who in Chloe's experience were few and far between. Despite the undoubtedly harrowing experience he'd had being interrogated by DS Atkins, terrified at the prospect of being officially arrested and charged, he'd assured her she wasn't to blame and that he bore her no ill will. He'd even offered to get the locks on her house changed while she was in here. Chloe had been so grateful. She'd been worrying herself sick about going back to a house that Steve had access to any time he felt like it, something Dom had intuitively picked up on without her having mentioned it. The man was a saint. If only Eve had realised it and stopped keeping him at arm's length, making it obvious she didn't trust him even with his own son.

She would feel bad for Eve, of course she would, but she'd decided that after so many years going along with everything her friend had suggested to make sure the truth never came out, she'd had enough. She hadn't been complicit in what had happened to Eve's father, after all, only in what had happened afterwards. It was time to take her life back. She had to make sure that Dom knew she would be there for him, that she would be unencumbered and that she wanted to be. She'd thought he didn't want her, but it was clear now that he did. He'd been torn, quite obviously. He had his dear little son to consider, plus he plainly felt responsible for Eve, as Chloe always had.

Eve, though, was a survivor. She'd had to be. And it wasn't as if she would be left in Chloe's position, supporting two children on a meagre salary. She was quite capable of standing on her own two feet, something she'd made obvious to Dom. Chloe could only wonder how he'd stuck with her until now. Many men would have been long gone.

Waiting until the nurse had left, she picked up her pen and opened the notepad. She'd been badly mistaken about Dom being the person who'd attacked her. He might have been angry when he'd left her, but the man hadn't got an aggressive bone in his body.

Taking a breath, she pondered and then set pen to paper.

For the attention of Detective Atkins.

Further to our recent conversation regarding my attacker, I thought I should provide you with pertinent information that has come to light since then. You might recall that you told me my children weren't at the house when you arrived. The assumption was that they were with my husband, Steven Adams. However, I can categorically state that my children were there when I realised there was an intruder. I'd instructed my son to take his little sister into the bathroom, lock the door and stay there until I told them to do otherwise.

With the assistance of a nurse, I've recently spoken to my daughter, who told me that her brother came out of the bathroom to try to help when he thought I was hurt. The crucial point is that she says her daddy told them I was fine and took them from the house. It pains me greatly to bring this to your attention, but I can only conclude that my husband took the children before the emergency services arrived and after I was attacked.

As I stated previously, I did not see who was behind me, but I now feel certain that Dominic Howell was not the person who attacked me.

I would be grateful if you could inform me as to your own conclusions and keep me up to date with any further developments.

Yours,

Chloe Adams

There, that should make sure they left Dom alone. It pained her to point the finger at her husband – she could feel her heart breaking inside her for what they'd once had, for Thomas and Rose – but if Steve had been the person who'd done this to her and then just left her lying in a pool of her own blood, she couldn't ignore it. She didn't want him anywhere near her or the children ever again.

FIFTY-SEVEN

PRESENT

Eve

'We need to start slowly and build up, Lydia, remember?' The physical therapist sounded as if she were mollifying her patient as Eve poked her head around the bedroom door. 'Baby steps to start off with,' she went on encouragingly as she helped Lydia back onto the bed after a faltering walk with two sticks along the landing.

Eve couldn't help feeling that her mother wouldn't be impressed by the childish tone the woman seemed to have adopted with her. 'Hi, Claire, how's it going?' she asked, tapping on the door and then going in.

'Not too bad. As long as we don't try to do too much all at once, hey, Lydia?'

Lydia managed a smile of sorts, but Eve was sure she saw a flash of irritation in her eyes. She couldn't blame her for being impatient. Eve would be too, in Lydia's shoes, with only a daughter she didn't care for to look after her.

'Everyone is different. You need to find out what works for you,' Claire continued breezily. 'We have to build up your muscular and cardiovascular strength with simple exercises and then work on your stamina, stability and flexibility, but slowly. Just remember, when you can walk ten steps unaided, you'll be well on the way to doing all those things you previously enjoyed.'

'Can I help her work on her exercises in between sessions?' Eve asked, giving Lydia a bright smile. She wasn't offered the same courtesy Claire was, she noticed. Her mother simply stared at her with that same guarded look in her eyes she'd had since she first went to see her at the hospital, and then glanced away.

'Absolutely.' Claire nodded enthusiastically. 'I have some videos from the Stroke Association I can send you. You could have a look at using the swimming pool programme after a week or two. Simple squats or walking through the water will really help improve calf and thigh strength. Would you like that, Lydia?'

Lydia drew in a breath as Claire looked expectantly at her. She mustered up another smile, but it was a very thin one.

'She'd love it. She used to swim in the local canal as a child, didn't you, Mum?' Eve wondered if her mother would understand her implication: that it was she who was now holding the cards, that she could easily embroider facts that Chloe, even though they were now estranged, would corroborate for her own sake. Eve had been just twelve, after all. Lydia had been the responsible adult. 'Probably best avoided now, though,' she went on. 'There'll be all sorts of unimaginable things lurking down there,' she added, making sure that Lydia got her point. That prison, or even the threat of it, wouldn't be a pleasant experience.

'Ugh.' Claire curled her lip, playing along. 'I'd stick to the swimming pool if I were you, Lydia.'

'Good idea.' Eve laughed and went across to her mother. 'Don't worry, I promise not to drown you,' she said, giving her shoulders a firm squeeze.

Lydia's eyes, she noted, were pleading as she looked up at her, and she felt a lurch of sympathy. She hadn't meant to be quite so cruel, but her mother had to know what Eve needed from her, and that was simply to do what she'd always done and stay silent.

'Right, I'll get off then,' Claire said, collecting up her things. 'I'll be back on Thursday, Lydia. Keep up those left-side exercises we talked about meanwhile.' She turned to Eve with a smile. 'I'll see myself out.'

'I'm going to grab Mum a cup of tea anyway,' Eve said. 'She's bound to be parched.' Her mum would probably view the tea with deep suspicion, as she did everything Eve offered her, but she had to eat and drink. She was just going to have to learn to trust her.

Reaching the hall, she paused before opening the front door. 'Is she making good progress, do you think?' she asked, her brow furrowed in concern.

'There's no quick fix, as you would know,' replied Claire, 'but yes, I think she's coming along.'

Eve nodded thoughtfully. 'It's just that she's been pressing her hand to her chest. She hasn't admitted she's in pain – too scared of going back to the hospital, I think – but I might get them to run a few more tests. Just to be safe.'

Claire nodded and reached to give her arm a comforting squeeze. 'Good idea,' she said. 'She's lucky to have you.'

Eve emitted a rueful sigh. 'I'm not sure she's feeling lucky.'

'Understandable.' Claire smiled sympathetically. 'Don't worry, we'll soon have her enjoying life again.'

'I hope so.' Eve smiled back and opened the front door. She blinked in surprise as she saw Dom outside, lifting Kai's carrier from the car.

'Hey,' he called, giving her a wave.

Claire widened her eyes, clearly impressed. 'Husband?' she asked.

'For his sins,' Eve joked.

'Heart-melting, isn't it?' Claire sighed longingly as Dom set Kai down, talking reassuringly to him as he crouched to check his straps. 'Seeing a man so hands-on with his child, I mean.'

Eve nodded in agreement. 'He's a good father,' she said, watching as Dom got to his feet, picked up the carrier and walked towards them with a smile.

Claire was definitely enamoured. Eve noted her gaze twanging backwards as, having stood politely aside to let her pass, Dom carried on up the path towards the house. He'd clearly melted Chloe's heart too. If he was to be believed, though, he had no reciprocal feelings for her, despite having kissed her, which was all he claimed had happened between them. Eve still wasn't sure she believed him. It would make her fight for him that little bit harder. And she would fight. She would do whatever she had to to make sure that anyone who might threaten her life was eliminated from it. What choice did she have, after all? She hadn't had a life worth living until she'd met him. If secrets from her past came out, she would lose him. If Chloe had got her claws into him, she might still. She couldn't bear that. Couldn't bear to lose the only man who'd looked at her with care and love in his eyes.

FIFTY-EIGHT

Eve smiled and leaned to plant a kiss on Dom's lips as he walked through the front door. 'To what do I owe the pleasure?' she asked him. Kai was supposed to be coming to stay with her for a while, but she hadn't expected Dom to bring him today.

Dom looked taken aback, possibly because she appeared to be so carefree here at Lydia's house, then he threaded an arm around her. 'The pleasure's all mine,' he assured her, returning her kiss, a lingering, sensual kiss, his tongue gently seeking hers, which was both pleasurable and reassuring – until she caught a waft of perfume that wasn't hers, and definitely not the after-shave Dom usually wore. 'How's things?' he asked, drawing away to place the carrier on the floor.

'Okay.' Eve's stomach squeezed painfully as she watched him crouch to unbuckle Kai, smiling and talking softly to him as he did. 'How's he been?' she asked, trying hard to quash the suspicion blooming in her chest as he lifted him into his arms and straightened up.

'Amazing.' Dom gazed lovingly at his little boy, which really was a sight to melt hearts. 'He came with me to see Auntie Chloe, didn't you, little man?'

Chloe? Eve felt as if he'd just slapped her. The perfume was Chloe's. She couldn't be sure, but who else's could it be? 'You went to see her?' She stared at him in astonishment.

Dom nodded apprehensively. 'I wasn't sure whether I should with Atkins all over me like a rash, but then I thought that one of us should make an effort to show her some support.'

Which meant what? Eve swallowed back a knot of incredulity. Was he saying that *she* should have gone to see her? Did he really think she would want to, knowing Chloe had her sights set on her husband? She couldn't believe he wouldn't have considered how she might be feeling through all of this. However much Dom tried to play it down, the inescapable fact was that her husband and her so-called best friend were attracted to each other. Could he really be so insensitive?

'I'm glad I did now, though,' he went on, oblivious to her bewilderment. 'She texted me shortly after I left. She's contacting Atkins, apparently.'

'But...' Growing more confused by the second, Eve tried to digest this. 'Why would she?'

Dom frowned in confusion. 'Why wouldn't she? Atkins has clearly told her I'm a suspect. Chloe obviously thinks she can provide information that might be helpful.'

To her or to you? Eve couldn't help her cynicism. She would have liked to think that Chloe had had a fit of conscience, that she was trying to help out of a sense of friendship and kindness, but bearing in mind what had happened between them, the resentment and jealousy that had been festering away inside her friend for a long time, she very much doubted it. 'Did you ask her to contact him?'

Dom paused before answering, then shook his head wearily. 'You mean did I go there with that specific aim in mind?' he asked, eyeing her disappointedly. 'No, Eve, I didn't. Because knowing that she hadn't seen who her assailant was, that would be asking her to lie for me, wouldn't it? Thanks for reminding me how highly you rate me, by the way.'

'That's not what I meant.' Eve felt her heart drop. Arguing with him over this was the last thing she wanted to do. She didn't want to appear not to be supporting him while Chloe was. 'I just wondered, that was all.'

'Right,' Dom said flatly, and Eve felt the void that had opened between them since Lydia had invited herself into their lives growing wider. 'For your information, I went because I was concerned about her. I wanted to check how she was doing. It doesn't mean I fancy her *or* that she and I are involved.' Sucking in a terse breath, he fixed his gaze on the ceiling.

Doesn't it? Eve dropped her gaze, her cheeks burning, a fresh wave of uncertainty unfurling inside her.

Dom looked back at her. 'She's your best friend, Eve,' he pointed out, attempting to curb his frustration. 'I thought *you* might be concerned about her. That you might want to know yourself how she was.'

Eve raised her eyes, saw the sincerity in his and was torn between disbelief, jealousy and guilt. 'I am. I do. It's just...' She faltered. 'I'm concerned about *us*, too. We need to be open with each other, Dom, there for each other. I'm worried we won't get through this if we're not.'

He gave her a look somewhere between bemused and cynical. 'I'm all for the openness,' he said, a definite scornful edge to his voice. 'As for the "with each other" bit, I'm not sure that's easily achievable with you staying here.'

'I have to be here.' Averting her gaze, Eve reached for Kai. 'Someone has to.'

Dom acquiesced with a reluctant nod. 'I suppose I've got Lydia to thank for being able to spend more time with my son at least. I doubt that would have happened but for this. How is she?' he added, before Eve had a chance to say anything.

Not that she knew what to say. It was true that she had

excluded him from much of Kai's life, though she hadn't meant to. Knowing now there was no way to make that right, she felt her heart drop another inch. 'Not too bad,' she said in answer to his question, smiling at Kai and turning finally for the kitchen. She needed to get him out of his coat. She needed to cuddle him and breathe in the comforting smell of him. 'She seems to be having a few chest pains, which is worrying, but the therapists are pleased with her progress.'

Glancing back, she noted that Dom had stopped in the hall. 'I should probably go and say hello,' he said, and she felt her stomach lurch. 'At least poke my head around the door.'

'That would be nice.' Her voice was strained, even to her own ears. She didn't want him up there on his own with Lydia, but what reason could she possibly give? 'She might be sleeping, though,' she suggested feebly.

'I won't disturb her if she is.' Dom was already mounting the stairs.

Eve felt panic rise so fast her head swam. It would be fine, she tried to tell herself. Dom wouldn't want to linger, and her mother could barely talk. In addition, the damage to the part of her brain responsible for language production meant she had problems with reading and writing as well. She wouldn't be able to communicate with him, though Eve guessed she would dearly want to.

'Let's get you out of this coat, shall we, sweetheart?' She forced a bright smile onto her face and focused her attention on Kai. She would give them a minute and then go up.

Her legs feeling distinctly wobbly beneath her, she sat at the table and eased his little arms free. 'There, that's better, isn't it?' she asked him, then hoisted him up, holding him while he chuckled and danced on her lap.

'Who's a strong little boy, hey? There'll be no stopping you soon, will there?' She pressed a kiss to his button nose, then laughed as he gave her the biggest beautiful smile and reached a hand out to her face.

'Mama,' he cooed, and Eve caught her breath, her chest swelling with a love for him so powerful she felt herself inwardly reel.

'That's right, darling, Mummy.' She laughed delightedly and cried all at once, hugging him close as an almost feral urge to keep him safe consumed her.

She *would* keep him from harm. If she'd ever needed a goal in life, something to live for, her child's need for her was it. Blinking away her tears, she kissed his peachy cheek and gathered him to her again. She needed to make sure she was there for him, always. She couldn't allow her past to creep back and come between them. Couldn't allow anything or anyone to take him away from her. She *wouldn't*.

'Shall we go upstairs and see what Daddy's up to?' she whispered, making excited eyes at him. Could she take him away from Dom if she had to? Rob him of his child? It would destroy him, but if that was her only choice, she would have to. She would need to disappear, make another life for herself, become someone else. She could do that. She would do that for Kai. She would kill for him.

But it wouldn't come to that. As long as the past stayed buried, her life needn't unravel. Even as she thought it, though, she could feel the foundations rocking, her world crumbling. As hard as she might try, she seemed to have no way to stop it, other than by doing something she had contemplated but wasn't sure she would be capable of. What were the alternatives, though? She couldn't live years of her life trapped in this mausoleum with her mother and fake brother. She couldn't bring Kai here permanently; that was unthinkable. She heard it again as she reached the landing, the haunting child's cry, and her blood ran cold. She couldn't be here, stuck in this prison without bars, slipping silently into madness, her mind taking her to places she could never remember having been. There was no way she would survive going there again.

Her heart slowed as she neared the open bedroom door. She could hear it beating, a dull thud at the base of her neck. Sweat prickling her skin, cold fear and nausea swirling inside her, she stopped as Dom's voice reached her, muffled as if through water. 'Lydia, I'm sorry.' She heard the frustration in his voice she'd heard so often lately, because of her, because of her mother. 'I don't understand what you're trying to say.'

Her mother's voice as she struggled to answer was drawn out and slurred, but Eve could sense her determination, her desperation as she made a renewed effort to communicate.

Holding Kai close, she nudged the door further open. She felt dizzy, disorientated as she realised that everything beyond it was distorted, as if she were viewing it through the eyes of the wasp that seemed to be buzzing dementedly in her head. Anger rose like a viper inside her as her gaze swivelled from Dom to her mother. Lydia was clutching his jacket with her good hand, yanking him to her, demanding his attention. Eve saw her mouth move as if in slow motion, the words that escaped hammering three sharp nails into her coffin. 'David. Jacob,' she rasped. 'Eve.'

Dom tried to pull away. Eve could see him struggling to unfurl her fingers.

But Lydia wasn't about to let him go. '*Eve*,' she repeated hoarsely – and Eve felt the room shrink, the walls whooshing suffocatingly in on her. In that second, she saw with clarity what she had to do. If Dom hadn't yet guessed, it wouldn't take him long to do so.

FIFTY-NINE

Dom had taken Kai from her. He was clearly agitated. Her mind a whirl of confusion, Eve couldn't understand why.

'Where are you taking him?' she asked, following him across the kitchen.

'Home,' Dom answered shortly, collecting up the carrier.

'But why?'

'Why?' He ground to a halt, shaking his head. 'What's going on here, Eve?' he asked, his eyes narrowed as he searched hers.

Her heart leapt. 'Nothing,' she answered quickly. 'My mother's not well. Things are bound to be a little stressful. I'm just trying to care for her. I need to see Kai, though, have some contact with—'

'She was trying to tell me something.' He cut her short. 'What was she trying to say, Eve?'

'I have no idea.' She glanced away from his penetrating gaze. 'She doesn't make much sense. You can see she doesn't.' She moved towards him to take Kai, who was fractious, clearly having picked up on the tension. Terrifyingly, she couldn't remember everything that had gone on upstairs. She recalled going into the bedroom, but it felt as if she were watching herself in a movie, looking in from the outside. Other than that, there was nothing bar the three words that reverberated loudly in her head. *David. Jacob. Eve.* Had Lydia said something else? Something Eve had missed? Did Dom know something?

'She was just rambling,' she tried. 'She gets frustrated, confused. She was groping for familiar words, that was all.'

'It was more than that.' Holding on to Kai, Dom walked with him back to the hall. 'She was petrified. It was right there in her eyes.'

Her mouth running dry, Eve followed him. She didn't want him to leave like this. She'd barely spent any time with Kai. And now Dom was taking him from her. That thought landing like a stone in her chest, she felt a new wave of panic spiral inside her. 'She wasn't making any sense, Dom. She can't. She has damage to areas in the left hemisphere of her brain. She struggles with finding words. None of what she said is likely to mean anything.'

Bending to strap Kai into his carrier, Dom didn't respond.

'Why are you taking him so soon?' Eve's voice quavered. 'You've only just arrived.'

He drew in a breath. 'It's not a healthy environment for him here, Eve, let's face it.'

'But I've hardly seen him. He doesn't have to spend time in my mother's company. He can stay down here with me.'

'He doesn't have any of his things here,' Dom said without looking back at her.

'You have his bag in the car,' Eve reminded him. They never travelled without the essentials. 'We can improvise. Please leave him for a while.'

He hesitated. 'And if your mother has some kind of a turn?' Standing, he looked questioningly at her. 'Another stroke? You said she's been having pains in her chest.'

'Then I'll call you, obviously. Kai's my priority. He'll always be my priority. He's not going to come to any harm with me, for goodness' sake.'

Dom scanned her face. He wasn't happy. She understood why he wouldn't be, but surely he wasn't going to deny her access to Kai because she was here caring for her mother. 'And if it's an emergency?' he asked. 'What then? Your focus will be on Lydia. It will have to be. I'm sorry, Eve, I just don't think it's a good idea him being here.'

'You can't stop me seeing him.' She straightened her shoulders, ready now to fight if she had to. She shouldn't have to negotiate to see her own child.

He arched his eyebrows. 'I'm not trying to stop you.'

'Then why are you trying to lay down the law?'

'Lay down the...' He squinted at her in bemusement. 'I'm not trying to do anything of the sort,' he retorted angrily. 'I just don't think this is a sensible arrangement. Your mother has had a stroke. You're having to devote a lot of time to caring for her. Then there's the issue around Jacob.'

Eve's heart stalled. 'What issue?'

Dom kneaded his temples. '*The* issue,' he said forcefully. 'At least it's an issue for me. I still have no idea what actually happened to him. There's also that bloody monstrosity sitting in the cot in the nursery. I don't want my child here. *I* don't want to be here. I don't think you should be here either.'

Eve hadn't heard past the words *my child*. What was really going on? Was he using the situation to alienate her from Kai? An excuse to keep him from her? To what end? So he could look like the perfect bloody father in *court*?

'You should get a professional care provider in,' he added, turning away to pick up the carrier.

Eve stared at his back. 'I can't,' she said past the lump in her throat she couldn't seem to swallow.

Dom faced her. 'You know, it strikes me that you actually could. That maybe you don't want to because you don't want to be with me.'

Her heart skidded against her ribcage. 'That's ridiculous,' she muttered.

'Is it? You've kept me at a distance, Eve. You're doing it now, for some reason I can't fathom.' He studied her, his forehead knitted in angry frustration. 'I don't understand any of it,' he went on as she struggled for something to say. 'The fact of the matter is, though, it wasn't just Lydia's behaviour up there that worried me. It was yours. You scared the shit out of me, if you want the truth. What I saw in your eyes when you looked at her wasn't caring. You looked terrified. What's more, when you looked at me, it was as if you couldn't even see me.'

Eve dropped her gaze. 'I didn't feel well. I have a headache,' she murmured weakly. How she wished she could confide in him. Tell him that she *had* been terrified. That the fear and disorientation she'd felt was exactly the way she'd felt as a child. It wasn't possible. If she told him some of it, he would want more. And she just couldn't give him that.

He studied her for a long, silent moment. Then, 'I'm leaving,' he said. 'I'm taking Kai with me. You know where I am if you need me. Not that you ever have,' he tagged on tiredly as he opened the front door.

Eve's heart went into free fall. She could hear the foundations shifting beneath her. She was losing him anyway. Her husband and her son, she would lose them both. Chloe would be there, wounded, waiting. Wasn't that what he wanted? That thought added another stone to the unbearable weight in her chest.

She wanted to call after him, tell him that she needed him, that she always had, that she wouldn't know how to be without him, but she couldn't formulate the words, couldn't focus on anything but the wasp that seemed to be boring a hole in her brain.

You have to stop it. It buzzed frantically. *Bring an end to all of it.* She did. She had no choice.

SIXTY

PRESENT

Lydia

Lydia blinked, disorientated, as she heard it again, a man's voice, calling her through the impenetrable red fog in her head.

'Lydia? *Lydia!*' It reached her, dragging her back, though she would much rather stay where she was. It was comforting somehow, the thick blanket of darkness. Safe. 'Lydia! Can you hear me?'

She wrenched her eyes open, fear piercing her chest like an icicle as she looked into the eyes staring down at her; dark, desperate eyes, drilling into hers. She blinked hard, tried to focus, and felt relief wash through her entire body as she realised they were filled with concern. Not hatred. There was no anger there. No malevolence. It wasn't him. The man crouching over her wasn't David come to take her to her grave with him.

Her mind flew back to that dark day at the foot of these very stairs. Paralysed for an instant, she'd looked from David to the girls standing trembling over him, and then sprung into action, easing Jacob away from him, then prising the poker from Eve's hand. She'd run quickly to wash it and place it back in the hearth before shepherding the two of them to the bathroom to wash the blood spatter from their faces. She'd protected her daughter in the only way she could think to. She would have taken the blame herself in an instant, but where would that have left her children? The thought of them in David's mother's care had made up her mind. The woman had created the monster David was. No, she couldn't allow that to happen.

It was Lydia's responsibility to protect her children, her natural instinct to do so. It always had been, though it seemed Eve didn't realise it. Her daughter had thought her as much a monster as David was. Lydia had hoped one day to explain everything to her, though she doubted she could ever have convinced her that everything she'd done was to protect her, that she'd loved her and her dear darling Jacob both, no matter how cruelly she'd seemed to treat them. She'd failed to keep Jacob safe, though. Failed in her fundamental obligation as a mother.

'What happened?' Dominic asked, reaching to brush her hair gently away from her temple. 'Christ,' he murmured, clearly noting the gash there. Lydia guessed it must be bleeding quite badly. She could taste it, a sour metallic tang in her mouth. 'What were you doing, Lydia? Why were you trying to get down the stairs? And where the bloody hell is Eve?'

Lydia opened her mouth, but nothing intelligible came out. If only she'd confided in him sooner.

Dom obviously realised the futility of his questions. 'Lie still,' he said, easing back to tug off his jacket and drape it over her. 'Try to stay awake, Lydia, okay? I'm going to call an ambulance. We need to get you to hospital.'

'No,' Lydia managed feebly, and twisted her head to the side.

'Don't move.' He placed a hand to her cheek. 'You need to stay still. You might have broken something. You could damage your spine.'

She didn't care. She didn't care about anything other than using these few precious moments she had alone with him to make him understand. She looked at him pleadingly, slid her eyes sideways, prayed he would follow her gaze.

A frown creasing his forehead, he looked at her in confusion, and then, mercifully, glanced to the patch of wall where, in the absence of a pen, she'd daubed her desperate message with her own blood. Could he read it? The words were stark against the white paint, like a child's scrawl. Would he make sense of them?

Jacob's illness, she'd written. *Beware Kai*. After calling Dominic's number, it had been all she could manage before her strength had failed and unconsciousness claimed her.

Her stomach churning with anxiety, she watched him as he studied it. Saw the incomprehension in his eyes as his gaze travelled from the wall back to her, and then something in his gaze shifted, giving way to hot, simmering fury.

He stared at her for a blood-freezing moment, seeming to assess her, and then, his jaw clenching determinedly, he jabbed at his phone. 'Stay still,' he instructed, his voice choked.

Lydia felt a tear slide from her eye as he calmly told the emergency services that she'd had a fall, that he was with her and making sure she didn't move. Finishing the call, he instructed her again to stay still, then raced upstairs, coming back down with a blanket. He'd left her once, but he wasn't the cruel man Lydia had worried he was, someone who might also have decided it would be better if she stayed silent. He was a good person. Her heart went out to him for all he might have to face, and then lurched violently as the front door opened behind him.

Eve's face was a kaleidoscope of emotion as her gaze pivoted from Lydia to Dominic and back: shock, confusion and palpable fear. 'Oh dear God, what happened?' she gasped, stumbling forward and dropping to her knees at Lydia's side.

'I would have thought that was pretty obvious,' Dominic answered. 'Why hasn't she got a mobile?'

'What?' Eve didn't look at him as she fussed around checking Lydia's limbs.

'She was trying to get to the phone,' Dominic pointed out, nodding to where it still lay on the floor to her side. 'Why did she need to do that, Eve? Why did you leave her?' he demanded, his tone tight with suppressed anger. 'I had to break a window to get to her. She might have died lying here.'

'I had to go out. To the surgery,' Eve answered falteringly. 'Her phone's upstairs. I've no idea why—'

'It's not.' Dominic cut her short. 'I checked.'

'She must have dropped it.' Eve's gaze was on Lydia, her eyes holding a warning, as if she might somehow contradict her. 'What were you doing, Mum? You knew I wouldn't be long. Come on,' she said, moving to ease her head from the floor. 'Let's get you back upstairs and—'

Dominic stepped towards her. 'Leave her.'

Eve glanced up at him. 'But she's fine. I just need to get her back to bed.'

'I've called an ambulance.' He looked dispassionately down at her. 'She stays where she is until it arrives.'

Eve laughed in bewildered astonishment. 'I'm a doctor,' she reminded him. 'I'm perfectly capable of looking after her.'

Dom continued to glare at her. 'Are you?' he asked, his gaze never leaving hers. 'She stays where she is, Eve. She has a head injury. She was unconscious. She'll need a scan.'

He wasn't about to give in, Lydia realised. She hadn't been sure he'd understood all that she'd been trying to convey, but when she noticed that there was nothing but a crimson smear where her message had been, she felt he might have. Prayed hard that he had.

SIXTY-ONE

PRESENT

Eve

'Where's Kai?' Eve asked as they sat in the corridor, waiting for Lydia to come back from her CT scan.

'With Chloe,' Dom said flatly.

Eve baulked. 'Chloe? I didn't even know she was out of hospital.'

'I collected her,' Dom answered, without looking at her. He'd hardly looked at her at all, in fact, since they'd left Lydia's house. 'I thought I should.'

'I see,' Eve said, her heart aching unbearably at the thought that he hadn't considered how she might feel about that. About his leaving her child with a woman who quite plainly had feelings for him, whether or not he reciprocated them. 'So you did that despite you being accused of attacking her.' She struggled to keep the anger and hurt from her voice.

'Chloe didn't accuse me of anything,' Dom pointed out. 'The police made assumptions. They were wrong.'

'Which they only realised because Chloe told them they were, even though she didn't see her attacker.' Eve felt obliged to point that out.

Dom said nothing. Eve noticed his tense body language as he dragged his fingers through his hair. What was his agitation all about? she wondered. His lack of eye contact. Was it because he was angry at finding Lydia the way he had, as if Eve were responsible for her mother taking it into her head to try to get down the stairs? Or was it because he felt guilty? 'Have I done something wrong?' she asked him, her throat tightening.

He exhaled a disparaging breath. 'Like leaving your mother alone, you mean?'

She stared at him in bewilderment. 'I have to leave her occasionally, Dom. I have to shop and collect her prescriptions. I have to breathe, for God's sake.'

'Why did she call me?' Dom asked, glancing sideways at her. 'Why not you?'

Eve knitted her brow. 'I've no idea. Perhaps my phone was engaged. Her speech therapist rang while I was at the surgery.'

'And you went there because...?' He looked at her full on. 'I assume it was some kind of emergency.'

He was scrutinising her as if he didn't trust her. Wasn't *she* the one who should be suspicious of him? 'It was actually,' she replied. 'My mother's online prescription hadn't been updated. I went to do it myself and collect some medication while I was there, rather than leave her in pain.'

Dom closed his eyes and nodded slowly. What had he been thinking? What might Lydia have communicated to him to make him so wary of her? Panic tightened her chest, her mind ticking feverishly as she realised that her mother would find a way to speak to him at some point. In addition, while she was desperately trying to prevent Lydia having contact with her husband, she was allowing Chloe free access to him. And Dom? She looked him over, wondering now if she'd ever really seen him. Was he playing unwittingly right into Chloe's hands? Wasn't it more likely that he *had* been involved with her, that he still was? That he was looking now for a reason to wash his hands of his wife, the woman who'd never fully trusted him?

'We'd been talking about the family photographs earlier. She keeps them in the sideboard. She might have been trying to get to those.' Swallowing her tears back, she attempted an explanation as to why her mother would have tackled the stairs. 'I don't know. I do know that you seem to be looking for reasons to blame me for something. I'm not sure what.' She jumped to her feet.

Dom followed her as she walked along the corridor. 'Eve,' he caught her arm, 'I'm not blaming you. I'm just confused, that's all. We need to talk. There are some things I don't understand.' He stopped as he spotted Lydia being wheeled back towards them.

'I want you to collect Kai from Chloe's house immediately,' Eve said coldly. 'I don't want him there, Dom. If you choose to continue to see her... Well, I can't stop you, can I? Quite clearly that sends out a huge message to me, though, doesn't it? It's up to you. Just so you know, though, I won't *ever* allow you to see Kai in her presence. She's a manipulative liar. A woman who seems quite happy to see the father of her own children go to prison. Maybe you should bear that in mind before you throw your life away for her and ruin your son's life into the bargain.'

'*What?*' Dom laughed incredulously as she snatched her arm away from him. 'Eve, I have no idea what you're talking about.'

'I think you do,' she replied without looking back. 'I'm going to take my mother home. I've organised a carer for her, by the way. It might cramp your style a bit, but I'll be home soon.'

SIXTY-TWO

She was glad her mother didn't try to communicate on the way home. Her CT scan was clear, but Eve had mentioned her concerns about her heart before she'd left. The consultant had been very understanding, suggesting that she put in a request for an electrocardiogram and he would try to hurry it through. She'd smiled gratefully at him. Her mother's face as she'd turned to her had been appalled.

She smiled at the patient transport staff, laughing at Tom's jokes, though she wasn't really hearing them.

'Hey, Lydia,' he said as he helped her into the stairlift once they were back at the house, 'what do you call it when an ambulance crashes into the side of a hospital? A medical breakthrough,' he answered when she didn't react. Her attention was elsewhere, her eyes full of apprehension as she looked upwards towards the landing.

'Don't worry, lovely, I won't drop you,' he assured her.

'He's stronger than he looks,' his colleague quipped.

Eve managed another smile, but she wasn't sure she could endure much more chatter. The wasp was back. This time, though, it felt as if there was a whole swarm of them buzzing angrily in her head. They were looking for a way out. *She* needed to find a way out before the house she was still trapped in stole the rest of her life from her, stole her son from her. She couldn't allow it.

'Thank you,' she said, once Lydia was securely belted into the chair. 'We can manage from here.'

'Sure?' Tom asked.

'Positive,' she assured him. 'I'm sure you have other patients to see to.'

'Right you are.' The two of them headed for the front door. 'Don't go doing anything I wouldn't do, Lydia,' Tom called with a cheery wave.

Eve breathed a sigh of relief as the door closed behind them. 'You really shouldn't have tried to come downstairs on your own, Lydia.' Using her name rather than refer to her as Mum, because she no longer regarded her as such, she sighed, following the lift as it carried her up. 'None of this would have happened if you hadn't been so determined.'

Lydia didn't respond. Her face was blanched of colour, Eve noticed as she helped her from the lift, her breathing laboured as she manoeuvred the rollator towards the bedroom. It was clearly taking some effort, but she held her head high and persevered. Eve noted her grim expression, and was instantly transported back to her childhood, watching her mother come towards her with the scissors in her hand. That had been the moment she had realised she would never feel safe and protected in her mother's care.

'Why didn't you stop him?' she whispered, her throat tight. 'You *should* have. You should have saved Jacob.'

Lydia didn't fight her as she got her ready for bed. Eve noted the tears welling in her eyes and thought perhaps her words had hit home. So many times she'd wished she could forget the events of her former life, the final cruel twist that had taken her baby brother's life. She never had been able to. She

felt a spark of compassion as she went to the nursery to fetch
Jacob.

He whimpered as she picked him up. 'Want Mummy,' he
cried, and Eve felt her heart tear inside her. Of course he did.
She hadn't understood when she was younger. She'd wanted
her mother's attention, her parents' love and affection, but Jacob
had been smaller and he'd needed it more. He'd been just like
Kai, so much like her darling baby. The attention she got at the
hospital compensated in a way. It was when Dr Kelman had
smiled at her, told her that she might well have saved her brother's life, that she'd made up her mind to try to keep him safe.

It had all gone wrong. The wasps buzzed more loudly,
planting their poisoned barbs painfully into her brain. Horribly,
tragically wrong. Seeing her father's eyes filled with vile
contempt as he'd looked up at her, recalling for the first time
each sickening crack of the poker as she'd tried to make it all
stop, she hugged her baby brother closer. 'I did make it stop,
Jacob,' she whispered tearfully. 'I didn't mean for you to get
hurt.'

Resting his head on her shoulder, one hand placed gently to
his back, she carried him to her mother's room, smiling reassuringly at him as she peeled the duvet down and pressed him to
Lydia's side. She hated that he'd been stuck all alone in that
nursery. The poor mite must have lived his nightmares over and
over, just as she had.

'He'll feel better here, secure, going softly off to sleep with
his mother,' she told Lydia, lifting her weak arm and making
sure he was snuggled close before tucking the duvet carefully
up to his chin. Then hesitating and lowering it a little. She
didn't want to restrict his airway.

She swallowed, trying hard to block it all out as she
prepared the syringe with enough diamorphine to make sure
Lydia would rest comfortably. Holding it up, she squinted at it

and flicked it with her finger to make sure there were no air bubbles.

Then she turned to the speaker. 'Alexa, play "Amazing Grace",' she instructed.

'You're clearly in pain. It will all be better soon,' she assured Lydia, readying her other arm as the sweet, mournful melody filled the room, soothing her mother and her baby brother. Soothing her too. The wasps had stopped buzzing. The butterflies were finally still. 'There won't be any more nightmares, I promise,' she whispered. 'Sleep tight, Lydia.'

SIXTY-THREE

'Eve!' Dom yelled behind her. 'What the hell are you *doing*?' He gripped her hand hard, forcing her to drop the syringe.

'Stopping her!' Eve cried, and tried to wriggle away from him. 'I have to. You *know* I do. *You* tried to stop her. You came here on the night she was taken ill.'

'Jesus *Christ*.' Dom stared at her, astonished. 'I came to *talk* to her. I wanted to stop her hurting *you*. I didn't try to fucking well kill her!'

'She'll be b-better off,' Eve stammered. 'She'll be with Jacob. That's what she wants, to be with her baby. That's why I bought her the doll, because he looks like Jacob, because I thought it would comfort her. She stuffed him in the nursery. Can you imagine how lonely he must have been in there all on his own? She *ignored* him, just like she ignored *me*.' She banged her chest with her free hand. 'She tried to take Kai, but I wouldn't let her. I *can't* let her.'

Dom studied her, horrified. 'You've lost your mind,' he said, his voice hoarse with shock. 'You need help.' Retrieving the syringe from the floor, he looked her over cautiously, then turned his attention to Lydia. 'Lydia, you have to sit up.'

Eve backed away as he pulled Jacob from under Lydia's arm, tossing him uncaringly to the floor. She hesitated, and then snatched him up, taking another unsteady step backwards as he helped Lydia to sit, supporting her with his arm, pulling his phone from his pocket with his other hand. Her blood froze as he jabbed in three digits. 'Who are you calling?' she asked, her mouth parched.

Dragging disdainful eyes over her, Dom spoke into his phone. 'Police,' he said, and Eve's heart turned over. With Jacob clutched to her chest, she spun around, flying to the landing and thundering, half stumbling, down the stairs. She'd almost made it through the front door when Dom caught up with her. 'Where do you think you're going?' he grated, grabbing her arm.

'To get my son! Let go of me.' Eve struggled to pull away as his fingers dug painfully into her flesh. 'I have to get to my baby!'

He yanked her around to face him. 'You have to be joking.' He looked her over, thunderstruck. 'Do you honestly think I would let you anywhere *near* him?'

Eve felt her world tilt dangerously, her chest constrict violently. She couldn't breathe. Her emotions colliding – deep visceral hurt, confusion, above all stone-cold fear – she stared at him in disbelief. This wasn't the man she knew, the man she loved, the man she'd thought cared for her. This man was an imposter! She held Jacob closer. 'You're going to take him away from me,' she murmured.

'I won't bloody well *need* to, will I?' he spat furiously. 'Do you think for one minute any court in the land would allow you to keep him?'

She squirmed as he gripped her arm tighter. 'You can't *do* this,' she seethed. 'I won't let you! Kai is my *life*.'

Dom looked at her through narrowed eyes, his expression contemptuous and bone-chillingly familiar. 'I don't think you know what love is, Eve,' he said cruelly. 'I should have got out sooner. Taken Kai as far away as possible from this *madness*. At least this way I won't have to fight you. I wouldn't have stood a chance before, would I, you a doctor and me without even a steady income?'

Eve's stomach lurched. Had he been *planning* it? *Aiming* to leave her, to take her son from her? 'You're in love with Chloe.' She stared at him, stunned.

Dom said nothing, merely continued to glare at her, which gave her her answer.

'Is Kai with her?' she asked, a new petrifying fear settling inside her.

Still he didn't answer, drawing in a terse breath instead.

'Is he *with her*?' she screamed.

'Yes, he's with her!' Dom yelled back. 'At least she won't bloody well *smother* him.'

You should put a pillow over his face while he's sleeping, a distant voice whispered. The wasps buzzed.

'You've finally been revealed for who you really are, Eve. It was you, wasn't it, who made your brother sick?'

'No! I tried to make him stop crying! That's all I ever did. He was always crying. I tried to make him *stop*. Chloe—'

Dom clutched her shoulders and shook her. 'It was *you* who hurt him.'

She squeezed her eyes closed. '*Stop*. Please stop,' she begged him.

'*You* who *killed* him!'

'*No!* He hit his head! He had a subdural haematoma!' She tried desperately to explain. 'It was an *accident*. I didn't mean it to happen. I *didn't*.'

'Lydia wasn't responsible for Kai getting sick,' he seethed. 'It was history repeating itself, wasn't it? A glimpse of what you're capable of when you feel threatened or frightened. You were petrified when she showed up. But you weren't scared she would take Kai, were you? You were scared she would alert me to what *you* might do to him.'

'*No!* That's not true. It's not!' Pressing the heels of her hands against his chest, Eve shoved herself away from him. 'You're wrong,' she cried, panic climbing suffocatingly inside her. 'It was *her*. This is all because of *her*.'

He eyed her stonily. 'You tried to kill Chloe, didn't you?'

'What?' She stared at him, shocked and disorientated. She couldn't think straight. Couldn't understand. The noise in her head, Jacob crying, the constant buzz, buzz, buzzing, it was too loud.

'You're the one who attacked her.' He jabbed a finger in her direction. 'It was *you*, Eve. All you!'

'No. You're lying. It's all lies!' she sobbed. 'You can't leave me. You can't leave my baby with her. You *can't*!'

'But I can, Eve. It's what you wanted, isn't it? Let's face it, you pushed me away hard enough. No man in his right mind would stay, would he?' He twisted the knife another inch. 'The thing you didn't factor in is that Kai is my life too. I wouldn't have left him, Eve. Not with you.'

Feeling the last vestiges of her world crumble, Eve staggered backwards. It wasn't Lydia who was taking everything away from her. Reality sank in sickeningly. It was *him*.

She took another faltering step, and then froze as the distant wail of a siren broke through the cacophony of noise in her head.

'It's over, Eve.' There was nothing but pity in Dom's eyes as she stumbled another step back. 'Your past has caught up with you.'

SIXTY-FOUR

As Dom grabbed at her arm, trying to hold onto her as the police car drew up, Eve reacted with the most base instinct of all, that of a mother protecting her baby. Gouging her fingers into his flesh, she kicked his shin hard, screaming with all her might as she did, 'Let *go* of me! Don't *touch* me!'

The police were on him in seconds, forcing his arms behind his back and pushing him to the ground. She could hear him protesting, shouting her name as she left him and ran. They weren't listening to him. It would buy her some time.

Tears blinding her, she had no idea where she was going until she got there. Clutching Jacob tightly to her breast, she inched closer to the edge, her toes jutting from the bank as she stared down into the murky depths of the water.

The poker had sunk easily. A shudder shook through her as she recalled how it had plopped smoothly into the water, taking the clumps of congealed blood and bone with it. The rolled-up carpet, tied and taped, weighed down by concrete Steve had fetched from her father's factory, had sunk along with it, eventually. Slowly, slowly, a few bubbles rising, and then it was gone.

Except it wasn't. It had surfaced constantly ever since. Every night she would see his eyes, pinpricks of pure hatred, peering out from the dark as she woke from her nightmare with a start. From the day he'd disappeared to this day, this moment, he'd called out to her. Icy fingers trailed the length of her spine as she heard him: *I see you, Eve. I know who you are.* Perhaps he did. Perhaps the man who was supposed to love her as a father should love a daughter simply couldn't, because he had known her, known what she was capable of.

She looked across the water to where a narrowboat manoeuvred precariously, its bow and stern nudging the bank either side as the man at the helm tried to steer it around. A woman stood on the steps up to the deck, holding a toddler safely in her arms.

Eve hugged Jacob closer and turned her gaze to the young girl standing in the well at the front. 'You hit it again, Dad!' she shouted, gripping the gunwale for support as the boat bumped the bank. 'You should let Mum steer. You're rubbish at it.'

'He is, isn't he?' Eve whispered to Jacob, her eyes still on the girl, who was around the same age as Eve had been when her father had wanted to shear the hair from her head. *It won't be long before blokes come sniffing around and her belly's filling out too. Can't have that, Lydia.* She heard him, felt his loathing, hugged her baby brother tighter.

This little girl was clearly loved. She was confident, unafraid. Why hadn't Eve's parents been able to love *her*? With Dom, she'd had a glimpse of what happiness could be. What normality could be. She'd experienced love. It shone from the eyes of her baby boy whenever they fell on her. Dom had loved her. She'd felt it. And now she'd lost him. She would lose her dear, sweet baby boy when the police caught up with her. Dom was going to entrust his care to Chloe, a woman who couldn't be trusted. Eve should have told him, yet she hadn't. The wasps buzzing, buzzing, buzzing had drowned out any coherent thought in her head, and she'd run. Her heart tearing wide open, terror driving her, she'd come full circle and ended up here – fittingly, she realised. If she did this, though, ended the unbearable hurt now, she would have failed to keep her baby safe. Just as she'd failed to keep her brother safe. *I'm so sorry.* She caught a ragged sob in her chest, nestled Jacob closer.

No, she couldn't do this. While she had breath in her body, she would fight. She had to get to her baby. Kai was hers, *her* child. Dom wouldn't keep him safe. He wasn't to be trusted either. She would not let him take him. Would *not* let that woman hurt him.

'Daddy!' the little girl called. Eve glanced back to her. She was still at the front of the boat. 'Daddy!' she shouted again, her voice filled with alarm. 'You need to reverse! You're going up the bank!'

'What?' The man's voice was drowned out by the chug of the engine. 'Louder, Lily! I can't hear you.'

'You're going up the bank!' the little girl yelled. 'The front end's coming out of the water!'

She was right. Eve glanced towards the bow of the boat. It was lifting, mounting the towpath.

The woman screamed and clutched the toddler to her. 'Ryan! The back end's going down.'

'*Shit.*' Glancing at the rudder behind him, the man cursed. 'There's something wrapped around the propeller. It's weighing us down. Go to the front, Emma,' he instructed his wife. 'Grab Lily and climb off.'

Eve's gaze travelled down the tiller to where the propeller would be, just under the surface. She saw it before the man yelled again. 'It's a carpet! A whole bloody carpet from the looks of it. Blimey, the things people throw in here.'

The ripples were growing wider. Her father had come for her, like she'd always known he would.

She wouldn't let him take her. She backed away. This time she would be strong. This time she *would* save the child she loved more than her life.

SIXTY-FIVE

Dom's car wasn't on the drive when she arrived at the house. He was still busy trying to explain to the police, Eve assumed. She needed to hurry. Chloe was inside. She'd seen her peer out of the lounge window. *Her* window. *Her* house. She'd moved in on him. Now, rather than struggle in her own home as a single parent, she was no doubt planning to move in *with* him. Sleep in Eve's bed with *her* husband. Squeezing Jacob tight to her chest, Eve emitted a strangled laugh. God, how blind had she been? How needy for love that she hadn't been able to see beyond his good looks and too-good-to-be-true caring nature. Chloe was right. Dominic Howell was the whole package. In other words, there was more than one side to him. Chloe would have realised that in time. Sadly, Eve couldn't allow her that time.

Chloe had known where her spare key was. Eve's eyes drifted to the stone lion at the front door. She'd bought him because he was smiley. Not fierce at all, more welcoming than frightening. Chloe had been with her when she'd spotted him at the garden centre; she'd been with her when she'd placed the key underneath him. Chloe alone had known where it was, in case of emergencies. She had also known that Lydia had arrived at her house on the dreadful night Kai had stopped breathing and Eve's world had started crumbling.

Why hadn't Eve realised all this sooner?

She would thwart her vile little plan. She *would* keep her child safe. After what she'd done to her father, Chloe really should know that she would do whatever it took.

The back gate was open. That was remiss of her friend. After checking through the kitchen window, she went to the back door and found it locked. Deep, visceral rage burning steadily inside her, she pulled her keys from her pocket. 'She hasn't bolted it,' she whispered to Jacob. That was remiss of her too. Surely Dom would have alerted her to the fact that his mad wife was on the run and unaccounted for? Perhaps this was the last place they thought she would come.

Opening the back door quietly, she stepped into the kitchen and listened for sounds of Rose and Thomas. Her plan would be thwarted if they were here. She would never scare them. Physical scars weren't the only scars that stayed with you for life. Eve knew that too well. Hearing nothing, she guessed they were with Steve's mother. She felt sorry for him. He was no saint, far from it, but knowing that his wife was in love with another man, lying through her teeth, blaming him for all that was wrong in their marriage, his life must have been purgatory. She could understand why he would have lost his temper so badly. He'd clearly also seen Dom at their house on the night of his wife's fall, Chloe wrapped around Dom wearing only her bathrobe. She'd pushed him to his limit. Finally, he'd snapped.

Chloe was in the lounge, talking on the phone, Eve realised. *To Dom.* Her heart skidded to a stop in her chest, then started beating again as Chloe said, 'The house is secure. How far away are you?'

She needed to be quick. Quick and quiet. As quiet as the mousy little girl in the school playground. The little girl Chloe had adopted like a pet dog. Did she not know that dogs could turn vicious if treated cruelly?

Making her way quietly up the stairs, she paused at the spare bedroom. Grabbing a pen and a sheet of paper from Dom's makeshift desk, she scrawled the message she needed to, then collected up a paper clip and headed silently on to the nursery. She found Kai sleeping soundly in his cot, his eyelids softly fluttering as his mind chased his dreams. Eve prayed they were good dreams. She would never allow him to have bad ones. Placing Jacob on the chair, the note she'd penned pinned prominently to his chest, she eased Kai gently up and into her arms. He whimpered briefly as she breathed in the special smell of him, the unique smell that bound baby and mother together for ever. *I won't let them hurt you*, she silently promised him. *I won't let them take you.* As if he could hear the thoughts in her head, his beautiful eyes flickered open and settled trustingly on hers. He knew she was his mummy. He knew she would keep him safe.

She'd made her way back down to the kitchen when she heard the front door bang open. 'Did you throw the bolt on the back door?' Dom asked tightly.

'I... No,' Chloe answered falteringly. 'But I've been here the whole time. She couldn't have—'

'Eve!' Dom yelled over her, his voice frantic, furious. 'Eve!'

He was bounding up the stairs, his mood dark. Eve could always sense dark moods. Realising Chloe was following him, she pressed Kai closer, kissed the top of his sweet downy head. As she slipped out of the back door, she could hear Chloe's hot denials. Dom had found her note, clearly. It was a little cryptic: *Do you remember what you said, Chloe? 'You should put a pillow over his face while he's sleeping.' Do you remember what you did?* She hoped he was able to read between the lines.

'It's absolute rubbish!' Chloe cried. 'She's insane, Dom. You must know that by now.'

EPILOGUE

A nurse comes into the corridor. Her uniform is purple and lilac, not like those the nurses in the hospital wear. 'Lunchtime, folks.' She claps her hands, smiling cheerily.

My visitor turns his gaze towards her, then looks back at me. 'We'll leave you in peace,' he says. 'Try to eat something. You're losing weight.'

I study him, staring intently into the soulful eyes that hold mine. I *do* know him. I'm sure I do. There's something in his tone, kind and caring, that tugs at the periphery of my memory. It's gone, though, flitting away like a wisp of smoke before I can capture it.

The woman with him gives me another smile. It's tinged with sadness and regret, as if she's trying to convey something. I'm not sure why she's sad, and I don't ask. I've found it's easier to stay quiet. The incessant questioning soon stopped when the police realised I wasn't able to answer any more questions. They were quite kind, but persistent. They asked me if my husband had hurt my little boy. I answered yes, immediately. It was a gut feeling, primal. I don't remember much about him, apart from the eyes I see when I close mine: thick-lashed and so dark they're almost black. There's no compassion behind them, no caring or empathy. I know they belong to my husband. They showed me a photograph. He's dead, apparently.

They asked me if I'd killed him. I was about to deny that emphatically when something stopped me, an image of a little girl standing forlornly at a window watching raindrops trickle down it like tears. Something compelled me to say yes, I had killed him. Something deep inside me, touching the very core of me, told me to say that in order to protect this little girl who clearly needed protecting. I feel I know her, such a sad little thing, treading silently through my dreams. I don't recall how, though. So many things taunt me in the dark hours, never tangible enough to hold onto. It's because of the last stroke, I suppose. The doctor tells me I've had three, the third quite serious. The disruption of the blood supply to my brain has resulted in mental confusion, causing thoughts to ping-pong incoherently around my head. I don't mind now that I'm used to it. My eyes are a window to the world, where I watch people come and go to pass the time.

'I'll just have a quick word,' the woman says, nodding towards me. My eyes drift towards the ring on the third finger of her left hand as she rests it on the man's arm, and I gather she's his wife.

'I'll give you some space. I have a phone call to make.' The man smiles, looking between us. 'Bye, Lydia.' His gaze, thoughtful and reflective, lingers for a second, and then he turns away.

'I can't stay long,' the woman says, crouching in front of me and taking my hand. 'I have to pick Kai up from the nursery.' *Kai.* The name whispers through my mind and I feel a sharp tug inside me. Is Kai their little boy? I guess he must be. Do I know him? I feel I should, but I can't place him. I hug Jacob close, glad that he doesn't go to nursery. I suppose I should allow him to mix with other children, form relationships, but I'm not ready to let him go yet. He's very shy, doesn't talk to strangers at all, and he's such a sickly little boy. The fear that someone will harm him is always with me.

Smiling sadly, she looks at Jacob, then back at me, her dark eyes scanning mine curiously, as if quietly assessing me. There's something about her. She reminds me so much of the little girl who looks sadly out of the window, the little girl who was lost to me, I feel my heart wrench. I can't recall how or when I lost her. I do know why – because I was neglectful. I wasn't there for her as a mother should be for her child. I squeeze Jacob closer.

'Dom knows what Chloe did,' she says, and pauses.

Chloe. I try to place her. An image returns to me, fleetingly, two little girls sitting together under the shade of tall trees. Whispering. Colluding. *Chloe.* It comes to me. She stole my little girl away from me.

'Do you know?' the woman asks me. 'It was Chloe who hurt Jacob on that last day at the hospital, do you remember?'

'While he was sleeping,' I whisper. I can hear them, monitors pinging, doctors and nurses panicking, barring me from seeing my own child. That had been the day Jacob had fallen silent.

Relief floods her features. 'Dom said she shouldn't get away with it.' She waits a moment. Then, 'He says he loves me, that he'll stand by me. I think he will. I think I want him to. What do you think, Mum?' There's a question in her eyes, also quiet pleading – and I realise she's seeking my advice. That my answer might help make things right in her life.

I don't have much sensation in the hand she holds, but I think she feels it as I try to squeeze my fingers closed.

Her face registers surprise for a moment. Then she leans towards me to brush my cheek with a kiss. 'I know what you told the police about my father. Thank you for protecting me,' she whispers.

Did I? I wonder. In the end, did I protect her? I think I did. I hope I did.

Easing away, she stands, smiling down at me, and a flutter of uncertainty runs through me as I see it again, unmistakably, the spark of triumph in her eyes as she reaches out to stroke my little boy's cheek.

A LETTER FROM SHERYL

Thank you so much for choosing to read *Her First Child*. I really hope you enjoy reading it as much as I enjoyed writing it. If you would like to keep up to date with my new releases, please do sign up at the link below:

www.bookouture.com/sheryl-browne

Her First Child is a story about a family struggling under the tyrannical rule of an abusive father. The story is told from the point of view of the mother, Lydia, and her daughter, Eve. They are able to tell their story; they both have a voice. Sadly, the tiniest member of the family is not yet old enough to have one. Who is to be believed: Eve, who goes somewhere else in her head to escape her reality, or Lydia, who is very present in hers? Lydia seems to take great care of her ailing son, miraculously gaining the respect of her husband for doing so, but appears to care little about her daughter, punishing her with long silences, making her feel invisible. For a short while, whenever her baby boy becomes ill, her husband's dark moods seem to disappear. Who in this dysfunctional family would fabricate illness in a child? Why? To ward off the dark moods? To be seen? As you might gather, *Her First Child* looks at Munchausen syndrome by proxy, a condition that I found both fascinating and harrowing to research. It looks at the desperation a person might feel when suffering abuse from which there seems no escape. From the point of view of a child, it examines the profound effects and unconscious reactions to traumatic incidents such as illness in the family, severe emotional upset, difficult or abusive relationships and being bullied.

It also looks at love in some of its many guises, which can sometimes be transient and painful, twisted or possessive, driving those who are unable to cope to all sorts of madness – even murder. Silence can be used as a weapon in such coercive relationships. Once again, I'm asking: are people who they seem to be? Are their actions being misinterpreted?

We leave one of our main characters in self-inflicted silence. I'll leave you, the reader, to judge whether she will ever find her answers.

I hope the subject matter doesn't cause any reader anxiety. I love you all so much for supporting me.

As I pen this last little section of the book, I would like to thank those people around me who are always there to offer support, those people who believed in me even when I didn't quite believe in myself. To all of you, thank you.

If you have enjoyed the book, I would love it if you could share your thoughts and write a brief review. Reviews mean the world to an author and will help a book find its wings. I would also love to hear from you via Facebook or Twitter or my website.

Stay safe everyone, and happy reading.

Sheryl x

facebook.com/SherylBrowne.Author
twitter.com/SherylBrowne

ACKNOWLEDGEMENTS

Heartfelt thanks to the fabulous team at Bookouture, whose support of their authors is amazing. Special thanks to Helen Jenner and our wonderful editorial team, who work so hard for me. Huge thanks also to our fantastic publicity team. Thanks, guys, I think it's safe to say I could not do this without all of you. To the other authors at Bookouture, I love you. Thank you for being such a super-supportive group of people.

I owe a huge debt of gratitude to all the fantastically hard-working bloggers and reviewers who have taken the time to read and review my books and shout them out to the world. It's truly appreciated.

Final thanks to every single reader out there for buying and reading my books. Knowing you have enjoyed my stories and care enough about the characters to want to share them with other readers is the best incentive ever to keep writing.